# Praise for the novels of Andrew Grey

"*Dragged to the Wedding* is a laugh-out-loud romantic romp that, in classic Andrew Grey style, doesn't skimp on emotions or sugarcoat hard truths."
—*USA TODAY* bestselling author Roz Lee

"From start to finish, *Dragged to the Wedding* by Andrew Grey is a sheer delight! This charming rom-com is laugh-out-loud, giddiness-inducing, toe-curling fun."
—Brenda Lowder, author of *Keeping the Pieces*

"An emotional, sexy and fun contemporary romance."
—Terri Brisbin, *USA TODAY* bestselling author of *The Lady Takes It All*, on *Dragged to the Wedding*

"Andrew Grey knows how to tug on the heart strings."
—*Sparkling Book Reviews* on *Lost and Found*

"A beautifully touching story."
—*Under the Covers Book Blog* on *Love Comes Silently*

"I am unashamedly a massive fan of Grey's books, [and] he has a great knack for writing stories of tough men in uniform."
—*MMGoodBookReviews.com* on *Heartward*

"This is a sweet and low-angst romance...a quick, sweet read, with just a hint of spice."
—*Joyfully Jay* on *Least Resistance*

**Andrew Grey** is the author of well over one hundred works of contemporary gay romantic fiction.

For a full list of his available titles, please visit andrewgreybooks.com.

# DRAGGED TO THE WEDDING

## Andrew Grey

carina
press®

Recycling programs
for this product may
not exist in your area.

ISBN-13: 978-1-335-50813-3

Dragged to the Wedding

For questions and comments about the quality of this book, please contact us at
CustomerService@Harlequin.com.

Carina Press
22 Adelaide St. West, 41st Floor
Toronto, Ontario M5H 4E3, Canada
www.CarinaPress.com

Printed in U.S.A.

For Dominic,
my husband and the man who always makes me laugh.
I could never do this without him.

# Chapter One

"Damn! Hell! Crap! I am so screwed," James muttered under his breath, running out of swear words he could use while thinking about his mother. There was no way out of this. He was just going to have to take his lumps.

"God," Randy said as he slipped into the chair across from him. "What has you throwing the world's biggest pity party? Did your dog die? Wait, you don't have a dog. It can't be that damned bad."

James Petika lowered his hands and raised his gaze slightly. "Screw you." James knew Randy would give him shit—it was part of his annoyingly quirky personality. "Why are we friends again?"

"Because you love me, and your life would be dull and dreary without my brand of fabulousness." Randy motioned to the server, who hurried over. "I'm just parched. Could you bring me a dry Sapphire martini, two olives, with a glass of water?" He gave her his signature smile, then leaned toward James. "What are you drinking, darling?" James hadn't even had time to think about it. "He'll have the same thing."

Randy added a few watts to his smile and then turned back to James. "You weren't going to order one of those awful beers you keep in that apartment of yours, were you?" He leaned over the table, lowering his voice, as if sharing a secret. "I know you're a police officer and all, but there is no excuse for drinking Miller Light."

James actually felt his lips curling upward. "You are such a snob."

Randy glared across the table. "Do not confuse good taste with snobbery. It's just gauche." He sat back in his chair, thanking the server when she returned with the drinks. He took a sip, then flashed her another smile. "Perfection." Randy handed her his credit card. "Please start a tab. I think my friend over here is going to need a bit more fortification."

"Of course," she said. "Let me know if you need anything else." She left the table, and James took a second to look around while Randy made sexy noises over his drink.

"Have you been here before?" Randy asked.

James shook his head. The Grand Riviera Club was not the kind of place that James would think of stopping by for a drink. The bar was rich wood, the tables polished, the chairs plush and comfortable, and the prices steep as all hell. "Have you?"

"A few times. Mostly with clients I'm trying to impress. After I got your call for help, I figured you deserved a little spoiling, so here we are." He motioned around. "I really love it." He sipped his drink once more and slipped an olive off the pick with his tongue. "Okay, dish. Tell me what has you so broken up."

James sighed, a finger tapping the stem of his glass. "I have to go to my sister's wedding in three weeks, and my mother is expecting me to bring a date."

Randy set down his glass. "What kind of date?"

"The only kind my mother would expect—a female date. One that's suitable for my sister's vision in white wedding perfection in Missoula, Montana." Just thinking about it made James's stomach churn. He could stare down a suspect without flinching, work a crime scene, and collar a suspect on the run. As an officer on the Schaumburg police force, James had been in numerous firefights, and had even been called in to back up the Chicago PD. But the thought of facing his mother's disappointment was making him ill.

"You mean to tell me that your family still doesn't know you're gay?" Randy asked, his mouth gaping open.

"Of course not. Have you ever been to Montana?" James drank some more to steady his nerves. "I love my family, I really do, but they have expectations… Well, my mother does."

"I've heard the stories," Randy told him, completely relaxed. "So what did you tell her? Did you promise to bring someone with you?"

James hated feeling like a little kid in the principal's office. "Not in so many words." It was hard to explain without getting into the screwed-up details. And James hadn't had enough alcohol for that. "I told my mom I was with someone named Terri a couple of years ago. I thought it would make her happy and keep her off my back. And I never specified if Terri was male or female, but I knew what she'd assume, so I let her." He was so screwed six ways from Sunday. But this was all his fault for opening his damned big mouth.

"Okay. So, your mother is expecting Terri to be at the

wedding?" Randy was having way too much fun at his expense. "Only you would get yourself in this kind of bind."

"No. But she is expecting me to bring a date. I asked all of my single female friends. Stacey agreed to go with me because her wife, Phoebe, was going to be out of town. But she tripped over one of Phoebe's dogs and broke her foot. Apparently she's going to need surgery, so that leaves me out in the cold." James finished the martini and was tempted to order another, but it was only four in the afternoon, and starting on a good drunk this early probably wasn't a good idea.

"Just tell them. Rip off the duct tape from your closet door and be done with it." He shrugged as though that were the answer to everything.

"How long have you known me? You met my parents, remember? Four years ago. You came with me to my grandmother's funeral. How do you think they'll deal with the fact that their son is gay? Do you expect us all to go skipping merrily down the Yellow Brick Road?" He knew he was being flip, but it was true. "Besides, it's for six days. If I can find someone to go with me, Mom will stop worrying about me being alone forever, and I can come back to my life here. It's that simple. Or it would be, if I could find someone to go." James ate his olives, enjoying the alcohol mixed with the brine. "Maybe I could tell them that my date got sick or something. But—"

The smile slid off Randy's face. "That will probably get you a pass at the wedding, but it won't keep her off your back for long. She'll want to meet your girl eventually, and if you don't come through, she'll start fixing you up." Randy understood the situation better than James thought he would. "I can see her signing you up for ChristianMingle.com or something," he added, finishing his martini. Then he leaned back and stared up toward the ceiling.

"What are you doing?"

"Thinking." He waved his hands, which told James he wanted him to be quiet and just sit prettily. James drank his water and reached for one of the snack menus.

Randy pulled it out of his hand. "That stuff will sit on your hips and take root." He leaned back once again, then scratched his head and grinned. Pulling out his phone, he sent a message, stood, and held up a finger to say he'd be right back.

James looked out the large front windows as Randy spoke with someone for a few minutes, before he returned and sat back down. "You owe me big-time for this. But I think I found someone." Randy motioned for the check, and their server brought over the charge slip. He signed the bill, thanking her again.

"You need to go home and dress up a little. Wear something nice. I'll be at your place by seven to pick you up." Randy seemed so damned pleased with himself, and James started to sweat.

"Who is it?"

"Don't ask questions, just do it. I'll see you in a few hours." Randy made shooing motions, and James left the bar. He had learned a long time ago that Randy thought outside the box and had a flair for the dramatic. That was the reason he'd called him in the first place. James was desperate, after all.

At seven, he was ready, dressed in a navy blue polo shirt and chinos. When Randy messaged him, James went down and got into Randy's BMW sedan. "Where are we going?" James asked. "Did you find someone for me? Maybe your sister?"

"Just hold your horses." Randy pulled out of the driveway and drove toward the freeway. "Do you want to do this or not? If so, then put yourself in my capable hands."

James sat back. Randy would tell him sooner or later. And there was nothing James could do, short of a formal police interrogation, to get him to talk before he was ready. "I just wondered why I had to dress up." Hopefully, if he got Randy talking, his friend might let something slip.

"It won't kill you to wear something other than jeans and a T-shirt. You look nice, by the way." Randy turned onto the freeway on-ramp heading toward the city. James loved Randy's car. It rode as smooth as glass and the seats were plush. He squirmed a little to get comfortable and then watched the familiar scenery outside the windows.

Traffic slowed as they approached the bypass and then sped up again when they were past it. Most of the cars were heading out of the city, and Randy exited the freeway, taking side streets to avoid the inevitable tangle of traffic near the downtown exits. "Are we going to a club?"

"Just sit back and put your cop curiosity on hold for a little while. Trust me. We're going to have a good time." Randy glanced over at him and grinned, making James a bit nervous about what Randy had up his sleeve. "We're going to meet someone who might agree to go to the wedding with you. Just be cool, and I'll introduce you… I promise. Now chill out so we can have a little fun."

James put up his hands in surrender. "Okay."

Randy seemed pleased as he pulled up to valet parking near a Greek restaurant. They got out, left the keys with the attendant, then went inside and were seated. James looked around, expecting someone to join them. But apparently it was only going to be the two of them for dinner. "Don't be so nervous. This isn't going to hurt, I promise," Randy said.

"My mother called while I was getting ready. She wanted to know what my girlfriend liked to eat, and if she was allergic to anything. Apparently I neglected to specify a meal for us on the RSVP." He closed his eyes and tried not to think of the mess he had gotten himself into. "She also questioned me about a number of other things, like what color my girlfriend would be wearing at the wedding. As if I know..." He rolled his eyes. "She's driving me crazy."

Randy grinned. "She wants to make sure your girl is real. Your mother has never met anyone you've dated, so she's not taking any chances." He patted James's hand. "Don't worry, everything is going to work out. Now, let's have a nice meal and then we can go on to the main event."

Dinner was amazing, James had to give Randy credit for that. And by the time they were done, James needed a walk to settle how full he was, which seemed to be what Randy had in mind as well. He motioned to the right once they left the restaurant, and they ambled down the sidewalk for a couple of blocks.

"Is this where we're going?" James asked as he craned his head upward to the marquee.

"Yes. A friend is going to be joining us here, so I got us tickets for the show." Randy took his arm and led him inside the small cabaret and down through the rows of seats, which were already filling up. They took their places one seat off the aisle, with Randy on the inside. "You're going to love this."

"Is that seat for—?" James swallowed nervously as he watched the last few couples file in and take their places.

"Yes," an almost sultry voice said from nearby. Randy turned, and James stood up as a stunning woman in a red dress that fit her like a glove walked over to them. As she got closer, James's eyes widened. Her makeup was flawless and her eyes sparkled in the theatrical lighting. She was beautiful in every respect, and James couldn't take his eyes off her.

"Are you James?" she asked demurely, extending her hand. James shook it lightly. "I'm Daniella. It's a pleasure to meet you. Randy," she said, inclining her head regally. James motioned to the empty seat, and she sat down. Only then did he sit as well. "Before the show starts and we have to be quiet, maybe we should talk. Randy said that you need a date for a wedding?" She placed her small clutch on her lap.

"Yes. My sister is getting married, and my mother insists that I bring a date. And, well…you don't disappoint my mother. Not if you know what's good for you." He tried to make it seem like a joke, but Daniella simply nodded.

"My mother can be quite demanding as well. Believe me, I understand." She curled her lips upward, and James relaxed a little. "Randy told me the date of the wedding, and luckily enough, I find myself between work engagements during that period. Besides, I've known Randy long enough to trust that he wouldn't steer me wrong."

James breathed a huge sigh of relief. Daniella was perfect—she was nice, classy, and seemed to know how to behave. Not that he thought women should need to behave, but his mother was going to love her.

"Let's deal with the business so we can enjoy ourselves." She smiled again, and James found his heart beating just a little faster. He leaned forward slightly. There was something captivating and almost intoxicating about her. And it scared the hell out of him, because he wasn't attracted to women. He never had been anyway. But Daniella drew him closer as she turned slightly in her seat, her dress riding up to show more of the legs that seemed to go on for miles. He blinked as Daniella cleared her throat, and pulled himself back into the conversation. What was happening to him? "Randy mentioned that you would pay for my airline ticket and take care of the expenses while we're there."

"Absolutely. I'll also show you around and see to it that you have a nice time." This was turning out better than he had hoped. "This will be strictly platonic. You'd be helping me out and I wouldn't expect anything more than maybe friendship. I'm a police officer—you can trust me. I'm not going to take advantage of you or anyone." That was the last thing on James's mind.

"Of course." She nodded and lowered her attention to the clutch in her lap.

"James," Randy added, "Daniella is responsible for her elderly grandmother, and she will be away from work for that week, unfortunately without pay, and…"

James nodded as the lightbulb went on. "Is a thousand dollars for your trouble satisfactory?" Lord knows he wasn't paying for sex, just her accompaniment on the trip, so there was nothing illegal about what he was doing. But he went through it in his head. The last thing he wanted was to get fired.

"More than enough. Thank you. That will help me out greatly." She relaxed and sat back in the seat. As the lights went down, a man in a theatrical tuxedo covered with more

sparkles than Dorothy's Ruby Slippers stepped onto the stage.
"Excuse me. I need to use the ladies' room while they make
the announcements." Daniella patted James's hand and stood,
slowly making her way up the aisle toward the back. James
watched her go, still not able to pull his gaze away. He'd
admired beautiful women before, but none had ever turned
his head and made him wonder if he truly was gay before.
Women certainly didn't get him excited…at least they never
had, until now. He returned his attention to the stage.

"Ladies, gentlemen, and those who have yet to make up
their minds," the sparkly man onstage said. "It is my pleasure to introduce you to our ladies of the evening—Bella
Fontaine, Candy Cain, Carmen Merengue, and Creamy
Sugar." The audience hooted as the entertainers paraded
down the aisles, each taking a turn and bowing as they were
announced.

"You didn't tell me this was a drag show," James said as
he leaned over to Randy.

"Does it matter?" Randy challenged, and James shook his
head, sitting back in his seat and wondering where Daniella
was. As the "ladies" gathered on the stage, James checked
to see if Daniella was going to rejoin them. She was going
to miss the show.

"It goes without saying that no show at Cabaret Candide
would be complete without our star," the man onstage continued. "It's my pleasure to present the one, the only, the
amazing… Lala Traviata." The curtain in the back of the
stage parted just enough for a figure to emerge, wearing
an ermine-trimmed cape, a towering tiara, and long white
gloves…and James almost swallowed his tongue.

# Chapter Two

Daniel, aka Daniella, aka Lala Traviata, loved the applause. It was why he got up every afternoon and looked forward to the day. The room rang with it, and Lala Traviata in all her splendor took a bow, accepted the offered microphone for the closing number, and swept center stage. The music began, and she belted out a signature rendition of "Que Sera, Sera." It never failed to bring down the house, and as the last note rang through the theater, the curtain lowered, the others stepped off the stage, and Lala Traviata took her final accolades of the night.

Under normal circumstances, Lala would return to the dressing room, change clothes, remove makeup, and quietly leave by the stage door, joining the people on the sidewalk as they hurried home or to their final stop of the night. But not tonight. Lala removed her jewels and slipped off the shoes she'd worn onstage, perching on the edge of the sofa against the dressing room wall and leaning back.

A knock announced the visitors, and then the door opened, with the other ladies entering to talk and discuss the performance. They came in still dressed but without wigs—and in some cases shoes, because the damned things hurt. Lala knew that beauty was a process—painful and a great deal of work.

"I think we were fabulous," Candy Cain said in her usual bright tone. Sometimes Candy was too perky for words.

Lala sighed, and Bella Fontaine glared before going in for the verbal kill. "Honey, you need to work on your timing, and tomorrow you're going to be here two hours early so we can go over the 'It's Raining Men' number," Bella said. "You were all over the place, and if you step on my feet one more time, you're going to get a high kick and take a flying leap off the stage." The staredown was priceless, and Lala was pleased to keep quiet. "All you gotta do is count. Looking pretty isn't enough."

"Don't be bitchy with me, Miss Cellulite City." Candy glared right back.

Lala cleared her throat, and both of them quieted instantly. Being the queen did have its advantages. "Candy, you need the help. And, Bella, your pirouette looks more like a dying bird. I think you could both use some work. Tomorrow we'll *all* be here early to make the number perfect and ready for when the place reopens after the renovations."

A knock paused the chatter of protest from all of them. "I got…" Carmen began.

"We all know what you got tomorrow, Carmen. Your weekly check-in at the clap clinic," Candy interrupted, and the group snickered.

"Enough," Lala snapped. "I'm tired of the bitchiness and the sniping. The reading room is closed, and I have some real visitors. Now get out, go home, and get some beauty sleep. You all need it." Lala smiled, and each of the others kissed her cheek and got a hug in return. No matter what was said or done, Lala's rule number one was that they were sisters and the camp stopped at the dressing room door.

They filed out, and Lala lowered her gaze as Officer James cautiously entered the room like he was checking it for weapons. Lala stood and embraced Randy tightly when he followed.

"Great show, lovely, and the vocals…amazing." Randy could gush with the best of them. "You were spectacular. Wasn't she, James?"

James didn't seem to know what to say, but finally he smiled. "I will admit that I've never heard a Doris Day song with BDSM lyrics before."

"Thank you, darling." Lala stepped closer and presented her cheek. James actually kissed it, and Lala's heart beat a little faster, just like earlier in the theater. And holy hell, James had intense eyes that sparkled in the makeup lights from around the mirror. What Lala could do with those cheekbones. The urge was almost too much to keep from fanning herself. On top of that, as he leaned forward, the light cologne gave way to a deep, musky, heavy scent that sent a zing of heat through her. If the aroma of James could be bottled, Lala felt she would never need to work again. "Please sit down."

Motioning to a single chair, Lala made herself a little more comfortable. James turned to Randy and stepped back.

"No, honey, you and I need to talk. Randy is going to step out and find something or someone to amuse himself." The long day was quickly taking its toll.

Randy snickered and tossed James his set of keys. "I have a date with Creamy Sugar tonight, and I'll make my way home eventually."

Lala knew Randy's look and decided to bring out the claws. She wagged a single finger in his direction. "You treat her right. That one has had more than her share of heartache. If you hurt her, I'll see to it that you sing a hell of a lot higher than I do."

Randy coughed. "Understood, sweetheart. My balls are safe, I assure you." He was at least two shades paler, as he should be.

"See to it they stay that way." Lala flashed him her best warning glare, and Randy left the room, silently closing the door.

Lala took close stock of James as he tried not to fidget in the chair. "Let's talk." Lala stood, taking off the wig, setting it on the stand. Next came the zipper on the dress. "I know Randy and I played a little trick on you earlier." Daniel dropped the affectations and spoke as himself.

"You certainly did," James agreed and cleared his throat. "Do you really think you can do this for six days?"

Daniel slipped out of the dress, hanging it up, watching James watch him as more and more of his boy-self emerged from the trappings of his onstage persona. "I have been doing this all my life." He paused, hands going right to his hips. "I was sixteen the first time I did drag. My mother found me in one of her dresses and full makeup. She told my dad. They had hissy fits worthy of Candy and Bella fighting over Benedict Cumberbatch."

James's lips curled upward and his eyes warmed. Damn, Daniel loved a man who could smile at him like that—perfect teeth, with those small lines that went almost all the way to his eyes. Genuine and warmer than Daniel would have expected.

"How long have you been on the stage? I noticed that the others didn't sing, but you did, and it was beautiful."

Daniel rolled down the pantyhose and sat down to take them off, laying them out to prevent runs. Taking care of the clothes and other items was almost as important as the performance. "Five years, and I'm glad you enjoyed it." He slipped behind a screen and removed the cincher that provided a narrower waist. "The fact is that Lala Traviata is just as much a part of me as Daniel Bonafonte." He slipped out of the undergarments and untucked the boys. Taking a deep breath, Daniel let his skin breathe before pulling on a red robe decorated with a huge golden dragon, wrapping it all around himself. Stepping from behind the screen, he let James get a look before sitting at the makeup mirror to remove the last vestiges of Lala.

"Why did you and Randy pull that little stunt?" James asked, and Daniel knew he had a right to the truth. The urge was to fluff it off with a little flouncing and maybe a dose of camp, but this wasn't the time for that.

"Because Randy wanted you to see me how your family would see me. I'm not going to dress the way you saw me onstage. Lala is probably way over the top for a family wedding in Missoula." Daniel projected confidence as he watched James in the mirror. He had always subscribed to a "fake it until you make it" philosophy. And quite frankly, he could hardly believe he was actually considering this entire situation anyway. "Let's make a deal. You consider what you want to do, and I'll do the same. We can meet tomorrow for breakfast…what you call lunch…and if either of us wants to back out, no harm no foul. Okay?" He closed his eyes and worked to remove the layers of makeup and glitter.

When he opened them again, James was watching him, seemingly fascinated. "What is all that stuff for? Do you really use it all?" He pointed to the top of the counter, which was covered with his immaculately organized bases, contours, shadows, lipsticks, and powders.

He thought of being offended, but pulled it back. If James was curious, there was no harm in answering. "Not all at once, but yes. Each look requires different makeup." He continued removing the base and then used a baby wipe to cleanse his face. At home he would shower and remove anything that remained, but for now, he turned to show James the man beneath the drag. "I'll see you tomorrow, okay?" He pushed back from the mirror.

"Give me your number, and we can figure where to meet for lunch."

Daniel was tempted to write his number on the mirror in lipstick, but he jotted it down on a Post-it and handed it to James. Then he saw James to the dressing room door and kissed his cheek. Hell, he was being forward, but he wanted to get close enough for one more dose of intoxication.

"I'll see you tomorrow," James said, his voice a little deeper and his intense blue eyes with their green flecks a little darker.

Daniel pulled into the restaurant parking lot a few minutes before one, just on time. He sauntered toward the door in perfectly pressed tan pants and a persimmon silk shirt that shimmered in the sunlight. He might not be here as Lala, but there was no way that some of her showiness didn't make its way into the other aspects of his life.

James sat just inside the door, standing as he approached. "Thank you for coming." There was none of the lightness or amusement that there had been the evening before. "I know it's quite a drive out from the city."

He shrugged. "My grandmother and I live in Rosemont, so it was no trouble." They waited for the hostess and then were seated at their table. Daniel placed his napkin on his lap and leaned forward slightly. "Why don't we get down to business. You need a date for your sister's wedding to keep your mother off your back, and I need to work while the theater is undergoing renovations. This can be a simple business relationship and nothing more." Daniel could definitely keep from acting on any sort of attraction toward James, no matter how many cop uniform stripping fantasies he'd had last night. Which was a little shocking, given the fact that the last time Daniel, a cop, and stripping were concerned, it hadn't been a pleasant experience.

"Will your grandmother be okay without you for a little while?" James asked, the concern in his voice pleasantly surprising Daniel.

"One of the neighbors will be able to spend time with her while I'm gone for a few days. They get along well so Gran won't get too peeved at me."

"Good. And if you want to see a hissy fit, you should have been around my mother when she wasn't happy. Bras involved or not." He leaned a little closer over the table, eyebrows cocked wickedly.

"Oh really." Daniel could play this game. "After my mother found me in her clothes, she asked me if I was gay. Duh. I told her I wanted to do drag. She had a fit and spent the next three days in mourning because her son was going to become a girl. At least I had my grandmother."

James snorted with derision. "Please, that's nothing. When

my mother figured out why I was spending so much time in the bathroom…" He paused for dramatic effect. "She took me aside and told me that good boys didn't do that type of thing, and that if I kept it up, I would run out of juice and would never have children." His eyes did this little laughing dance.

Daniel rolled his eyes. "You think that's bad? When I met Tulane Highway, my drag mother, and brought her home, my mother spent half the night ignoring her, then she asked for makeup tips, and the last part of the evening she shared pictures and stories of me as a child, including one with me apparently eating watermelon and peeing at the same time. In one end and out the other." Daniel could not believe he had actually shared that little tidbit of nostalgia with James and gulped from the glass of water at the table. "I'm lucky Tulane didn't run screaming from the house."

James waved his hand. "At least your mother warmed up to her. If my mother found out I was gay, she'd, I don't know, maybe want to book me into some program to change me. That's probably an exaggeration, but still…" He shrugged like he wasn't quite sure. "She could tell me that it was okay as long as I didn't act on my gay feelings, or never speak to me again for the rest of my life. I'm actually starting to wonder which would be worse." James sat back, crossing his arms over his strong chest, prominent jaw set, a smile hinting at his lips.

He was trying to make light of it, but Daniel saw the fear in his eyes regardless and he waited, holding James's gaze, giving him a chance to put his thoughts together.

"Growing up, there was a lot of fear in our lives. 'Behave or you're going to hell' kind of fear. We heard it at church and it was just part of the way we were raised. I love them, but being gay… Do you know how many Sundays I had to sit in church while the minister railed against the evils of homosexuality?" James shook his head as if he were trying to get rid of the very idea. "Okay, that's enough of me being a wet blanket. We should talk about something happier, like my last root canal."

Daniel grinned as the mood lightened. "You know, if my mom was still with us, we could get her to meet your mother, and maybe they'd short-circuit each other. Though eventually mine did come to understand my life before she died." In the end, his mother had been wonderful and had even come to see his show on a few occasions. Those were memories he held dear.

"If that could happen, I swear the nuclear blast that would be my mother's head exploding would send the western half of the country cascading into the ocean, never to be seen again." James smiled. "I really do love my mother a lot, always have, but it's a whole lot easier when I'm two thousand miles away from her expectations. I don't like playing tricks on her, but this will make her happy, and I want that."

Daniel liked that James had a sense of humor. "I think you're exaggerating. You have to be. Twenty bucks says your mom isn't that bad." Daniel was pretty sure James wasn't going to take the bait.

"You're on. I'll take that bet." James held out his hand, and Daniel shook it.

"Are we really going to do this?" Daniel asked. He was willing. The money for the week would go a long way toward helping cover the gap in income, and he could use some time out of the city. It would also be a chance to develop a whole new persona to use onstage. Maybe the up-tight Christian drag character on her way to hell. Now, that would knock them dead…?

James bit his lower lip. "Yes. Let's," he agreed. The server came over. James ordered a beer, and Daniel a cosmo.

"Good. You make all the travel arrangements, and I'll put together some outfits." His mind was already running forward at a fast clip. This would probably be a lot of fun, if James didn't suddenly look completely terrified.

"What?" Daniel asked, tilting his head slightly as James's mouth hung open, his eyes as big as saucers. Daniel got up and patted James on the back. "Breathe, honey, don't forget to breathe. In and out…that's it. Always breathe." He waited a few seconds and sat back down. "Now tell me what's got you having heart palpitations." He sipped his drink and pushed James's beer nearer to him.

James drank the beer in a few huge gulps and set down the mostly empty mug. "I'm going to my sister's great big family wedding in conservative Montana, with a drag queen," James said as though it was just beginning to sink in.

Daniel smacked James's hand to get his complete attention. "Oh no, buster. You are not going to this wedding with *just* a drag queen. You are going with the most talented and amazing drag queen within five hundred miles, and don't you ever fucking forget it." He raised his glass, and it took James a second, but he raised his as well. "Here's to a wedding to remember…or maybe one we'll wish we could forget."

# Chapter Three

James refused to be nervous. He sat at the gate at O'Hare, looking up and down the concourse for Daniel before returning his attention to the book he was trying to read. What he should have done was plop himself in one of the bars and have a drink...or three. He needed to calm his nerves. It was only for six days, and then he and Daniel would return home and go back to their regular lives. His mother would be happy, and then a month or so later, James could report that he and Daniella had broken up. James could go back to his life, and his family would be none the wiser.

"There you are," Daniel said, stepping into the gate area, coming around to sit next to him, placing his Louis Vuitton bag on the empty seat. Daniel handed him a coffee cup. "I figured you could use one."

"How did you know?" James closed his book, slipping it into his carry-on, and took the cup, sipping the coffee. He didn't ask how Daniel managed to spike it with whiskey. He was simply grateful.

"I'd need one if I were you," Daniel said, leaning back in

his chair and crossing his legs. He looked great in tailored jeans and a magenta polo shirt. Even dressed as a man, he had style. "But you have nothing to worry about. Just relax. I'll change once we arrive. Your family is going to look at me and see only Daniella, an attractive woman. I do this all the time." He seemed so damned calm, and that only made James wonder if he didn't understand the gravity of the situation.

"What if they look too closely, or if later in the day you develop shadow or something?" James took another sip of the drink and let the alcohol flow through his system, warming him from the inside.

"First thing, I don't grow much hair on my face at all, and you sat right next to me in the theater and had no clue. Relax. If things get too close, I'll simply excuse myself to use the ladies' room." Daniel shifted in his seat, watching him. James felt his gaze, turning to see what was wrong. "Everyone at that wedding is going to see me through you. Remember that. None of them knows me or has ever seen me before. They will never see me as a man unless you give them a cause to."

"You know that's bullshit. They're going to be looking at you the entire time we're there." He could just imagine the microscope his family was going to put Daniel under. "They will want to know everything about you."

Daniel sighed. "Stand up," he said gently, and James complied. "Now look at me." James turned and watched Daniel, wondering what the hell he was getting at. "Not like you want to punch me." Daniel didn't break the slightest smile.

"Then how?" he snapped, and for a second Lala made an appearance in Daniel's cooled gaze. "What do I do?"

Daniel didn't answer, his gaze instantly morphing into one

of warmth and gentleness. "James," Daniel said with just a hint of breath and seduction. For a second, James could imagine being the very center of Daniel's world, that Daniel truly cared for him. "Look at me as though you care deeply for me. That you want me to be happy." He widened his eyes and willed them to grow more intense. "Not like you're constipated. Look at me as though you love me," Daniel whispered. "That's a little better, but it still needs work."

"They're going to see through this," James said, even more worried now.

"No, they're not. It's your family. As I said, they are going to see me through you and how you treat me. If you open car doors, take my hand, speak gently and kindly to me—basically treat me like the queen you know I am—they will follow right along. Because if I'm someone important to you, then I will be important to them." Daniel drew a little closer, and James wasn't sure if some of his calmness transferred to him, but the butterflies in his belly finally stopped flapping like they were trying to escape the clutches of hell. "Once you've done that, short of me dressing completely as a boy, they won't think anything of it." Daniel held his gaze, and James did the same, Daniel's eyes pulling him in, and damned if he didn't want to dive into those deep sea-blue eyes and go for a long swim. "That's exactly the look." Daniel licked his lips, and for a second James parted his own.

The agent called their flight, the announcement booming through the gate area. James snapped back to himself like a rubber band and nearly spilled the last of the drink Daniel had brought for him. He backed away, blinking, and finished the last of the whiskey-laden coffee, dropping the cup into the trash and heading to the gate.

Daniel cleared his throat loudly from behind him. James pivoted to Daniel, who had his hands on his hips, glaring at him. "Remember, I'm your girlfriend and I'm to be treated like a queen." Daniel stepped forward. "You always let a lady enter the room first, and you always watch out for her." He went right ahead, and they took their places toward the front of the boarding queue, Daniel standing in front of James. "Maybe we should review some basic manners during our flight." The mischief in Daniel's eyes was delightful.

"As long as there isn't a quiz. I always freeze during tests," James said as the few people in front of them began to move. James motioned for Daniel to go ahead, and he patted James's cheek and then handed the agent his boarding pass and stepped toward the Jetway. James following him with his gaze. There was no turning back now. One thing was certain—this trip was going to be anything but dull.

The plane taxied to the terminal in Missoula. "Daniel," James said gently, wondering how Daniel could sleep through all that activity. Those blue eyes slid open, and he unlatched his seat belt, smiling and standing up.

"Let's go."

"You're like the Energizer Bunny. You slept the whole way here and I bet you'll be raring to go for hours now." James, on the other hand, was exhausted. It was only four in the afternoon and he was already tired. James stood, got their bags from the overhead, and stepped out of the way once he was in the aisle so Daniel could exit ahead of him. He sure as hell didn't want another Daniel glare-fest. One of those was more than enough.

James turned on his phone once they were in the terminal

and heading toward baggage claim and the rental car counter. It buzzed, and James read the messages, groaning. "Shit," he growled under his breath. "My family is here. I sent them our flight schedule, and they decided to meet us." A cold sweat broke out on the back of his neck. "What the hell are we going to do?" It killed him that he could be calm under fire when on the job but his family made him completely nuts.

"It's okay," Daniel soothed, patting his arm. James tensed at the touch, but didn't pull away. "Give me a few minutes." Daniel strode across the concourse as though this was no big deal, going into the family restroom and closing the door.

James leaned against the wall, waiting, wondering what they were going to do. After ten minutes, he took a seat at the nearest gate, watching the door, wondering if he should knock to see if Daniel was all right, when the door opened and Daniel dressed as Daniella stepped out in slacks, a blouse, auburn wig, and even makeup. James stood and approached, extending his arm to him. "Thank you for being prepared." He sure as hell hadn't been.

"I wasn't planning on changing in the airport, but this will have to do for now. My makeup is a little thin, but I put on some base to smooth out my skin." Daniel tied a scarf around his throat, tucking it into the top of the blouse.

"You look beautiful," James said without even a hint of hesitation. He extended his elbow, Daniel looped his hand through, and they sauntered arm in arm toward baggage claim. It seemed a little strange, and a touch wicked, to be walking like this through the airport knowing that he was with a man, but he was the only person there who would know.

"I can feel your tension," Daniel told him softly. "Just relax and act like everyone else." They went through the security barrier of no return. "Where's your family?" Daniel asked warily, looking from side to side.

"Jimmy!" They both turned as James's mother, father, sisters, and future brother-in-law all marched down the hallway, his mother picking up speed as she got closer. She came to an abrupt halt right in front of Daniel. "Look at you." She pulled Daniel into a hug.

"Mama, this is Daniella Bonafonte," James introduced, his mother still hugging Daniel.

"It's so wonderful to meet you," his mother told Daniel and finally stepped back. James had been worried he was going to have to call in the jaws of life. "I have been looking forward to this for sooooo long." She took Daniel's hands and stepped back. "Isn't she lovely, Phillip?" She looked to James's dad and then right back to Daniel. "She's just beautiful."

"Grace, she isn't a race horse, for Pete's sake. Let the young lady breathe and have a minute before you scare her away."

She released Daniella, and James stepped closer. "You've met my mama." *Boy, had he ever.* "This is my dad, Phillip, and my younger sister, Margot." They both shook hands with Daniel. "And of course, this is my older sister, Holly, and her fiancé, Howard." Holly hugged Daniel much more gently.

"I'm so glad you're both here," Holly said with a strained smile. "All the arrangements have been so stressful." Holly glanced at her mother and then back to James.

"Oh, honey, don't worry about it," Daniel told her. "Your day is going to be magical, and we're all here for you. I've been part of many wedding ceremonies, and believe me, the day is going to be a whirlwind preceded by five days of sheer nervous hell. It's completely normal."

Holly brightened considerably, and James put his arm around Daniel. "We need to get our luggage, and then I have to pick up the car. Do you want us to meet you at a restaurant for lunch?"

"I thought we'd surprise you. Get your luggage, and Phillip will bring up the van. Then we'll head back to the house. On the ride, Daniella and I can get to know each other," his mom pushed. "I'm sure you can wait a little while before you eat." James's dad seemed taken aback, and Margot turned away, studying the departures and arrivals boards like she was going to be tested on them.

Thank the stars for Holly. "Mom, I'm hungry too. James and Daniella can get their things, and we'll go on to Mastriano's," she offered. "It's right on the way back into town, and they can have a few minutes to decompress from the flight." She stepped forward and hugged James. "I got your back, bro. Just return the favor later, I'm going to need it." James squeezed Holly a little tighter and then hugged his younger sister and mother.

"We'll be along in a few minutes." He swore his heart only began beating once again when his dad led his mother toward the exit and the rest of the family followed. They walked to the baggage claim area, finding the carousel for their flight.

"Holy shit," Daniel breathed from next to him. "Your mother is a force of nature."

"Like a hurricane," James deadpanned. "The luggage seems to be arriving." They wandered over to the carousel, and James grabbed his bag when it came by. "Which is yours?"

Daniel smiled and pointed to the lavender hard-sided luggage. "All of them are that color."

James swallowed. "All of them?" He knew he was in trouble when Daniel's hands returned to his hips. "Let me guess, queens never pack light."

"Damned straight," Daniel said as James began pulling bags off the carousel. "Now you're learning."

After a long line at the car rental, where James wished he could have flashed his badge just to make the young man behind the counter move a little faster, and once they'd filled the trunk with lavender luggage, James drove to the restaurant. "Last chance to back out. I could tell them that you got a call and had to go home."

"Or we could fake a riot in Schaumburg because Ikea ran out of Swedish meatballs and you have to go home and mediate a standoff outside the store between vegans, meatball fanatics, and the board of directors." Daniel wagged his eyebrows slightly. "I think it's full speed ahead."

James made the turn into the restaurant, parked, and walked around to Daniel's side of the car, opening the door for him. "My family is watching us through the window," James told him. Daniel got out of the car, and James closed the door.

Daniel took James's hand, drawing him nearer. "Then let's give them something to watch." He slid his hand around the back of James's neck, pulling him nearer until their lips met. Daniel's lips were warm and smooth, tasting slightly sweet, with undertones of rich heat that sent a zing racing down James's back.

"We should go inside," James whispered, blinking a little to clear his head. Damn, that was unexpected. He extended his arm, letting Daniel take it, heading inside the restaurant while he tried to figure out what the hell was going on. This was a business relationship, nothing more. James had to get his head in the game if he was going to pull this off and go back home to his own life at the end of it all.

As they approached the table, James's father stood, as did Howard. "Daniella can sit next to me," Mom said, and James took his place on the other side of the table. "How long have you and James been heating up parking lots?"

James opened his mouth to answer and didn't know what to say. Daniel answered as cool as a cucumber. "We've been dating about three months. He and I met when he came to my little cabaret show in Chicago. I'm a singer, and after the show, he and a friend came to my dressing room. He had the audacity to ask me out for a snack after the show, and I agreed." Daniel patted his hand. "I love a man in uniform." James felt a flutter of excitement at his smile.

"You're a performer?" Mama's eyes grew as big as saucers, and James reached for his water glass, taking a huge gulp, wishing to all that was holy that it would suddenly turn to vodka. "What sort of music?"

Daniel took Mama's hand. "One of my best numbers is a rendition of a Doris Day song."

James nearly snorted water out his nose and put down his glass. Holly patted his back and handed him a napkin while Margot sank further into whatever she was watching on her phone.

"Put that away at the table," Mama scolded, and Margot lowered the phone, sliding it into her purse. "This is a nice family meal." She glared at everyone around the table, waiting for them to argue with her. No one did, but the immediate effect was that everyone stopped talking and stared at one another, drinking their water. James only breathed again when the server came to take their orders.

"Where do your people come from?" Mama asked.

"I grew up in Chicago," Daniel answered, daintily lifting his glass to his lips, and James found himself watching every movement.

"She cares for her grandmother," James interjected. He could tell Mama was settling in for a third degree that would put the FBI to shame. "Have you decided what you'd like?" James asked Daniel, hoping to change the subject. Daniel nodded, and they shared a brief, strained smile before Mama started her interrogation once again.

Poor Howard. He was exhibiting that "deer in the headlights" look, and James wondered if the poor guy had a clue what he was getting himself into.

"We should go over the schedule," Holly said, and James was growing more grateful for his sister by the second. "There's nothing today. Tomorrow evening there's a couples' wedding shower. Thursday my dress should be ready, and we meet with the minister. The bridesmaids all have their dresses, so they're good. James, I was hoping that you and Daniella would go with me to pick it up. Mama has a ladies' circle meeting at the church."

"Of course," Daniel agreed before James could come up with an excuse to get them out of it. "I can't wait to see your dress." He was amazing, and some of the tension dissipated, only to return full force as Holly's eyes darkened.

"Mama and I picked it out." Damn, that was code for Mama picked it out and probably rammed her decision down Holly's throat.

"I'm sure it will be amazing," Daniel said, and Holly's lips curled upward once again.

Holly took a deep breath before continuing. "We're supposed to meet with the minister at one." She pulled a face.

"What's wrong with the minister?" Daniel asked as the server arrived with their drinks, and the conversation halted until she left. Mama shot Holly a stern look.

"He gives me the creeps," Margot piped up, and Howard nodded his agreement.

"Reverend Peterson is a fine man," Mama said more loudly than was necessary, to cut off any further dissent in the ranks. "He's a real defender of the faith and he's trying to make a difference in the community."

Margot shivered, and Holly leaned closer. "I don't like him either, but Mama insisted." James got the feeling that he was going to hear more about this later. "Thursday night is also the bachelor and bachelorette party. I was able to find a dance instructor to work with Howard and me on Friday morning so we don't make complete fools of ourselves for the first dance."

"I have two left feet," Howard explained.

"Dancing is fun," James tried to reassure him.

"Not for me," Howard whispered. "Would you come with us?"

James shifted his gaze to Daniel, who inclined his head slowly. "Of course. Whatever we can do to help make this special." All James wanted was for Holly's day to be the best it could possibly be and then to be able to go back to his life afterwards.

Holly bumped his shoulder. "Thank you," she added softly, then cleared her throat. "Friday evening is the rehearsal and dinner. Saturday afternoon is the wedding and reception, and Sunday we all sleep it off."

"Where are you going on your honeymoon?" Daniel asked.

"I don't know. Howard says he wants to surprise me." She leaned against Howard's shoulder, and he put his arm around her. He obviously adored her, which was one less worry for James.

"Daniella," Mama began, but thankfully the server arrived with their food, and Mama's renewed third degree could take a break…for now.

"Jesus," Daniel breathed once they were safe in the car. "I thought you were kidding about your mother."

"Nope. Not for a second." James started the engine and pulled out of the restaurant, heading toward his parents' home.

"And this wedding. Is your mom getting married or your sister? It seems your mama either made a lot of the decisions or forced them." Daniel fanned himself. "I sure hope all this comes together, because it sounds like a disaster waiting to happen."

James sighed. "Why do you think I live two thousand miles away? I love my mama, but I can only take her in small doses."

"But your sister's wedding?" Daniel asked. "She's the one getting married, not your mother, and yet apparently your mother picked out her dress." Daniel seemed so shocked. It was hard for James to explain that things had always been this way.

"Sometimes it's easier to just give in rather than fight her."

That was why he'd moved halfway across the country. It was better than dealing with her in his life on a daily basis.

"But it's your sister's wedding, and that's the one day that should be all about her."

James rolled his eyes. "Every day is about Mama and her expectations. She has these ideas of how things should be, and we all have to somehow live up to them. I swear Mama has been planning Holly's wedding day since the moment she was born." He paused when he heard how whiny he sounded. "I don't want you to think I don't love her, and I know Mama means well and wants the best for us. She was always there for our school programs and activities. She chaperoned field trips and volunteered for room mother. She cooked barbecue for hundreds to help raise money for Cub Scouts. It's just that we're adults now and her expectations feel like none of us can quite measure up."

Daniel grew quiet, watching out the windows, biting his lower lip nervously. "I wish I could help."

James patted Daniel's knee gently. That was one of the kindest things James had heard in a long time. "I hate to say this, but I think all of us may be beyond help when it comes to Mama. At least Holly's getting married and will have a life of her own with Howard."

Daniel nodded as they continued driving to the house. Getting out a bag, he pulled down the mirror in the visor.

"Can you do that in the car? I can pull over if you want."

"I'm fine. I just want to touch up my face and make sure I look okay." Daniel pulled out some base and fixed his makeup. James wanted to watch, but he kept his eyes on the road. He would never have thought that someone putting on makeup would be so fascinating. Eye shadow followed the base, and then a fresh application of lipstick.

"Why that color? A lot of women wear red, but you use a lighter pink."

"It's a color that works for me, and I thought that something subtle would be better for the occasion. I didn't want to draw too much attention to myself." He finished and closed the makeup case, flipping up the mirror. "Do you want me to wear something different?"

"No. I think you look great." James let his gaze flow over him before returning his attention to the familiar road ahead. "I really think this is going to work." Maybe he could finally relax. His mama clearly bought that Daniel was Daniella, so all they had to do was get through the next six days.

He and Daniel talked lightly, with James answering questions about the scenery outside the windows. James had grown up with the mountains and rugged landscape around them. "Do you think we'll have a chance to explore some of the area?"

"I'll do my best. I know you're doing me a real favor here, and I want you to have a good time." He turned off the main road, and after winding through a residential area, they arrived at the ranch-style home he had grown up in. Pulling into the drive behind Holly's Toyota, they got out, and James led Daniel up the walk.

The front door opened, and Holly motioned them inside. "Mama's in the kitchen."

James hugged Holly tightly, and she held on to him. "She's got me wishing Howard and I had gone to Las Vegas and bypassed all this. But you know her…"

He nodded and held her tightly. "Mama's commandments," he said softly, Holly hugging him again before letting him go.

"At least I'm complying with the damned things. She should be thrilled." Holly hugged Daniel as well. "Let's get you both something to drink and then you can rest for a while."

James nearly bumped into Daniel when he stopped on his way into Mama's ultimate domain, following his gaze to the far kitchen wall. The damned needlepoint had hung on the wall there for as long as he could remember, and he hadn't thought of it until this moment. He'd have thought she would have taken it down, but no… Daniel slowly turned around, a little paler under the makeup. Reaching slowly into his pocketbook, he pressed a twenty-dollar bill into James's hand. This was one bet James wasn't so happy to win.

# Chapter Four

*Holy freaking hell, what have I just walked into?* Daniel thought as he stared, unable to pull his eyes away from the wall. This was like an episode of *The Twilight Zone* and Daniel had been dumped in some alternate universe. "Mama's Ten Commandments." Jesus Christ. His mind skipped a beat and Daniel found himself completely mesmerized and horrified by the sight in front of him.

"Daniella," Grace said gently as she moved through the kitchen. "Coffee or tea?" Slowly the world came back into focus and he remembered why he was here and what he was supposed to be doing, and it wasn't being shocked out of his gourd. *Get it together. It's just for a few days.*

"I'm sorry." James whispered from behind him, then moved past him to pull out a chair at the table. She couldn't be serious.

"Daniella," Grace prompted again, and he shook his head slightly to bring himself back from la-la land. "Coffee or tea? Juice?"

"Tea would be lovely," Daniel managed and turned as

James sat down, cocking his eyebrows. The sampler had obviously been done some time ago; the fabric behind the stitches had yellowed with age. James's mother very clearly had expectations, and she wasn't at all shy about them. There they were for the entire world to see.

Daniel accepted the cup of tea and tried not to stare, but it was difficult as his mind processed the visual. Some made perfect sense, in a way: "Thou shall work hard, Thou shall call thy mother, Thou shall not fight with thy brothers and sisters, Thou shall finish school…and college." The college part was in a slightly different color, so it had probably been added later. A couple actually had him smirking, but he managed to aim it in James's direction, especially "Thou shall keep it under lock and key until marriage," and "Thou shall go to church." Daniel sipped the Earl Grey, giving the sampler a final review. "Thou shall not lie to thy mother and father…" Well, that one was already out the window. "Thou shall not embarrass the family." Okay, they were well on their way down the road to hell there. The last ones bordered on frightening. "Thou shall get married, Thou shall give thy parents grandchildren." He turned away to stop looking at the thing, his gaze settling on James.

"Sorry," James mouthed once more, and Daniel shrugged. He was here, and he had to make the best of it.

Daniel finished his tea and thanked Grace, who whisked the cup away. "Maybe we should bring in our luggage and get settled?" he prompted, figuring if he and James had something to do, then they could avoid round two of Grace's upcoming interrogation, at least for now.

"James, I have you in your old room, of course, and I figured Daniella could share with Margot." She wiped the table of nonexistent spills as a groan went up from the living room. Daniel expected that this development had been discussed with James's younger sister and was not popular on that front either. Daniel glanced at James, who had paled considerably as he stared alternately at his mother and then at him.

"Please excuse me a minute," Daniel said. "James, could you tell me where the bathroom is?" His throat constricted slightly as panic welled up inside.

"Of course," James said, practically jumping to his feet and motioning Daniel to go first. "It's just down the hall here to the left." Thankfully James took the hint and followed him.

"Could you be a sweetie and bring my makeup case in from the car for me?" He was trying to think quickly because this was going downhill fast.

"Be right back." James hurried away, filled with tension. Daniel entered the bathroom and left the door cracked, running some cool water and dampening a cloth to cool the back of his neck, trying to calm his racing heart and hopefully clear his head so he could think.

"Honey," James said from outside and then stepped in, closing the door.

"What are we going to do? I can't share a room with your sister. Yes, I can be convincing as Daniella, but I can't stay in makeup constantly for six days, and I have to sleep, and…" He took a deep breath.

"I know. Let me think a minute." James put both hands on the worn Formica countertop, staring into the huge mirror. Daniel opened the case, using the opportunity to check his makeup.

"I…" James sighed, and Daniel hated that his family made him feel this way.

"Somehow it will be all right," Daniel soothed, even as he tried to figure out how the hell it could be possible. His skin would look like he was allergic to everything after a while.

"We'll go to a hotel. That's the only solution. It will put some distance between us and my family and give us some privacy. Mom will probably be upset and get worked up, but there's nothing we can do about it." Daniel liked the determination in James's intense eyes and shifted closer, running a hand up and down James's strong back and up to his shoulders, which rippled under his shirt. Wow, he wanted to feel closer and see if the rest of him was as hard and hot.

Daniel pulled his hand away. This was a job—a working arrangement, nothing more—and he needed to keep his thoughts and wandering hands where they were supposed to be.

"We'd better get back out there or your mother is going to check to see if we aren't breaking her 'lock and key' commandment." Daniel couldn't resist, and James groaned, a deep, resonant sound that rumbled off the light blue tiled walls.

Daniel closed his makeup case and opened the door, stepping out and following James down the hall and back to the kitchen.

James cleared his throat and seemed to get ready for battle. "Mom, Daniella and I have been seeing each other for a little while now. Do you really think that we—" His voice trailed off as Grace turned around. Daniel expected her eyes to shoot fire and smoke to come from her ears at any second.

"Under my roof…" She emphasized each word, and Daniel knew the exact speech that was coming. He'd seen it in multiple movies. Daniel wondered at the way James seemed to pull away a little, like he was pondering what she was going to say next. The guy was a cop, he stared down criminals on a regular basis, and yet his diminutive mother had him practically cowering in the corner. Maybe it was time for a Lala moment.

"Of course, James." Daniel patted his hand with a huge smile that he flashed in Grace's direction. "This is your mother's house, and she needs to feel comfortable with what's happening in her home. I'm sure that she and your father have talked things over and have given every consideration to the fact that I'm a guest here and they only want me to be at ease." He flashed the brightest, most innocent smile possible at Grace before standing up. "You're the only person I know here, but if she feels it's important that I stay with your sister, whom I've just met, then I will be okay with that." Grace's stance and expression had already softened…a little. "It's been a long trip, and I'd like the chance to freshen up and maybe relax for a little while and get off my feet."

"But we can just go to a hotel, then, and…" James sputtered softly, most likely confused. Daniel watched Grace yank open the refrigerator door with more force than was necessary.

"I won't hear of it. Your mom and dad have been so generous and gracious to invite us to stay here with them. It would be rude of us to decline. This is your sister's wedding, and I don't want to do anything that will add to an already stressful situation." He turned toward the hallway. "Can you show me which room I'll be using and then we can bring in my bags?"

"Oh, for god's sake, Grace," Phillip called from the living room. "James has a life of his own back in Chicago, and if you think that he's a perfect little angel and doesn't go out and have a good time, then you're fooling yourself." He shook his head from his chair in front of the television where he was watching baseball.

"Phillip…" she snapped.

"Get over it, Grace. We're in the next room. What do you think they're going to do?" He rolled his eyes, and Daniel tilted his head toward the hall.

"Strike while the iron is hot and show me which room is ours," he whispered, and James drew his lips upward and strode back down the hall, pushing open the bedroom door right across from the bathroom.

"I'll be right back with our stuff." James raced away, and Daniel grinned as he watched that damned tight backside haul ass.

"That was brilliant." James beamed softly as soon as he set the bags down on the floor.

Daniel had taken the time they were alone to slip off his shoes and scout out the room. It seemed to have been recently painted an off-white, and while the bed was probably the one James had used growing up, the rest of the room was bright and cheerful. So not the childhood room he'd envisioned for James. "Thanks." Daniel sat on the side of the bed, wiggling his toes to get the blood flowing to them again.

James pulled open the closet and tossed his suitcase onto the side of the bed, popping it open before hanging up some of the most wrinkled clothes in the history of mankind. "What are you doing?" Daniel stopped him. "Those poor shirts look like they want to hide away in shame—either that or just do themselves in and have it over with." He snapped the shirts and smoothed out some of the wrinkles before opening one of his suitcases, pulling out his portable steamer.

"Thanks. I was going to ask Mom to iron them for me," James told him, and Daniel shook his head. "What?"

Daniel shrugged. It wasn't his place to spout his opinion about everything James did. "Nothing." Daniel helped James hang up his clothes and then unpacked as well.

"How much do you need?" James asked as Daniel proceeded to pretty much fill the small closet.

"There's day wear, evening wear, sportswear. I need things to sleep in as well as a robe and scarves so I can hide some of my features. I had no idea what sort of activities there were going to be, so I had to pack for most every occasion." Daniel put his hands on his hips, giving James that glare like he was being ridiculous and smiling when he simply nodded. "Guys have it easy." He pointed to the closet, and James put his hands in the air.

"I will never complain about my sisters or mother taking too long to get ready again. I promise." James closed his mostly empty suitcase and slid it under the far side of the bed. "How much longer will you be?" James asked. "I thought that after all that drama, you and I could get out of here and drive up to Glacier National Park. We'll travel through one of the mountain passes. The views are amazing, and it will give us a chance to have some time away."

From the wedding schedule ahead, it seemed like this could be their only chance. "Let me get my jacket and some sensible shoes and we can go."

"Thank you for an amazing afternoon," Daniel said when he and James were once again behind the closed and locked door of their bedroom for the night. Finally, Daniel felt he could relax a little, releasing the tension from his shoulders and back.

"I sometimes forget how breathtaking it is up there," James said as he sat down on the far side of the bed, tugging off his shirt. "Oh, I forgot," he said, and handed Daniel a small bag.

"What's this?" He opened the white paper bag, pulling out something wrapped in tissue paper.

"I wanted you to have a memento to remember our day together." He leaned across the bed, showing off acres of muscle and honey-gold skin that Daniel ached to touch. "I stood in the gift shop, looked all over, and realized I know so little about you." He drew nearer, and Daniel was reminded that everything was still tucked. He turned away and, as discreetly as he could, released the family jewels before things got painful, because certain parts of him were reacting to that smile with gusto. "Most everything I saw was for women, and they had these high heel and purse Christmas ornaments, but I didn't want to get you something like that." James swallowed, and Daniel found himself leaning closer, being pulled toward him simply by the intensity in his eyes.

"Why not?"

"Because you're more than the shoes, purses, and dresses." He motioned to the package, and Daniel slowly opened it to reveal a small, detailed, leaded glass light catcher with a mountain scene. "This is a rendition of a view from the Going-to-the-Sun Road, and the color they used for the sky reminded me of your eyes, with the highlights of purple that run through." James looked deeply into Daniel's eyes as though he were trying to verify that he was correct. Daniel held the piece up to the light, sending sparkles onto the wall.

"It's beautiful," he whispered.

James leaned a little closer. "I'm glad you like it," he breathed. Warmth flooded through Daniel. Was James going to kiss him? Daniel licked his lips and felt his breath hitch in anticipation, the sounds from the rest of the house receding until only the rush of blood through his ears remained. James slowly stood, Daniel's gaze following him around the bed as he drew closer, his shoulders hunching slightly, flat belly flexing as he moved. Excitement built as the air in the room filled with tension and anticipation. "Do you want to use the bathroom first or should I?"

Jesus, that was a buildup to nowhere, and not at all what Daniel had been expecting. "Umm, you go ahead." Daniel waited until James left the room and fell back on the bed. What an idiot. James was being nice, and he let his attraction for the guy run away with him. Daniel needed to get his head on straight and stop this nonsense. He pushed himself upright and removed his wig, tying a scarf around his head to cover up his hair. Then he stripped off his clothes, sighing as the layers came away and he was unrestricted once more.

Barefoot and covered in a robe, he was ready when James returned, and Daniel checked outside the door before zipping across to take his turn in the bathroom.

The real danger was when he returned without his makeup, so Daniel made sure there was no one nearby when he returned to the bedroom and shut the door.

A single light burned next to his side of the bed. James was already under the light covers, his cannonball shoulders and muscled arm resting on top of the covers, with a hint of powerful back also showing. Daniel hung his robe on the doorknob just as James rolled over.

"Pink pajamas." James chuckled softly. "In all my life I never expected to sleep with someone in pink pajamas."

Daniel climbed onto the bed and smacked James on the shoulder. "What did you expect me to wear to bed with your mom and dad in the next room?" He met James's gaze and lifted the covers, because what the hell? James had on a pair of baby blue boxer shorts, nothing else, and Daniel got a tantalizing look at the rest of him…and he liked…definitely.

"Hey…" James protested, but held the covers in invitation. Daniel shrugged and got into bed. What the hell else was he going to do, sleep on the damn floor? He didn't think so, and making James sleep on the floor just seemed mean. He pulled the covers up to his chin, and James rolled over once again. Daniel turned out the light and stared up at the ceiling.

"You know this has to be the craziest thing I have ever done in my life," Daniel whispered, unable to relax even though he was tired.

"Somehow I doubt that," James retorted softly. Daniel glared at his back.

"Ass."

"You're going to have to do better than that," James quipped, still facing the other way.

Daniel poked his shoulder. "Do you really want to go there? I am a drag queen, and I've spent more time in the reading room than you can imagine." He scooted up, resting against the headboard, crossing his arms over his chest. James turned over, propping his head on his hand. "Think before you answer."

James laughed again, his face free of the tension it seemed to carry so much of the time. "You need to do that more often."

"What?" James whispered.

"Smile. You're so serious. And you have a great laugh, deep and rich. It suits you. Too bad it seems to be missing a lot of the time." Daniel slid back under the covers. "You knew how to laugh when we were back in Chicago."

James sighed. "I know. There's very little to laugh about here." The humor seemed to leach out of the room in seconds. "I'm continuously tense and on edge. Will I say the wrong thing? Is Mama going to be disappointed? It's like I'm walking on eggshells, and I always seem to be the only one. Give me a good old-fashioned firefight any day of the week. Those I can handle. I just don't seem to have been able to figure out how to manage the crap with my family."

"You know, I could sing for you. Maybe that would cheer you up." Daniel watched as light from the cracks in the curtains played across the walls. "When I was just a little gayboy," he sang, and James chuckled once again.

"Oh no. Now I'm going to have naughty Doris Day ringing in my head all night long." Still, his voice held amusement. "Go to sleep. We have a busy day tomorrow, and god knows what sort of drama we're going to get dragged into."

"Pun intended," Daniel said because he couldn't help it. James snorted softly and shifted closer, sliding an arm around him.

"You make me smile, and anyone who can do that while I'm here with my family is pretty damned special." James leaned close, kissing Daniel on the cheek before rolling over once more. It seemed like seconds before James was asleep, while Daniel lay awake for what seemed like hours.

## Chapter Five

James woke alone and with a headache. He groaned and slowly got out of bed, wishing he could sleep for the rest of the damned day, but he was sure there were things he had to do, and this pain wasn't going away on its own. James popped a couple of ibuprofen and sat still, willing the pressure to abate.

He pulled on a pair of light sweatpants and opened the bedroom door, hearing voices drifting down the hall from the kitchen. "That was awesome yesterday," Margot was saying. "Maybe I'll have a chance to have a little fun before I'm old and gray."

"Don't count on it," James said, shuffling into the room where Daniel and Margot were talking. Daniel was already dressed and looked his usual million bucks in a pair of light slacks and a simple blouse. As usual, Daniel had style, and it showed through as Daniella.

"Are you okay?" Daniel patted his arm. "You look like hell."

"I feel like it too." He got a mug for coffee and felt more

than saw Daniel's gaze following him. He liked that Daniel noticed him.

"You're really into my brother?" Margot asked in a stage whisper.

"Your brother is pretty hot," Daniel stage-whispered back as though he was sharing a secret.

Margot snickered. "Please, he's my brother. I don't notice if he's hot or not."

"I'm right here," James growled, pouring a mug of coffee and sitting down at the table next to Daniel, kissing his made-up cheek. "Good morning." He did his best to smile as he waited for the pills and caffeine to do their magic. "What are we doing today?" James asked. "I'm sure Holly gave you a printed schedule with everyplace you were supposed to be." He was only thankful that she hadn't made one up for him.

"Mother," Holly bellowed from the front door. Daniel jumped and squeaked a little as she barreled into the room, her eyes blazing, slamming a box down on the table. James closed his eyes and put his hands over his ears.

"She's at the store," Margot answered. "What crawled up your butt?"

"Look." Holly half collapsed into the chair. "These are the programs for the service, and everything is wrong. I picked out the hymns, and they're all different. Howard's parents' names are spelled wrong, and..." She lowered her head to the table. "The florist called this morning. Their shipment of white roses went bad somehow. They're trying to get some more, but they wanted to know if they could use white carnations instead." Holly rubbed her eyes. "This isn't a prom from the eighties or a funeral. It's my wedding, and I want roses."

"Of course you do," Daniel said, jumping up and coming around to Holly. "What did you tell the florist?"

"To get roses," Holly said, the tears starting now that her anger was spent.

"Give James the number of the florist and a copy of the order for the wedding. He can use that policeman voice of his to put the fear of god in them and you'll get your roses." Daniel met his gaze, and James nodded. "Thanks, sweetheart," Daniel added with a smile, and James's mind skipped a thread for just a second. Damn, he loved that smile.

"I'm back," his mother said as she came into the kitchen through the garage. "What's wrong?" she asked, and Holly pushed the box across the table. Mom opened the box. "These look fine to me."

"Mom! You did this?" She whirled on their mom in a second.

"These are great hymns, and what you had didn't seem like you, so I thought this would be better." She set her jaw, and James braced for a fight.

"How could you? That isn't what I wanted," Holly said softly, the tears running down her cheeks.

"I thought you'd made a mistake and would want the hymns you grew up with." His mother pursed her lips as though she were going to argue, then sighed dramatically. "You do what you like. It's your wedding." James had heard that guilt-inducing tone many times before. Their mother always thought she knew what was best.

"It's okay, we can fix it," Daniel said gently, lightly tapping his long nails on the table. James was so grateful for Daniel's calmness in the wake of the crisis. "Do you have your original program?" Holly nodded. "Then come on. Let's you and

I fix everything up. There has to be a printer nearby." Daniel was already on his phone, looking up what was in the area and making calls. James returned to the bedroom to dress, and by the time he came back out, Daniel was sending the files to the printer. "They'll email a proof in an hour, and we can have the updated programs by tomorrow." Daniel smiled.

Holly wiped her eyes. "Oh god, thank you." She hugged Daniel, who gently patted her back. "You saved this."

Daniel glanced at him over Holly's shoulder, smiling slightly. "I'm glad I can help."

"Tomorrow when we meet with the minister, we can make sure that he knows exactly what you want for the service. That way there won't be any mix-ups," James offered.

"Just relax. Little issues will come up, but you have plenty of people to support you," Daniel comforted her, and glanced around the room. "Where's Howard?"

"Today is his last day of work before the wedding," Holly said, grabbing a napkin from the holder in the center of the table to dab her eyes.

Mom had said nothing more through this entire exchange and clearly wasn't happy. "Is anyone hungry?" She didn't wait for an answer before getting started with eggs, sausage, and a platter of bacon. Dad joined the rest of them, and once the food was on the table, everyone sat.

The lunch yesterday was a veritable party compared to the strained conversation around the table now. Holly glared at their mom, who pretended not to notice. Dad just ate and said nothing. Margot grabbed her plate and left the table, closing her door more loudly than was necessary. Poor Daniel looked like he had no idea what was going on. "Is this normal?"

James shrugged. There was no normal when it came to

his family…and especially his mother. "When we're done, I'm going to call the florist."

"What's wrong with the flowers?" Mom asked a little snappily.

"You didn't change those, did you?" Holly retorted and pushed her plate away after eating just a few bites.

"It's fine, Mom. Just a mix-up in an order. I'm going to take care of it. Holly has enough to do." James hoped to calm the waters. Daniel patted his hand, fingers resting on his skin for longer than was necessary. James turned his hand, sliding his fingers into Daniel's. It was strange to him. Daniel was dressed as a beautiful woman, and yet James found it hard to see anyone but Daniel. The clothes didn't matter, and neither did the makeup. The features were Daniel's, and that was what mattered.

James slowly pulled his hand away, not wanting to draw attention to the movement. He needed to keep his head on straight and remember that Daniella was a character that Daniel was playing, and that they both had roles to play. He was here for Holly's wedding, and Daniel was someone he had an arrangement with to be his "girlfriend" for the duration of the trip. Anything more would be a bad idea.

He got up from the table, taking a deep breath, needing to handle the florist issues for Holly and taking the opportunity to put a little distance between him and Daniel for a few minutes. It was so damned easy to get carried away, and it needed to stop.

"What can we expect at this shower?" Daniel asked in his normal voice once they were within the safety of their bedroom, just the two of them. He spoke softly and sat on the edge of the bed, pulling on nylon socks.

"I'm expecting it to be casual—some games, talking, and plenty of wine," James explained. "Mom apparently wasn't thrilled about the alcohol, but Holly's friends planned the party, and thankfully Mom was polite enough to keep quiet for once."

"Are your parents going to be there?" Daniel asked, lying back on the bed, probably enjoying a few minutes of quiet. James knew he was, and sat next to him, lying back as well.

"I don't think so. This is supposed to be for Holly and Howard's friends. There's going to be enough to keep Mom and Dad busy for the next few days." He sighed. "Shit..." he swore under his breath. "I don't have a present to bring." He had the wedding present covered, but he had completely forgotten about a gift for the shower.

"Don't worry about it. Holly and Howard probably aren't expecting anything. They're happy that you came to the wedding. Showers aren't usually about presents as much as they're about a chance to have fun with friends before all the formal wedding activities drive everyone nuts."

James agreed and slowly rolled onto his side, Daniel meeting his gaze with those intense eyes that James could so easily get lost in if he allowed himself to. "What's your family like? You've met mine and seen the levels of craziness."

"There isn't much to tell. I was a late-in-life baby. Mom and Dad had given up on having children. Mom was apparently told that she wasn't able to have children, and then in her forties, she thought she was going through the change of life...instead—surprise!" He smiled, showing perfect white teeth, small lines reaching to bright eyes. James basked in the warmth of that gaze, forgetting about his earlier reservations, at least for now.

"That must have been a shock," James whispered.

"To say the least. Mom was thrilled, and I can honestly say that no child was loved more. I sang, danced, and Fosse'd—" he made jazz hands above them "—my way into their hearts. Mom took me to acting and dance classes, vocal lessons, you name it. She came to every school performance or recital, sitting in the front row."

"Did they know about you being gay and the drag?" He was curious how Daniel's family took it. He could already imagine the uproar in his own family, the yelling, the ridiculousness, and the threats that would follow because he didn't measure up to what his mother thought he should be.

"They knew I was gay." Slowly Daniel turned toward him. "Lala has always been part of my life, but I didn't acknowledge that part of me until five years ago. Before that, I modeled as a way to try to break into the theater. As a guy, I don't think I was special enough. I didn't have something that really set me apart." He shrugged, and James felt himself being pulled closer, like some invisible cord tugging him.

"I think they were crazy," James whispered, holding Daniel's gaze until he blinked and turned away. He instantly missed being the subject of such intensity. "I believe you said your mom has passed?"

Daniel hesitated. "Mom contracted cancer while I was in college. She fought it with everything she had, but it was too much. Dad nursed her though the entire ordeal and followed her a year later." Daniel stared at the ceiling, and James slid his hand along the bedding until their fingers met. "I don't think he could bear to be without her."

"So, your grandmother, the one you care for..." he prompted.

"You remembered." Daniel forced a smile. "She's the only family I have left, and she isn't able to care for herself and needs medical attention. The social worker wanted to put her in one of those homes most likely to appear on the national news, so I pay what her benefits won't for her to be in a place where I can see her regularly and where she gets treated better." Daniel's eyes darkened. "Yes, she knows about the drag, and Lala has taken her show to the care facility more than once."

"What about Candy and Creamy...all the other people in the show?"

"They're my drag family; that's very different. We look after one another and have each other's backs, but as much as we use the word *family*, in the end it's really a job and we all have to work together. Sometimes there are especially close relationships, just like with anything else. Creamy Sugar is my drag daughter, I helped her learn the ropes and helped hone her raw talent into the performer she is today, just like my drag mother, Tulane Highway, did for me." James couldn't help chuckling at the name. "She's in New York now and has been doing amazing things." The pride in Daniel's voice was unmistakable, and he lightly squeezed James's fingers.

James rolled onto his side, propping his hand under his head. "I have to ask, and it will probably sound stupid." He shrugged. "But why drag? You're really talented and have a real gift. Your voice is amazing, and I'm sure you could do whatever you wanted."

Daniel's expression hardened. "I am doing what I want." He sat up, turning toward him, tugging his hand away. "This is part of who I am." His jaw set and his eyes grew stony. "I don't play at my craft. I work hard, and I'm damned good." Daniel stood and went to the closet, moving clothes aside, the hangers scraping on the rod. "Look, I get it. You're a cop. Your work is gritty and you live a hard life that could get you injured or killed every time you make a mistake. You have to be tough." He whirled around like a damned ballerina.

"Lower your voice," James interjected.

"Yeah…" he whispered. "You may not see me the same way you do the guys you work with, or the men you fuck, but I'm true to myself and I don't play a bunch of games. I'm not the one who hired a drag queen to play my girlfriend at my sister's wedding. I know the person that I am on the inside, and believe it or not, I like myself." He turned away and began tossing clothes onto the bed. "I need to get ready for this party, and so do you. I suggest you use the bathroom to clean up and dress, because I need some time to let this urge to rip your nuts off pass. Otherwise it's going to be one hell of a party tonight, and me having a screaming hissy fit will end up as the damned entertainment."

"I didn't mean…" he began and clamped his mouth shut at the way Daniel bared his teeth.

"You did. You're a dragophobe. What you really meant was that I'm talented, so why don't I go out and get a real job?" He heaved for breath, eyes blazing with fire, and James alternated between fear and all-out desire. Damn, that energy was smoking hot. Daniel's lips, slightly pursed, both drew and pushed his away. James got his clothes for the evening and found himself on the other side of the bedroom door with it closed and locked behind him.

Margot peered out of her room, rolled her eyes. "What did you do?"

James shrugged, and Margot disappeared back into her room. He hurried into the bathroom, shutting the door and setting his clothes on the counter.

"Are you ready?" James asked from outside the bedroom door a while later. He waited and hoped he wasn't going to have to go to the party alone. The door clicked open, and Daniel emerged. James still wasn't sure whether his balls were safe.

"Yes."

"Okay. I'll meet you at the car."

The glare he received would freeze water on the equator. Those delicate hands went to lush hips as Daniel glared at him. He paused and rethought his plan. James had figured he should keep his distance, but it seemed that was the wrong course of action. Instead, he offered his elbow, and he smiled and took it. "You're learning," Daniel whispered. "Let's go."

The shower was being held at the home of Kiersten, Holly's matron of honor, and the party had already started by the time they arrived ten minutes later. The street near the house was parked up, so James found a spot on the next block, and they walked in the breezy evening air.

"Tell me about these people," Daniel said.

"Kiersten, the hostess, has been Holly's best friend since middle school. Her husband, Kyle, is a nice guy. I don't know him very well, though. I really have no idea who is going to be here. I hope it's just a chance for everyone to get to know each other, and we can mingle and have a few drinks, then leave before it gets too late." He slowed and then came to a stop. "This is Missoula, not Chicago. I'm not really expecting this to be a blowout or anything. Some food, wine, and a lot of standing around and talking. That sort of thing."

They approached the house with all the lights on. The front door opened, and a pounding musical beat poured out into the night. James turned to Daniel, who smirked back at him. "No blowout?" Daniel quipped. Obviously he had no clue whatsoever. James tensed as they approached the house. "This should be a lot of fun." Daniel's hips already swayed to the beat. "Just go with whatever is happening. Have some fun. This is supposed to be a party, a chance for your sister and her fiancé to have some fun and let loose a little before the wedding." Daniel was right, and James nodded, heading toward the door, glad he had Daniel and his bright energy to go with him.

# Chapter Six

This was unlike any couples' wedding shower Daniel had ever imagined. These people were wild. Oh, there was no breaking of stuff, but the wine and cocktails flowed freely, the furniture in the large family room had been rearranged to accommodate the small band, and people were dancing… well, at least what seemed to pass for dancing. It looked more like a lot of flailing chickens in their death throes…at least as far as the guys were concerned. Maybe eye protection should have been provided at the door?

Everyone seemed to be having fun, though. Daniel took pity on James and went to get a few drinks, returning to where James still stood near the set of large patio doors, as rigidly as if he were standing guard in full uniform on a presidential schmooze tour. "Loosen up," he said lightly, pressing a martini into James's hand. "I take it you aren't much for this sort of thing."

"Not really." James seemed ready to bolt at any second.

"Some sort of party trauma?" At least that got him a smile, as well as a small nod. "What the hell happened? Knife fight, gun battle, two queens fighting for the last chicken leg? Believe me, if it was that, I can understand the trauma. That's something I wish I could unsee." He cocked his eyebrow, and James finally broke a smile and let go some of his "impending doom" tension.

"I'm always nervous around large groups of people who are drinking. Things can get out of hand and…" He sipped from the glass. "I know I'm being dumb. Do you want to finish these and dance?" James downed the drink, and Daniel handed his glass to James, who set it aside.

James's hand was warm, and they moved to the dance area just as the music died away. A woman stepped up to the mic. "That's Kiersten," James whispered by way of introduction. Daniel had learned so many names and made enough small talk that remembering them was impossible.

"I want to thank all of you for coming, and the Mountain Boys for playing for us tonight." Everyone applauded. "They're going to pack up, and then we're going to play some games, so get your lips warmed up, couples. It's going to be a fun night." A murmur went through the group, and Daniel met James's gaze, hoping for some sort of explanation, but his shrug said he didn't have a clue either.

"I'm going to use the ladies' room. I'll be right back," Daniel said, figuring now was a good time to check and refresh makeup. The group moved through the house, some to the bar and others outside to the smoking area.

"Hey, gorgeous." A tall man smiled, and Daniel continued on until a light tap on the shoulder caught his attention. "I mean you, sweetheart." Daniel whirled on his toes. This man was stunning, with shiny black hair, the perfect scruff beard, intense, almost black eyes, high cheekbones, and a golden tan. "Kiersten is about to start one of her patented couples' games." He cocked his eyebrow. "Do you want to be my partner? We could burn up the house." He leaned a little closer, his cologne cloying at Daniel's nose. Did this guy bathe in the shit? "I'm Weston, Howard's best man, and maybe you could be the best woman." His gaze grew more intense.

Daniel leaned closer, lips parting slightly. "That has to win cheesiest line of the year. Does that really work for you? Because if that's the best you've got, it's no wonder you're at a party trying—in vain, I might add—to pick up women outside the bathroom." Weston at least had the courtesy to blush. "I'm with someone. Excuse me." Daniel would have gone into the bathroom, but it was occupied.

"So am I," Weston countered.

"Then I feel sorry for her. She deserves to be treated better than this." Daniel caught James's gaze from across the room, and he made his way over. "James, do you know Weston?" Thankfully, James slid his arm around Daniel's waist and met Weston's gaze with a glare.

"Excuse me," Weston said hurriedly before heading across the room.

"What was that about?" James asked, instantly filling with tension. "Did he give you a hard time?"

Daniel turned away and tried to keep from laughing. "He hit on me. The guy is a scummy lech, and I wouldn't go anywhere near him without a tetanus shot and maybe a course of antibiotics, but he actually tried to pick me up with some awful line."

James glared cross the room as Weston continued making his retreat. "Bastard."

Daniel wasn't sure if he should be flattered or not. "Hey, think a minute. He'd have been in for one hell of a surprise."

"Everyone, let's gather around," Kiersten called as the bathroom door opened.

"I'll be right out." Daniel hurried inside to take his turn, using the toilet, which was no fast process, and then checking his makeup in the mirror. After reapplying lipstick and making sure everything was in place, he washed up, left the bathroom and stepped over to James, who had taken a place toward the back of the room. He was just in time to hear the rules.

"Are all the couples here?"

"James, you and Daniella need to play," Holly said, with everyone turning toward them. "No chickening out."

"Come on," Daniel said, leading him up to join the other couples.

"There are two stacks of cards. The first one is a trivia question, and the second stack is what you have to do if you can't answer the question." Man, that woman looked evil, and Daniel wondered just what she'd come up with. "We'll start with…" She glanced around the room, pointing at James. "You." Her manicured claws flashed in James's direction. "You can answer as a team, but if you're wrong, you have to pick from the stack of shame." Someone brought a pair of chairs, and they sat down, joining the inner circle. The single friends apparently got to watch.

"Okay," Daniel said, genteelly lifting the first card.

"Read the question and answer if you can," Kiersten encouraged.

Daniel cleared his throat. "What author created such characters as Little Nell and Estella Havisham?" he read and turned to James, who paled slightly, his eyes growing wide.

"I have no idea," he said quietly.

Daniel knew this was all about fun and a little theater, so he reached toward the stack of shame and then pulled his hand away. "Charles Dickens." He set down the card and turned to the next couple.

"Oh, I forgot to explain," Kiersten interjected. "Once you get a question wrong and pay the price, you're out and another couple will take your place. The last couple standing at the end of the night wins the wedding night prize package." She motioned to the other team, who had no idea who the German leader during World War I was, and they had to kiss, which was lame.

"Is that all?" James asked, and they watched until the next couple missed their question and a woman had to paint her husband's lips with her lipstick. The next missed answer resulted in the couple French kissing. Thankfully, they played it up, to plenty of hoots and hollers.

That round, three couples were out, and others took their place before Daniella picked another card. "What movie featured Benedict Cumberbatch playing the codebreaker who helped usher in the computer?"

"Do you want to answer or just get this over with?" Daniel whispered.

"I wanna win," James growled softly, and Daniel shivered.

"No dirty talk over there," Kiersten said. "Save that for the walk of shame."

"*The Imitation Game*," James answered, and the turn shifted from couple to couple until there were only two left. He and James, and Weston and his date.

"We'll kick that ass's ass," Daniel told James and then picked the question. "What is the highest mountain in Europe?" He turned to James. "No idea. You?"

James shrugged. "Mont Blanc?" James guessed for both of them.

"Mount Elbrus," Kiersten said with too much delight. "Pick your card of shame." Daniel lifted the card, read it, and showed it to James before standing and kicking the now empty chair out of the way. Hoots grew behind him, but he locked gazes with James and heard very little else. Sauntering closer, slowly rocking his hips, Daniel put on one hell of a show. He straddled James's legs, lowering himself to his lap and wrapping his arms around his neck, slowly gliding his hips back and forth.

"Good god," he heard from behind him, but then the rest of the people at the party seemed far away. James's eyes practically glowed, and Daniel continued slowly gyrating before taking James's lips in a kiss that stole his breath away. James wrapped his arms around him, hands pressing to his back, and he kissed Daniel hard with heat and passion that left his head spinning.

Applause and catcalls pulled him back and he remembered where he was. James stiffened, not that parts of him weren't already standing at attention. Daniel pulled back, still gazing into James's blue eyes, the shade of the deepest ocean.

"Now, that was a winner if I ever saw one," Kiersten said.

"Ladies, that's how you get a man's attention…or standing at attention. Either one works." Daniel climbed off James's lap and demurely sat back down as the gathering roared with laughter. The other team didn't answer their question either, and since he and James had been in the game from the be-ginning, they were declared the winners.

James accepted the basket, and his eyes widened in sur-prise at the contents. "We're going to have to hide this from my mother." He picked up a box of condoms and placed them back in the basket, grinning. Damn, he looked amaz-ing when he smiled.

"I promise I won't tell," Holly quipped as another round of laughter went through the group. Daniel left James in charge of the basket and their loot, some of which was chocolate and a bottle of sparkling wine. The rest, well, yeah, they needed to hide all that from Grace.

"I wonder how many of your mother's commandments we broke tonight?" Daniel couldn't help whispering to James, who turned red and then rolled his eyes. "You really need to lighten up a bit and have some fun. Come on, I want a drink." He tugged James to his feet, waiting while he set the basket aside before weaving through people to the bar.

James got Daniel a martini and ordered a Coke for him-self. The air inside was stuffy, so they made their way outside onto the back patio, fairy lights illuminating the trees. The overlapping voices from the party dulled when they closed the door. "I wasn't exactly expecting that," James said be-fore gulping his drink.

"You wanted a show and you got one." He glanced around, making sure no one was within earshot. "Everyone thinks you have a wild girlfriend, and the guys all wish they were you. Isn't that what you wanted?"

James set his soda on the table and plucked the glass from Daniel's hand, setting it aside before leading him down the stairs and off the deck.

Out in the yard, the light fell away and darkness closed around them. "Look up. I used to come outside on nights like this when I was a kid. In the city you can't really see anything, but out here, all the stars are visible." He held Daniel's hand as they stood still, glancing upward, the evening mountain breeze as clean and fresh as any air Daniel could ever remember.

"I lived in the city all my life," Daniel whispered as the sky seemed to draw closer, the ebb and flow of the stars undulating around him as scale and points of reference faded into the background. It was almost like the two of them were floating through a sea of light on some journey that could take them to the ends of the universe. Daniel was tempted to try to reach up and touch them, but as soon as he did the illusion faded and the stars grew distant once again.

"And I grew up out here," James said quietly. "But I couldn't wait to get away."

"I suppose that living the life you want is worth not being able to see a few stars," Daniel whispered. "Though it would be nice to have both."

"As much as I may want it, I can't." James shrugged. "There are plenty of things that I can't have. You get used to it." He sighed and drew out his breath. "We should get back."

"There's no rush." Daniel slid a little closer. "The party is still going on, and I doubt anyone is going to miss us in the next ten minutes."

"James," Holly called from the balcony, as if to prove him wrong.

"I need to see what she wants. I'll be right back."

"I'll be here," Daniel said. He wasn't interested in returning right away and turned his attention back to the stars.

After a few minutes, footsteps approached, and Daniel smiled. "What did Holly want?"

There was no immediate answer. "Was that little show for my benefit?" Weston asked. "I saw you looking at me, watching me." He drew close enough that Daniel could feel the heat wash over him, but unlike when James stood close to him, all Weston did was make him sweaty. "I must say that was quite the performance. One I'm willing to bet you've done before." His alcohol-soaked breath ghosted over Daniel's neck, and he shuddered with revulsion.

"I don't know what's going on in that little pea brain of yours, but I'm starting to wonder if there's room out here for the three of us." He wished James would return. Daniel could take care of himself, but he didn't want to make a scene at Holly and Howard's party.

"Three?" Weston whispered.

"You, me, and your ego," he retorted. "Few things are as unattractive and ugly as a man who can't seem to see beyond the end of his dick. I suggest you stop thinking with yours and leave me alone." Daniel kept his voice light, because when he got angry his tone lowered, and he didn't want to give himself away. Daniel took a few steps, putting distance between them.

"I'm only an admirer. You have spunk and energy. I like that, and I'm used to getting what I want."

Who the hell was this guy and where in the fuck did he come up with these bad movie lines? Daniel shook his head slowly.

"Then get used to disappointment, because it just showed up," he said firmly. "Now, turn around and go back into the house. I'm saying no for the last time."

"So, the next time I ask, the answer will be yes?" Weston pressed. *Good god!* Daniel had dealt with aggressive patrons at the theater, and there was always the drunk guy who couldn't seem to take no for an answer, but this guy was delusional and really needed a well-placed high heel, probably in the center of his forehead.

Daniel whirled around. "The next time, it will be a strategically placed knee, and then you won't want to ask anyone for anything other than an ice pack to soothe your aching little balls. Do I make myself clear? I am perfectly capable of seeing to it that your family line ends with you." He started back toward the deck. Daniel had had more than enough of this conversation. Thankfully Weston didn't seem to be following, and hopefully he had gotten the message this time.

"Who was out there with you?" James asked as he stepped out onto the deck.

"No one," Daniel said.

"The two of you looked a little cozy."

Daniel glared at James for a split second before backing away. "Are you jealous?" He couldn't resist, and the way James shook his head rather violently told Daniel more than mere words. "You were." He wasn't quite sure what to make of that idea. The lines between them seemed to be blurring, but Daniel wasn't sure if it was just his imagination or if it was real. Not that it mattered. Daniel reminded himself that he was here to help James out and that was it. This was a business arrangement, and part of Daniel's job was to make James look good and to be convincing as his date for the wedding festivities. Nothing more.

It didn't matter that when he'd kissed James, he nearly lost himself in his firm soft lips, and when James had enclosed him in his arms, Daniel was damned near transported to another place and time, far away from the room filled with people. He'd simply let himself get carried away, and it was time to come back down to earth and fucking reality. It had been way too long since Daniel had had someone to spend time with outside of work, if he was getting his head all twisted around with James. Daniel reran his encounter with the police a few years ago, for a quick reality check. That threw cold water on any flights of fancy that he might have had. On top of that, James was still in the damned closet as far as his family was concerned, and Daniel was not going to be anyone's dirty little secret. Been there, got the T-shirt, and it wasn't anything he intended to repeat. They had a few more days until the wedding, and then Daniel would return to his life at the theater and James could go back home to his job as a cop.

"Are you ready to go?" James asked, cutting through Daniel's thoughts. He extended his elbow, and Daniel took it, letting James lead him back inside. The notion that just thinking about their kiss made Daniel's lips tingle all over again didn't matter in the least. Now who was delusional?

# Chapter Seven

"Are you still awake?" Daniel asked from next to him.

"Yeah," he answered without rolling over. He had spent the last hour with that kiss running through his head, trying to figure out if it was real or not. The fact that his body refused to calm down, and that he was too damned excited to roll over in case Daniel became aware of it, was another issue completely. Daniel had said that it was just for show, but it certainly hadn't felt like it...in any way. He liked to think he could tell when someone was being fake, but this had him completely confused. "I can't sleep while I'm here. Never can."

"Why?" Daniel whispered into the darkness.

"Could you? I keep wondering what my mother is going to do next. It's like walking through a minefield all the time." At least he was grateful that his mother hadn't brought up marriage yet during this visit. Usually it was first and foremost on her mind, like she was going to push and prod him down the aisle in order to complete commandment number nine.

Daniel rolled over. "I'm the last person on earth to tell anyone how to live their life, and I'm not going to do that to you. I have made my own way for years. Hell, my job and the way I dress and act are a big huge fuck-you to anything that most people consider 'normal.'" He made air quotes above them, his pink sleeves blazing the way. "But I can tell you that there is something...liberating...about living the life you want and simply telling everyone else to go screw themselves if they don't like it."

James swallowed hard. "I know you're right. That's the shitty thing. If I had just been honest with them years ago, I wouldn't have to put myself...or you...through all this." But now he was stuck. "I have to make a clean break, but I can't do that days before my sister's wedding." What a mess he'd made of everything.

Daniel took his hand. "I'm not going to leave you hanging in the wind. I promised you I would be your date and see you through this wedding, and I will." Daniel squeezed his fingers, and James tried to let go of some of the tension. "Try to get some sleep. We have plenty to do tomorrow, and your sister is going to need your help."

"Why do you think that?" James asked.

"Her wedding is just days away and she's going to be stressed to the gills. We need to be there to help and support her. Especially since we have no idea when your mother is going to play her version of *Mama Knows Best* next." Daniel let his words hang in the air, and in about three seconds, they smacked right into James like the proverbial backhand across the cheek.

"You don't think...?" God, what had she done?

"I don't know, but what do you think? You know your

mother better than I do." Daniel sounded so reasonable, and that was even more frightening. James hated to ponder it. Oh hell, now he had a real reason to lie awake and worry.

"I made coffee, and there are cinnamon rolls in the oven," his mother was saying as James padded barefoot through the house toward the kitchen. He needed something to perk him up after the sleepless night he'd had. How anyone could be near Daniel and not tell he was a guy just by the earthy, rich scent was beyond him, but Daniel was right. People saw what they wanted to see.

"Thanks, Mom," he muttered as he sat down next to Daniel, who looked amazing as always in a simple light blue blouse and flowing tan slacks, with a light scarf for color tied just so around his neck. "You look lovely," he whispered to Daniel and lightly bumped his shoulder.

Daniel smiled at him as he sipped his coffee, not noticing as James's mother sat in the chair across from them. Oh god, it was too early for the Spanish Inquisition, but James recognized the determination in her eyes. He knew exactly what was coming. His exhaustion flew out the window and James was instantly awake and on his toes.

"In all the rush around the wedding, we haven't gotten a real chance to talk. How long have the two of you been dating?" She sipped her coffee.

"A few months. Not too long," Daniel answered.

His mother's eyes widened. "Then why haven't I heard about you before?" Her Medusa-like glare shifted to him, and James wished he could turn to stone. That would give him an excuse to get out of this conversation.

"Because I asked him not to make a big deal over things.

I haven't had the best luck with men." Daniel leaned over the table as if to share a secret, and James let him take the lead. "Before I met James, I thought I had this loser magnet implanted in the girls, if you know what I mean. Any loser near or far would beat a path to my door. I dated this guy, Rodney. He seemed nice…until I found out that he was interested in me as a third for him and his wife." She rolled her eyes. "I am *not* that kind of girl." The emphasis in the voice couldn't be faked.

His mother nearly dropped her mug as she did a damned good impression of a largemouth bass. "No!" she gasped, and Daniel nodded slowly.

"Then there was Vincent…" Daniel rolled his eyes dramatically, leaning a little closer. "Let's just say that sticks and stones may break my bones, but whips and chains do *not* excite me." She shuddered. "I can be as kinky as the next girl, but there are definite limits." She sat back and took another sip of her coffee, and James tried not to grin as his mother nearly choked into her mug.

"Maybe I should get those cinnamon rolls," she said, practically jumping up from the table. Damn, that was one hell of a way to handle his mother. He needed to remember that. "You know…" She had her back to them as she pulled the rolls out of the oven, the entire kitchen filling with buttery, cinnamon heaven. He closed his eyes and was transported to the Saturday mornings of his childhood. "Phillip and I were quite adventurous when we were first married."

Like nails on a chalkboard, he came out of his food memory haze with a bang. He did not need to hear about his parents' sex life. "Mom…!"

"Oh, please… Your father and I were married, and we

were young. You kids like to think you invented sex. Where do you think you all came from?" She dished up the cinnamon rolls and brought plates to the table.

"You always told me the stork brought me, and I'm perfectly happy with that explanation, thank you very much." He grabbed a fork and dug into breakfast, humming with gustatory delight.

"That's the exact sound your father used to make when—" his mom continued, and James dropped his fork on the plate.

He started to choke and cough, and Daniel patted him on the back. "Breathe and take it easy, honey. It's just fine. Slow and steady breaths...in and out." He rubbed his back as James wiped the water from his eyes.

"Can we please change the subject?"

"Fine, I still want to know why you didn't tell me you were dating someone. You talk to me every few weeks and you don't think I know that you don't really tell me anything about your life?" She leveled another glare at him.

Daniel leaned close to his ear. "I guess you blew the 'call your mother' commandment." He took a dainty bite of cinnamon roll. "You have to give me this recipe. The girls I work with would die for these." He continued eating and sipping his coffee, talking cinnamon rolls and baking with James's mother while James tried to get this small part of his worldview back on kilter.

Margot breezed in, snagging a roll on a plate, and started back to her room. "Thanks, Mom. These are awesome. I'm going out with some friends in a few hours and I'll be gone most of the day."

"Did you get your dress fitted?"

"Ages ago."

"Well, don't eat too many of those or you won't be able to fit into it," his mother warned.

James cringed. "Mom, leave her alone. Margot is beautiful and she can eat what she wants. How would you like it if I said something like that to you?" He hated that sometimes his mother made comments like that about Margot. It wasn't right as far as he was concerned.

"Thanks, Jimmy," Margot said and hurried out of the room, their mother right behind her. James hoped it was to apologize for what she'd said.

James pulled into the parking lot of the bridal shop a few minutes before ten, sliding into a parking space. He turned off the engine, but the car still vibrated from Holly bouncing her legs. "I appreciate you coming with me."

Daniel turned in his seat. "This is supposed to be fun, not nerve-wracking, honey." They held hands a moment, and Holly seemed to calm somewhat. The three of them got out and approached the door of the shop as the woman inside was opening up.

"Clare, this is my brother, James, and his girlfriend, Daniella. They're here for moral support." Clare greeted both of them, ushering their small group into a mirrored area at the back of the store.

"It's a pleasure to meet both of you," Clare said. "Please have a seat, and Holly can come with me. I have the dress all ready for her to try on." She swept into the back with Holly, and James settled on the sofa.

"How much of what you told Mom this morning was the truth?" James had wanted to ask earlier, but they hadn't been alone.

"I sassed it up a bit for your mom's benefit, but basically it's true. I dated both those guys and many more. Losers beat a path to my door." Daniel colored under his makeup, and James growled.

"You deserve a lot better than that." He held his jaw rigid, wanting to take all those guys to task. Couldn't they see what a wonderful heart lay under the makeup and clothing?

James's anger completely derailed at the earsplitting howl that grated up his spine from the back room. He jumped to his feet with Daniel right next to him.

"Holly, who died?" James called.

She stepped out, tears running down her cheeks. "What happened?" Daniel asked, rushing forward. The dress hung on Holly, practically falling off her shoulders.

"It's too big."

"We ordered the size your mother told us to," Clare explained, and Holly went off again. James figured they were lucky all the glass in the front of the store didn't shatter. As it was, James wondered if his spine was ever going to be the same. Then the tears started again, this time deep, wrenching sobs.

"Can we fix it?" James asked.

Clare's complexion had paled by at least three shades. "We can make basic alterations, but our senior seamstress is on maternity leave. This was a special order and it was delayed." She looked heartbroken. Holly was devastated, her makeup running down her face. James pulled Holly into a hug to try to comfort her.

"Where's your sewing area?" Daniel asked.

"It's in back," Clare answered.

"Take me there," Daniel demanded, and Clare didn't argue, the two of them leaving the room.

"It's going to be okay," James told Holly.

Holly pulled back, her face a mess, and seemed two seconds from slugging him. "How in the fuck is this disaster ever going to be all right?" She lifted the dress. "It's at least a full size too big. What size is it?" She turned and James read the label.

"A ten," he read.

"Make that two sizes too big. What the hell did Mom think was going to happen? Why would she do this to me?" Holly alternated between explosion and tears. Not that James could blame her for either one.

"Okay," Daniel said, returning with a stool. "Holly, step up there. James, walk to that coffee shop a few doors down and get us all lattes. We're going to need plenty of fuel."

"What can I do?" Clare asked.

"Just stay out of the way." Daniel began pulling the dress this way and that, tugging it together in the back as James made for the exit. "Does your mother have a sewing machine?"

James carried the cup tray in one hand as he cautiously pulled open the door to the shop, expecting yelling, tears, or something in between, but it was quiet. Daniel stood behind Holly, still working on the dress, pinching and tucking fabric, adding pins and marking the fabric with chalk. James handed each of them their coffee and then took a seat in one of the chairs off to the side, checking email and messages on his phone.

There was nothing important, and once he slipped it into his pocket, he found himself watching Daniel as he moved around Holly, adjusting the way the dress hung. He also tugged at the square bodice of the dress, speaking softly to Holly, who lowered her gaze and shook her head.

"Don't worry. I can fix it. I've been making my own clothes for years." He flashed a bright smile in James's direction and nodded. It was truly going to be all right.

"I think that's it." Daniel stepped back and had Holly slowly turn around. "Why don't you go take off the dress. Just be really careful—there are a ton of pins." Holly carefully stepped down, and Clare went with her into the back of the store once again. Daniel drank the last of his coffee and tossed the cup in the trash before sitting down next to James.

"Thank you." He was so grateful for what Daniel was doing to basically save the wedding.

"Your mother really messed that up for her. I have no idea what she was thinking. But I will say this, the store certainly should have contacted her before they changed Holly's order." Daniel sighed. "I can make this work, somehow. I will, because I am not going to let your sister walk down the aisle on her special day in anything that doesn't make her look the way she deserves to look." The determination in Daniel's expression drew James closer before he realized it was happening.

Holly joined them, and Clare brought out the dress in a plastic protective cover, carefully laid over her arm, and handed it to Daniel. She clearly felt bad, but it wasn't her fault.

"Let's get back to the house so I can plan how I'm going to do this before we need to leave for your meeting at the church," Daniel told Holly gently. "It's going to be okay." Daniel handed the dress to him and then hugged Holly. "I'll do my very best."

"Are you really going to be able to fix this?" James asked, standing behind Daniel as he worked in the bedroom with the dress laid out on the bed, pins everywhere. "It seems like a huge amount of work."

"It is." Daniel turned to the open door, and James closed it for privacy, returning to where Daniel sat as he made notes. "I have to do something. This dress is all wrong for her." He sighed, and James massaged Daniel's shoulders.

"What can I do to help?" he asked. James was probably going to regret asking. He knew nothing at all about sewing, but the job just seemed huge.

"Believe it or not, you're doing it." Daniel set down the notebook and pencil. "At least now I know what I'm going to do." He rubbed his eyes. "When are we supposed to leave?"

"You don't need to come."

"We told your sister we'd go with her and Howard. Besides, I need a break before I tackle this thing. I'm going to have to pick apart the seams and resew them. It's fiddly work, but not the most complicated thing I've done."

James leaned down, hugging Daniel from behind. "You're a real lifesaver, you know that? Mom can sew, but I doubt she's up for this kind of project." Even though she should be the one fixing this mess.

"We have to get ready to go. Howard picked up Holly a little while ago. I think he's doing his best to keep her calm, and that's probably the only reason Mom hasn't been hung up by her ears." Why she had to meddle in everything and thought she knew better than everyone else was a mystery to him. She always seemed to think Holly exaggerated the size she wore. Mom was always sorry after she meddled, but she just couldn't seem to help herself. If she would have left things alone, none of this would be necessary. But on the other hand, Daniel had come to the rescue.

Daniel nodded. "Let's make this as quick as possible so I can get back here to work on this before we go to the parties tonight."

James nodded, but stopped Daniel with a light touch before he reached the door. "I want you to know that all those guys, the losers…were also complete fools to let you slip through their fingers." Daniel's eyes shone, and James nodded. "None of them had a clue." Daniel squeezed his fingers, and James felt that pull once again. Daniel's lips parted, and James didn't see the dress, the makeup, or the fake chest. All he saw was the man under the trappings, the one with the kind heart, hiding it under a veneer of sass and one-liners.

He was becoming more and more confused by the hour, not about his feelings, but by what was real. So many of the things between them were built on an illusion that James had no idea what the underlying truth was. The shitty thing was that he was responsible for the sleight of hand in this situation, and that settled in his gut like a lump. Even though his heart told him to just back away and think things through, put some distance between them, he still drew nearer, and felt Daniel doing the same.

"You're going to be late," Mom called from the hallway outside, interrupting the moment. She sounded more than a little subdued, probably smarting from the whole dress incident. There had been raised voices, more tears, and as far as

James could hear, even an actual apology from his mother. The bubble around them burst, and James stood straighter, turning away to adjust himself so he didn't flash a boner at his mother. In fact, that notion was enough to send things racing south...fast. This trip was turning into a marathon that showed no signs of ending, and the thing was, they had barely started. But, damn, he was so grateful that Daniel was here with him. Going through this alone would have been hell.

## Chapter Eight

Daniel wasn't quite sure what to think of the church. It certainly wasn't what he had been picturing in his head. Somehow, the image in his mind was of a white church with a steeple, reminiscent of a Currier & Ives postcard. This modern building with odd angles and a bell tower that jutted out like a misshapen ship's prow made him think that maybe the architect had smoked crack just before sitting down at the drafting table.

"This is it?" Daniel asked Holly in hushed tones, almost expecting her to tell him it was a joke and that they were really going to the church down the street.

"I know," Holly whispered, exaggerating her lips.

"The old church was very traditional, with wooden beamed ceilings and long pews. It was white with a traditional bell tower. The only thing left of it is the bell in that monstrosity." James pointed to the imitation of a ship's prow off the front.

"What happened to it?" Daniel asked.

"Reverend Peterson," Holly spat like the name was a curse

word. "They hired him, like, five years ago, and within a year he was raising money and got the board to knock down the old building and start work on that." She took Howard's hand. "It's still a sore spot. I liked the old church. It was the church I grew up in, and we used to play hide-and-seek in parts of the old basement." Holly shook her head as Howard pulled open the door and held it for the rest of them.

Lights came on inside, and Daniel turned to the left, practically taking a step back. He shared a moment with James; he couldn't see Holly wanting to get married here. The back of the sanctuary was a wall of glass, and beyond that was a huge open space, more like a theater than a church. The urge to say something naughty crossed his mind. The altar sat on what looked more like a stage than anything else, and to one side stood a platform nearly eight feet high with a glass lectern and microphone. "Someone really likes to be the center of attention, don't they?" Daniel whispered to James. "I could do one hell of a show in this place."

James snickered as the reverend swept dramatically down the aisle. "Howard, Holly, you're just in time." He smiled brightly, and a zing went up Daniel's spine. Daniel understood what Holly meant the other day. That smile, the energy—all of it was designed to impress and be warm, but something was definitely off. Daniel couldn't put his finger on exactly what it was.

"James, it's good to see you again." Instead of shaking his hand, Reverend Peterson drew James into an awkward hug. Daniel practically growled; it didn't seem to him like the fake intimacy was welcome.

"Reverend, this is Daniella," Holly said. "She's James's girlfriend and came with him to the wedding. They agreed to come along with Howard and me for moral support and because the two of us are a little overwhelmed right now."

"Of course. We welcome as much family involvement in our wedding festivities as possible. I love to make these occasions as special as we can, with as much joy and energy as I can. Weddings are the most important day in a couple's life. It's the start of a grand journey, and I love that I can help you begin that...together." He gestured down out of the sanctuary. "Please come to my office and we can go over the arrangements with all of you. Afterwards, I'll take Holly and Howard's testimony and prepare them for the blessing that is marriage." Everything the reverend said was true, but it seemed verbose and ostentatious.

The reverend glided down the hallway. His movements were theatrical. Daniel stayed close to James, sharing silent glances. "Is this guy for real?" he mouthed to James.

"Drama queen," James mouthed back, and Daniel chuckled silently, taking James's arm.

They entered the room, and it was unlike any minister's office he had ever seen. It appeared more like that of a CEO, with large windows, a conference table, and a large glass-topped desk that would have been at home on the pages of *Architectural Digest*. "Please take a seat at the table, I'll be right with you." No pictures hung on the walls, religious or otherwise. Diplomas were framed, larger than life, from prestigious universities, proclaiming the reverend's credentials and achievements for all to see...and admire, Daniel was sure.

Reverend Peterson went to the desk, posing behind it before lifting a folder, drawing their attention. At first Daniel couldn't understand why the reverend seemed taller, until he shifted slightly and Daniel realized that the floor was raised behind the desk in order to set him higher. That was bizarre. The reverend returned with the folder and sat down in the empty chair. "We made a little change to the program," Howard said as he slid over a copy of the updated program for the service. "Somehow some of the songs were changed."

The reverend slipped the program into the file, barely glancing at it.

"Reverend?" A soft knock followed.

"Yes, Bernice," he said, standing. She spoke quietly and looked something like the *Saturday Night Live* church lady, complete with pinched expression. He approached her and spoke softly for a few seconds before turning back to them. "Excuse me just a few minutes." He followed her away.

"See what I mean?" Holly whispered.

Daniel leaned forward, glancing at the door. "It's all about him. Did you see that platform in there?"

Holly snickered. "He gets up there on Sunday mornings and lays down the word from on high. There's no subtlety. It's all about getting everyone worked up and ready to race out to do the lord's work and the reverend's bidding." She pursed her lips. "The thing is, what he says isn't right sometimes. It's inflammatory and hate-filled." She shivered. "Mama insisted that we use him. But I wanted to just have a friend perform the ceremony and leave the church out of it altogether."

Howard leaned closer to her. "It's okay. Once we're married, we can live the lives that we want. We don't have to go to church here, we can find a place where you and I both feel comfortable." He held Holly's hand. "We're keeping your mother happy." He shrugged.

James got up and looked around the office. When he stepped behind the desk, Daniel snickered. James was already tall, but he looked like André the Giant looming over that desk. James checked the bookshelves and pulled out his camera, taking a few pictures of the room, and then slowly sat back down. Damn the man was calm and cool. Daniel hadn't been able to look away because confidence was sexy as all hell and James wore it as well as he did those thigh-hugging jeans.

"I'm sorry. There was a parishioner who needed my guidance." The reverend lowered himself regally into the chair once more. Daniel had seen drag queens perch themselves on a throne with less drama. "Shall we review the meaning of marriage?" He proceeded to go over what marriage meant in great detail, drawing each of them into the conversation. Reverend Peterson was charismatic as the devil, explaining the meaning of the various parts of the service, asking questions.

"I always wondered about that," Holly said in response to his explanation on the sanctity of marriage and the deep need for openness and communication, and how secrets could destroy a marriage.

Daniel half listened, watching the reverend and glancing at James, who looked completely enthralled with what the reverend was saying. The man was charismatic, that was for sure, and Daniel could see how people became enamored with him. He gave each person his full attention in turn, taking in every word they said and then skillfully turning them to his way of thinking without leaving anyone the wiser. If Reverend Peterson went into politics, the next stop would be the White House.

Finally, the reverend pulled the updated program out of the folder. He looked it over and seemed ready to comment. Having gone through enough drama already, Daniel was about ready to step in at any changes, but the reverend simply smiled. "This is not a problem." He set the program down on the table. "I wanted to talk about the vows. Many couples decide to write their own, but here, we use the traditional vows that have been part of the service for decades. We want to stay with tradition—it grounds the service in history." His expression hardened, and Daniel turned away to keep from laughing.

"That's fairly obvious," Daniel quipped and somehow managed to not roll his eyes. He meant it sarcastically, but the reverend didn't even flinch and sat up straighter, like he had an ally. James met his gaze, and the two of them had to turn away. Daniel took a deep breath to keep from laughing. This church and this particular reverend were anything but traditional, and for this guy to espouse traditional religion while housed in this white concrete monstrosity was ridiculous.

To Daniel's surprise, Holly didn't argue and watched the minister as though some heavenly light shone down from up above. Daniel turned to James, who nodded slightly, running a finger over his hand out of sight of everyone else. Daniel's heart sped up and this meeting could not end fast enough.

"Do you have any more questions?" the reverend asked.

"No. And you have all the information you need?" Howard asked, and Reverend Peterson nodded and smiled.

"I know everything I need to know," he said and stood up, indicating that the meeting was over. Daniel stood as well, waiting while the others got ready to go, and after thanking the minister, they filed out of the office, winding their

way back to the front of the church and outside the cavernous building into the fresh air.

"That was a total crock of shit," James spat once the doors
were closed.

"Why?" Holly asked, blinking like she was just realizing
what happened.

Daniel chuckled. "That guy has a Napoleon complex the
size of Montana. Did you see the floor behind that desk? It's
angled to make him seem taller and more important, like
he wants to lord it over everyone. That's just damned weird.
And fake…all those smiles and the way he paid attention…
he didn't give a crap what any of us said. He just twisted it
to his way of thinking."

Holly ground her teeth, swearing under her breath. "He
did do that, didn't he?" Damn, she looked about ready to
march back into the church and rip off the reverend's balls.
Not that Daniel could blame her for a second. Everyone
hated being played.

"Let's get something to eat somewhere and we can talk
someplace that isn't the church parking lot."

"Just relax and don't worry about it," Howard told Holly
gently as she continued raving about the minister.

"But I don't want to be married by Reverend Nutcase,"
Holly half wailed and half cried as she leaned against Howard's shoulder. "I know it's too damned late to back out now."
She turned to Howard, wiping her eyes. "Now you know
why I refuse to go to church with my mother." She shivered.

The server brought their coffees and hurried away to handle the myriad of other customers. Holly sipped hers and
sighed. "Didn't you meet with him before today to discuss

the basics of the service?" Daniel asked. That seemed a little strange to him.

"Mother insisted and arranged for him to perform the ceremony." Holly seemed calmer the more coffee she got in her, and Howard did his best to settle her down. Daniel couldn't help wondering how much more Grace could insinuate herself into this wedding.

Daniel leaned closer to James. "You looked huge when you were behind that desk."

James chuckled, his gaze heating enough that Daniel could feel it. "How do you know?" James shifted his view to a leer, and Daniel did roll his eyes.

"Leave it to you to turn this into a dick joke."

James howled drawing Holly and Howard's attention. "This whole thing is a dick joke. The reverend's full name is Richard Peterson."

He chuckled and sipped coffee, grateful for James lightening the mood. Daniel needed to return to the house and get to work on the dress once more. He had a lot to do to take that disaster of a dress and turn it into the gown that every woman deserved on her wedding day.

Thankfully, James seemed to understand the situation. "Daniella and I need to return to work on the dress, and you two need to figure out the situation with the vows and Reverend Narcissist." He lightly patted Daniel's leg under the table. "Why don't you and I get going? Mom and Dad had an appointment this afternoon so she isn't supposed to be home."

Daniel thought a second and then smiled and nodded. He understood. As long as Grace was out of the house, maybe he and James could avoid the next round of questions.

Unfortunately, that little notion turned out to be a complete fantasy. As soon as they returned to the house, they were met by Grace, who greeted them at the door and ushered Daniel into the kitchen. "We never got a chance to finish our conversation this morning. James, you go and help your father in the garage. There are some things he needs to get down out of the loft area, and Daniella and I need to chat." She took him by the arm, leading him into the kitchen. "It's time for you and I to have a little girl talk." Daniel and James shared a quick glance, and Daniel shrugged. He really wanted to grab James by the hand to hold him here, but it looked like he was going to have to face this particular round of questioning on his own.

"Would you like some cake?" She set a pound cake on the table with some plates. "My James is a wonderful man. I'm so proud of him."

"You have every reason to be," Daniel said without a moment's hesitation. James was a good person, and Daniel found himself attracted to him more and more.

"We're women, so let's just talk. Okay?" She leaned slightly over the table. "Men are clueless most of the time. My James is a caring, loving person, but he'll take his own sweet time and dither on the sidelines until the cows come home. I know you've been dating for three months…" She was picking up a good head of steam, and Daniel wondered where this was going. He had a pretty clear idea though, and lord, Grace had a one-track mind.

Daniel cleared his throat. "I think it's best for things develop in their own time." It was worth a shot to try to get her to back off.

"Pffft…" Grace said. "We girls have got to drive things.

Do you think I let Phillip make all the decisions when we were dating?" She rolled her eyes. "I let him think he was the one in the driver's seat, but hell, that man may as well have been in the trunk, because I wasn't going to let him get away. And you can't either. Men need a push if we're going to get them to do anything."

Daniel had the notion that Grace's idea of a push was the equivalent of shoving someone off a subway platform in front of the oncoming matrimony train and hoping it didn't kill them. "James and I are just dating." He did his best to seem a little frightened, because heck, Grace was more than a little frightening like this. Yes, he had known James's mother had expectations, but this went beyond that. He glanced toward the door, hoping that James would return and rescue him from this situation. "Important, life-changing steps like marriage take time, and both people need to be sure that they are making the right decision." Oh god, he was spouting crap just to fill the space. He shifted on the chair and hoped to hell the makeup he was wearing didn't melt away under the laser-like focus of her gaze. "I need to get back to work on the dress..." Escape, any sort of escape, was preferable right now.

Thank god James strode in the back door just then. Daniel had never been so glad to see him. He smiled and extended his hand. James strode over and took it, and Daniel slid his arm around James's waist as he stood beside his seat, leaning against him, suppressing a sigh of relief.

Phillip strode into the room. "Grace, were you putting the marriage screws to Daniella?" He shook his head.

"I was just lending a guiding hand," she explained. *More like a shove off a cliff.*

Phillip leveled a glare in her direction. "You and I talked about this. Leave James and Daniella alone. Holly is getting married, and you have more than enough to do." He leaned down to Grace's ear and Daniel glanced at James as Grace's cheeks grew red and her eyes widened to saucers.

James sputtered and tensed next to him. Phillip pulled his lips away from his wife's ear and left the room without another word. Grace seemed speechless, which Daniel figured was some sort of miracle from god, and he took the opportunity to get to his feet. James seemed to have the same idea, and they left the kitchen as fast as they could.

Daniel shut the bedroom door behind them and burst into laughter. "I wonder what your dad said to her."

James paled and shivered. "I never, ever want to know."

"Come on. Your mom and dad had sex, probably still do. And it's pretty clear that your dad still floats your mother's boat." He snickered when James paled even further. "Ya big baby." Daniel decided to let it go and turned his attention to the dress. There was a lot of work to do, and he tried to center his attention on the task at hand. But his body had other ideas, and his mind centered on James instead.

"Do you need some help?"

Daniel lowered his gaze. "Can you sew?"

James paused. "I can do a lot of things," he answered, voice growing lower as he drew closer.

"Really?" Daniel asked, unable to move as the energy in the room shifted completely. This was a bad idea, and he had to try to figure out a way to keep his head. He had to get this dress done, and James was becoming too close for comfort— and not just because he was only a foot away. This was a job. Once they returned to Chicago, all of this would end and they would go their separate ways. Daniel was finding it hard to keep things professional between them as every fiber in his being drew him closer to James. There was something about him that got under Daniel's defenses and…

This couldn't be real. It had to be all the proximity and the parts they were playing with James's family. It was getting to him and reading more into their act was going to get him hurt…again.

Daniel turned away, able to breathe once again as oxygen returned to the room. "I need to get this done." He picked up the dress and sat at the sewing machine, pointedly ignoring James as he let the task at hand take over his mind. It didn't completely block out James's presence, but James took care of that, the door clicking softly as he left the room, leaving Daniel all alone.

# Chapter Nine

James had never felt so clueless in his life. His head spun from the "come here, go away" feeling he kept getting. The thing was, the "come here" part seemed to be stronger, but maybe he was wrong and just being stupid. Usually he'd ask Randy for advice, but that was pretty much out of the question at this point, mainly because Randy would hold it over his head for the rest of his life. And because he wasn't supposed to be getting so churned up over Daniel. Maybe if he just concentrated and saw only Daniella. He wasn't attracted to women. Sighing, he recollected how that notion had already crashed and burned completely. James had been attracted to Daniella when he'd had no idea about Daniel. Besides, all he had to do was inhale Daniel's scent and he forgot all about the outward accessories and the man underneath came forward.

"Son, you seem perplexed," his dad said as he passed. "Troubles with Daniella?" He motioned to sit. "Let me give you the best advice I can when it comes to women. Whatever you did, just say you're sorry." He sat down in his chair and James did the same on the sofa.

"I didn't do anything," James explained, already feeling a headache coming on.

His father chuckled. "That's the time when you need to apologize the most. It took me ten years and three children to figure that out. She thinks you did, and that's enough." He turned on the television and settled in to watch baseball.

"I never heard you and Mom fight when we were growing up," James said.

His father turned his head away from the television. "We fought; everyone does." He turned back to the television and released a deep breath. "Talk to her."

"I can't…she…" James could not explain to his father exactly what was going on, and that was part of the problem. He didn't know what was real and what was an act any longer. This was all his fault, and now he had to find his way through this minefield of dresses, makeup, and deception all on his own.

"Ah, I see," his father whispered knowingly as he sat forward. "I thought that I recognized something was amiss. You're not telling us everything about Daniella, are you? You know, if you look closely enough, it's pretty obvious." His gaze bored into James, and for an instant he felt completely exposed and vulnerable. A cold chill ran up his back, and James held his hands together just to keep them from shaking.

"I…" He opened his mouth to try to explain, but his father continued. This was his worst nightmare. James's mind raced in a million directions at once.

His father looked toward the kitchen and motioned for James to come closer. "What were you thinking?" The tone was barely above a whisper and knife sharp, and James lowered his gaze. "I'm not stupid, and don't think for a second that I condone this type of thing. Lying to your mother…"

"Dad, I… There are things that you don't know." The ground beneath his feet turned to quicksand in a second, his heart raced, and James could almost feel the end of his life with his family approaching like a freight train.

His father's face transformed with a smile. "You really care for this girl," he said. "I can see it."

"What?" James tried to make his head shift gears in a second as relief warred with the idea that he should just come clean and tell his father everything. Still, he only had a few more days and then he could return to Chicago and everything would go back to the way it was. Though keeping his secret was taking its toll. His sisters might be okay with him being gay, but his parents…that was a different ball game. And no matter what happened, everything would change and James wasn't ready to be their gay son or their gay brother… marginalized because of part of who he was.

"Daniella's important to you. I see the way you look at her. And, son, you have to be careful. Your mother is on a tear to get you married. It's what that woman lives for, especially now that Holly is getting married. And if she sees the way you feel about Daniella, the pressure on the two of you will become completely unbearable."

"Oh god," James murmured. Why did he have to make everything so damn complicated? Now it wasn't just enough for them to keep up the charade that Daniel was really Daniella, but he also had to pretend they weren't too close in order to keep his mother from interfering in his relationship. Hell, with the way his mother had been acting about Holly's wedding, she would turn into a nightmare of epic proportions if she thought James might get married.

"Exactly. I'll do my best to keep your mother occupied with Holly's wedding and all the things that are happening the next few days, and you and Daniella do your best to stay out of her way and under the mama radar." He went back to watching baseball, cheering when the Colorado Rockies scored a run.

"Thanks, Dad," James said, his father unlikely to have heard as he skulked down the hall toward his old bedroom, the hum of the sewing machine penetrating the door. "How is it coming?" James asked as he went inside.

The machine stopped and Daniel lifted his gaze from his work, his lower lip between his teeth, eyes filled with concentration. James closed the door and hurried over to him, cupping Daniella's made-up cheeks in his hands, leaning over the machine and kissing him. Yeah, it was probably the wrong damned thing to do, but he couldn't help it. He needed to know what was real and what wasn't. The tingle that raced through him all the way to his toes and the way Daniel returned the kiss were real.

Damn it all, it would have been so much easier if the kiss had been a complete dud and they really were just pretending. But it was real, and now he had to figure out the rest of it. James wanted Daniel with everything he had, and his whole body shook with excitement. But like it or not, he had to tamp down his feelings in order to keep them from his mother or this entire situation was going to get a hell of a lot worse.

"You're really bad, James," Daniel said softly as he pulled back.

"But I'm really good when I'm bad." He wagged his eyebrows, and Daniel grinned widely, pink lipstick shining.

"I don't get it. Do you Missoula boys all take a class in cheesy lines? You and Weston could sure as hell use some lessons in smooth…" Daniel pointed in queenly derision with a long-nailed hand. "Maybe I should offer a class in how to not sound like a dork."

"I see. I thought I was being cute." He drew nearer.

Daniel stood, leaving the wedding dress draped over the sewing table. "If you want to be remembered, try a sincere compliment."

James nodded. "You mean, like your eyes are the same color blue as I imagine the ocean is from a cruise ship at midnight—dark and mysterious with just enough turmoil to be interesting?" He came even closer. "How was that? Or I could say that your lips always remind me of the sweetest chocolate, and I can never get enough chocolate, especially the dark smooth kind that I want to lick until it's gone." His breath came deeper, and James's chest ached. "I could compliment your shoes or the fact that you always look perfect, but that's what you're wearing. It isn't you. Your eyes are the same no matter how you dress, and so are your lips." James smiled. "Maybe I could say that I want to follow that strip of skin down your throat until that little crescent disappears behind your first shirt button." He backed away. "Is that closer to what you had in mind?"

Daniel swallowed hard, throat working, drawing James's attention to the scarf around a long, slender neck. He knew it hid one of the few visible indications that he was a man, but he didn't care, tugging the knot open, running his finger down warm, smooth skin until it slid over the silk blouse.

"I think you got it down." Their gazes met, electricity filling the room.

The moment shattered at a knock on the door and Daniel tugged the scarf out of James's hand, tying it in place once again. "Are the two of you busy?" Holly asked and then barged right into the room. "Mom said you were working on the awful dress." She paused in the doorway. "Did I interrupt something?"

"Just a private conversation." James sat on the side of the bed. "Are you only being nosy? Because I can arrange for certain people to be really nosy on your wedding night." James grinned at Daniel. "We could arrange a shivaree. It wouldn't be hard to find out where they're staying."

Daniel clapped his hands together in delight. "I could sing, and we could get all the groomsmen to bring pots and serenade the happy couple. I always wanted to do that. Doris Day has the most lovely songs."

Just like that, James lost it. Lala Traviata's rendition of "Que Sera, Sera" flashed in his mind and he was done.

"You do that and so help me god, I will…" Holly's expression was pure horror.

James put his hands on his hips. "What?" He was having fun with this. Holly's cheeks had turned bright red and her head seemed seconds from exploding.

"Come over here," Daniel said, changing the subject. "I'm making some progress, but I want to check a few things before I put the final seams in. James can step out so we can work, and you can tell me all kinds of stories about the things he used to do as a kid."

Daniel was completely wicked. Before James could protest, he found himself on the other side of the locked door with Holly giggling up a storm.

"What are you up to?" his mother asked, carrying a basket of laundry down the hall.

"They're checking the dress, and Holly is apparently telling Daniella stories about me as a kid." He took the basket from her and carried it to the master bedroom, setting it on his parents' tightly made bed. The army had nothing on his mother when she made the beds, that was for sure.

"Heaven help us," his mother muttered and then sighed. "Your sister doesn't know the meaning of the word *discretion*. Remember the time she told the entire school that you once sat on a plate of baked beans? It didn't matter that it was when you were three years old." She snatched a towel out of the basket and started folding it. "I like Daniella. I think she's interesting, and she certainly has no qualms about sharing. I bet she's fun, and she's really cute." Mom placed the folded towel on the bed and got another. "If you let your sister mess this up for you…"

"Mom, just relax. Daniella and I haven't been dating that long. There aren't wedding bells ringing in the foreseeable future." He leaned over the bed. "Daniella has been hurt before, and it's going to take some time before either of us is ready to make a commitment. Holly is getting married, and you're going to need to be happy with that for now." The words *back off* nearly bubbled out of his mouth. "I know you want us all to be happy, but you're not the arbiter of what that is." He held her gaze. Mom had this thing she did when she got really determined, and James leaned closer over the bed, meeting the gaze of steel.

"You need to find someone to make you happy and…"

He didn't look away. "I may never get married." Another one of those damned commandments bit the dust. "I certainly am not going to walk down the aisle just to make you happy." God, it felt good to stand up to her like this. "Or date someone of your choosing."

She smacked the towel down on the bed. "What do you expect me to do, sit back and wait? You're twenty-eight years old. It's time you settled down."

"And I will when I'm ready. You don't get to make these decisions. I'm sorry if it upsets you, but that's the truth." He strode out of the room, returning to his old bedroom, feeling buoyed in a way he hadn't in a long time. James had stood up to his mother. He had no illusions that his little conversation was going to do much to change her behavior. His mother thought that she had a right to interfere in her children's lives when they didn't do what she thought they should. It was that simple. Her expectations overruled everything else—they always had.

Holly opened the bedroom door. "I'm all done." She smiled. "Daniella has actually managed to fix the monstrosity that Mom's interference created." She narrowed her gaze as Mom came back down the hall, and for the first time James could remember, Mom pursed her lips and said nothing as she passed...well, almost nothing.

"What is it, pick on your mother day?" she finally snapped on her way to the kitchen.

Holly sighed and shook her head before checking the time on her phone. "I have to get ready for tonight." Holly stuck her head back into the bedroom. "I heard a rumor that Jane has arranged for a stripper. She promised me that he was really hunky."

"I see. And you're okay if Howard has one tonight as well?" James couldn't help revving her up.

She narrowed her eyes. "He'd better fucking not."

"Isn't that a double standard?" James was having fun with this. He wasn't interested in any stripper that Weston came up with. Lord knew the kind of taste that man had must be awful. What bothered James more was the fact that if there was a stripper, he was going to have to figure out a way to seem interested, and yet not too interested because he had a girlfriend. Some of the guys would get overly enthusiastic. He'd seen it before.

"You're damn right, and I made sure that Howard knows it. I can't control what Weston does, but I made it perfectly clear that Howard was to keep his hands and any other part of him to himself or there would be hell to pay." She was most definitely her mother's daughter.

"Don't worry. I'll keep an eye on him." He did his best brother voice. After all, if Howard did anything to hurt his sister, he was going to have to answer to James. "Maybe I'll take my handcuffs to the party just in case."

"Ooooh, kinky," Daniel said from inside. "I like the way you think." The motor of the sewing machine hummed, and James just smiled as Holly shook her head, leaving without saying another word. "She seemed happy with the dress so far," Daniel said as James closed the door. Daniel's gaze lifted when James stayed by the door. "What are you smiling about?"

"I told my mom to back off. I doubt it will do anything, but I did it nonetheless."

Daniel got up from the sewing machine and came right over to him. "That's awesome. I know that was hard for you."

"It was liberating in a way. Now I want to go out and run a marathon or something." He was all keyed up.

"You could do that. In fact, I have someone for you to look into." Daniel lowered his voice, coming even closer. "Apparently Reverend Nutcase is pushing for more financial control of the church. That's what Holly told me."

"Huh…" James commented. He really wasn't interested in getting involved in what was certain to be a complete mess.

"Is that all you have to say?" Daniel asked with an accompanying shiver. "The guy was creepy as hell. And now he wants control of all the church money. That should set off a bunch of alarm bells."

"It does. But I don't have any authority here." James really didn't want to get involved. "We're here for just a few days and then we go back to Chicago. I'll look into the guy," he agreed. "But there's only so much I can do, and remember, creepy isn't a crime." James had to agree that he hadn't thought much of the reverend either, but the guy probably just had a big ego and liked being the center of attention. "My mother can't find out about this or she'll be mad as a wet hen. You know that."

Daniel hugged him. "Like I'm going to tell her." He squeezed him tighter and then Daniel returned to the sewing machine. "I need to get as much of this done as I can before we have to go to the party." The motor whirred and fabric slipped under the sewing needle. "Believe it or not, I've never been to a bachelorette party."

James was surprised. "Really?"

The motor stopped. "Yeah. Carmen got married a year ago, and we had a shower for her. It was fun." Daniel leaned over the sewing machine. "You haven't lived until you've been to a party with twenty drag queens all preening to be the one to garner the attention. Talk about catfights. There was so much shade being thrown around, you'd have thought we were having an eclipse."

"Shade?" James had to ask.

"Bitchy insults," Daniel explained. "For some of the girls, it's part of the shtick. I try to stay above all that." The way Daniel looked up at the ceiling told James that was a bold-faced lie.

"Bullshit." He grinned and approached the sewing machine, careful not to step on the fabric. "I bet you are an expert on throwing this shade. Don't forget, I heard you in your dressing room with the other girls before we actually came inside. I wondered if that was normal or if you guys actually hated each other." He made sure to speak softly. "Ummm… I think you might want to check your makeup." Daniel paused and grabbed the bag off the dresser nearby, pulling out a mirror.

"Yeah… I don't grow much of a beard, thank goodness." Daniel pulled out some makeup and did a quick retouch.

"Doesn't that hurt your skin?" He tried to think of what it would feel like to wear all that and he couldn't really imagine it. "I went as the Hulk for Halloween when I was a kid, and the makeup drove me crazy." He had hated that. The makeup had seemed caked on his skin, and he couldn't wait to get it off.

"This isn't like that. What I use are high-end cosmetics, and they help moisturize the skin, rather than lie on the surface and dry it out." Daniel put the mirror back in the bag and set it aside before returning to work, sewing a seam and holding up the dress. "That looks a lot better. The basic dress is back together, and the size is right. Now I need to do some more work on the bodice." Daniel set the dress aside, standing and stretching, arms overhead, lithe body growing longer. James's fingers itched to feel. He wondered what those long muscles would be like under his hands. James had already broken the rules that the two of them had set down. Heck, they both had. He wanted to break them again, but held back.

"Are you hungry? I have no idea what sort of food these parties are going to have."

"No, thanks. I need to take a few minutes to rest and clear my head before I get back to this. I want it done so Holly can try it on a final time," Daniel replied and returned to work.

"Is there anything I can do?"

Daniel shrugged. "Keep me company."

Now, that was something he could manage.

"I know you're a cop, but I would never think of you that way first," Daniel said. They had been talking for almost an hour, and apparently the dress was nearly done.

"Am I that different?" James asked. "Have you met police officers before?"

Daniel released the pedal, stopping the machine. "I'm sure I have, probably multiple times. But the ones I've come in contact with weren't particularly helpful. Some have been downright cruel. Not like you at all." Daniel stared at him for a few seconds before started the machine once again, sewing a final seam and standing with a smile. "We should get ready for the parties."

"Nice change of subject?" James commented.

"It's not a pre-party story." Daniel placed a suitcase on the bed, rummaging through it. "I know you're curious, but I don't want to throw a wet blanket on the evening's fun. Just let it go. I shouldn't have said anything." Daniel pulled out a pair of leggings, a mid-thigh-length skirt, and a blouse. "What do you think?"

"It looks great to me. I was never a real connoisseur of women's clothing." He continued staring at the blouse. "I like that color blue on you. It really brings out your eyes." James opened the closet door, pulling out a white button-down shirt.

"Is that what you're wearing?" Daniel asked and moved him aside. "This is much better. Don't be afraid of a little color."

"I only brought that shirt because Holly gave it to me last Christmas and I thought I'd have it if she asked about it." James really wasn't sold on the plum color, but he pulled off his shirt and shrugged the plum one on. "I don't know…"

Daniel stepped right into his space. "I think you look stunning in it." Deft hands fastened the buttons, gliding up his chest with the softest of touches. "Don't argue with me. You'll be the envy of all the other guys tonight because they'll look dull and you'll be fabulous. Now let's see what pants we have to go with these…yummy…" Daniel snapped a pair of black jeans at him. "These."

"They're a little tight," James protested. Daniel waved that notion aside with a flick of a delicate wrist, and James toed off his shoes, slipped out of what he was wearing, and pulled the black jeans on. Daniel twirled a finger, and James turned around. "Hey…" James jumped slightly as Daniel gave his backside a pat.

"No protesting. You look edible. It's too damned bad that I'm not going to the same party you are because…damn…" Daniel sighed and stepped back. "Jesus, it's almost a shame to waste that look on a bunch of straight boys." His backside got another pat. Daniel chuckled and started getting ready. James sat on the edge of the bed, enthralled, and Daniel almost regally undressed and untucked. "That is the hardest part...no pun intended. The boys seem to think they're being ignored."

"Will you need to tuck tonight?"

"No, thank god. The skirt has two layers and I'll have on some extra underwear to keep things in place. That should make things much easier."

"Come here," James whispered deeply. Daniel standing in front of him, nearly naked, was damned close to his undoing. He was certainly glad he never had to tuck, because, fucking hell, there was no hiding his desire in these jeans. It was on clear display for Daniel.

"I shouldn't."

James held Daniel's gaze, sending *come over* vibes. When Daniel approached, James wrapped his arms around him, lightly stroking up his back. He felt drunk, his mind clouding as pure electric desire shot through him. He knew what attraction felt like, and this was a hell of a lot stronger than just that. "You're probably right," James agreed without letting Daniel go.

"We're going to be late, and your mother is going to start to wonder about her commandments," Daniel warned as he ran a warm hand under James's shirt and over his chest.

"If Mom decides to investigate, she's going to get the shock of her life." He groaned, but rested his head against Daniel's shoulder, inhaling his fresh scent with just a hint of muskiness.

"Okay..." Daniel prompted.

"I'm finally relaxed for just a few minutes." He didn't want to move. For what felt like the first time in days, he wasn't uptight, though his heart rate was still fast, but for a much more delightful reason than the fact that his family kept him on edge. Eventually he let his hands fall to his sides, and Daniel moved away.

"You know, this is a really bad idea from every angle I look at it." He turned away and began getting dressed, pulling on multiple layers of underwear and then the leggings. Slowly, before James's eyes, Daniel turned from the man he'd held in his arms into the image of a perfect woman. James still saw him as a man, even with the makeup and clothes. The important parts of Daniel were the same, especially the eyes.

James got up and adjusted his clothes, then checked himself in the mirror. "Are you ready?" Daniel asked from behind him, and James nodded. "Then let's go."

"The evening starts at the same bar for the men and the women, and then we go our separate ways," James explained as he pulled up outside the Irish pub in downtown Missoula. He parked the rental car and got out, opening Daniel's door.

"You're learning," Daniel said gently.

James shrugged. "It's easy when you want to do nice things for someone." He closed the car door and held Daniel's arm as they entered the raucous taproom.

"Daniella," Margot said as she came over from the restaurant portion of the establishment. "I'm here with Mom and Dad." She rolled her eyes the way only a teenager could.

"I take it this was how they'd let you be part of the festivities," James said as he hugged his younger sister.

"This whole wedding thing really sucks. Everything is too *old* for me."

James did his best not to chuckle. "Well, how about you and I have lunch tomorrow. Daniel and I want the dirt on the reverend, and I'm sure you have plenty you could tell us."

She pulled away, truly smiling for the first time this visit. "You bet, big brother. Is this an investigation? Mom would have a fit, but I want to be a police officer like you. She wants me to take home economics classes. Like I want to spend my entire life in the kitchen. Sometimes I wonder if she thinks it's still the fifties or something."

"Nope, no poodle skirts," Daniel quipped.

"You got that right." She shivered.

"Why don't you go on back to Mom and Dad before Mom comes unglued, and we'll all go to lunch tomorrow." James hugged her again, and Margot returned to the table.

"I thought you didn't want to get involved?" Daniel teased.

"I don't. Not really. But she's felt a little left out, I'm sure, and if nothing comes of it, then she'll have had a little intrigue." He really wasn't going to hold his breath on any of this stuff with the reverend no matter how much he felt the guy felt false. He motioned forward before guiding Daniella into the private room where their parties were supposed to begin.

James had to content himself with drinking soda for now because he intended to drive and had to limit himself to one beer, but he got Daniel the cosmo requested. "Don't overdo it."

Daniel lifted the glass before sipping. "Don't worry. I have no intention of letting my guard down…too much." With a wink, Daniel was off to join the girls, and James headed toward where the men had congregated.

"It's not too late, Howard," Weston was saying, an arm draped over Howard's shoulder. "You could still call this whole thing off and save yourself from a life of marital servitude." His words were slightly slurred, and James wondered how much he'd already had to drink. Judging by the way he threw back a shot and reached for another from the nearby table, quite a bit.

"Knock it off," one of the other guys said. He must have been a friend of Howard's. James didn't know him, but they shook hands and he introduced himself as Teddy. "I've known these guys since college."

"I'm Holly's brother." He narrowed his gaze at Weston. "We might want to get some food in him or he'll keel over in the next hour."

"Wes, go eat something, mate," Teddy called. "Or you're cut off." Thankfully, Teddy seemed to get through to Weston, and even though he grumped, he stopped a server and placed an order. Then he wove his way through the guys, heading toward the group of ladies…and right up to Daniel. James was ready to intercede when Daniel shook his head, jaw set, eyes hard. Then Daniel caught his eye just as Weston made his way back toward them.

"Either that one is one stone-cold bitch…" Weston muttered as he passed, heading back to the standing table as the server brought out his food. "Not much of a woman, if you ask me." The remark was probably made as a bad joke, but James felt a cold chill run up his spine. Hopefully Weston had had enough to drink that he wouldn't remember much of the evening, but just the idea was dangerous.

"He's had too much to drink," Teddy explained, pulling James's attention.

"That's my date he's insulting," James growled. He hated that Weston was hitting on Daniel, but to use that sort of language... "He's going to find himself missing some teeth if he doesn't treat her and all the ladies properly."

Howard nodded. "I'm going to call him a cab once he's finished eating. This isn't the kind of evening I had expected."

"Me either," James agreed. Howard excused himself and headed off toward Weston's table. The ladies had moved on to a room in the back of the pub, and James hoped Daniel was all right. It was clear that Daniel could take care of himself, but James and Weston were going to have a real problem if Weston didn't back the hell off. James ordered a soda and wished it was something stronger. He needed something to calm his nerves. Although what James really needed was to keep Weston away from Daniel. He took a sip and shook his head. Everything was becoming more complicated by the second.

# Chapter Ten

Daniel didn't spend a lot of time with women...well, at least not groups of women. His time in Chicago was spent with men who dressed as and imitated women. That was very different from being included in one of their rites of passage...as it were. One thing was most definitely true: these ladies were wild.

"Do you always act like this?" he asked, seated around a small table that was already piled with empty glasses. They were on their second, and hopefully final, stop while the guys had stayed at the pub. Daniel checked around the room, looking for the small handbag he'd come in with, but he didn't see it. A lot of the girls had placed their bags behind the bar, and he craned his neck to see and wondered if someone had placed his with the others. That was the one thing that made him nervous. Inside was his real ID, just in case there was trouble of some sort.

"Are you kidding?" Holly asked as the music changed, and she whooped, grabbing Daniel by the hand, dragging him out to the dance floor. "This is the most fun I've had in years."

"Really?" Daniel asked over the music, giving up on any sort of conversation as they danced to the thrumming beat. He loved to dance and would usually let go and be one with the music, but tonight, he felt as though he needed to be on his toes.

"This is awesome!" Holly called, lifting her hands in the air, whirling around as she rolled her hips. Daniel smiled and kept dancing, enjoying himself for a few minutes. It was wonderful being in the company of women. Sure, they could be catty sometimes, but he found a sense of acceptance with them that was more difficult with most men. It had always been that way for him. When he was in school, most of his friends had been women. He'd had a few guy friends, but mostly they were the boyfriends or people in the extended circle of the women. He always felt that women had few expectations of him. Guys wondered if he was interested in them, and had been plenty ready to beat the crap out of him if they thought he was. Even the gay guys had stayed away because he was just too gay, even for them. This was pleasant and fun, especially when more of the ladies danced into his orbit, and he simply let the pounding beat of the music carry him away. Suddenly, the music ended, and the women all drifted to the nearby chairs. The room went dark, and one corner of the private room of the bar burst to light with a stripper dressed as a police officer, muscled body bulging in his uniform.

"Damn, I want me some of that." Holly hurried over as the music changed to a pulsating beat and the police officer began to dance. Daniel let the ladies move around him to get closer, standing toward the back.

He smiled and then chuckled to himself. This guy could

most definitely benefit from dance lessons. Who in the heck hired a stripper who couldn't dance? Daniel snickered as the huge guy rolled his hips. The ladies cheered, but all Daniel could see were the awkward movements. Granted, the guy was stunning, deep tan, huge muscles threatening to burst out of the shirt that strained to contain them. The women didn't seem to care if he could dance or not, whooping and screaming when he pulled off his shirt, whirling it overhead as he finally got into the rhythm of "It's Raining Men." The yelling grew louder as a number of the ladies joined him. Thankfully they left their tops on.

"Not interested?"

Daniel hadn't heard anyone come up behind him. "Not really." He smiled at one of Holly's friends. "I have a cop of my own." The words were out before he could really think about them, and Daniel felt himself blushing under his makeup. The truth was that if James were up there, he would be enraptured, but while this guy was nice-looking—if a little too muscle-bound—he wasn't a certain police officer who had taken up residence in Daniel's dreams.

He shouldn't allow these kinds of thoughts to take root, for his own sake. James wasn't out to his family. That wouldn't be a problem in Chicago; they could be themselves there. But Daniel was not going to pull out the Daniella persona every time his family came to visit or when they were expected to return here. That wasn't going to happen. Daniel had spent a great amount of emotional energy coming to terms with who he was, and going back into the closet wasn't something he was prepared to do. Being here was a job, Daniel reminded himself, and once they left, the job would be over.

"I see." She sipped her wine. "I'm Rachel."

"Daniella."

Rachel nodded. "So you're James's date. I heard you were pretty." She took another sip and set her glass on a nearby table. "I've been wondering about the kind of girl that James would be interested in." There was something in her tone that left Daniel suspicious about her. She seemed too intent. "I had a crush on him through high school, and James never showed the slightest interest...in anyone. He dated a few girls, but his heart didn't really seem to be in it. I always wondered about the kind of person who would turn his eye."

Daniel nodded. "I see." Of course, Daniel knew the exact reason why James had behaved as he had. James wasn't interested in any woman, at least not the way Rachel had hoped he might be.

"Tell me, is James a passionate man?" She was fishing now and clearly had ideas about James and what he might be like. She probably figured that since he hadn't been interested in her, James wasn't interested in anyone. It was a dead-on conclusion, but one Daniel needed to dispel.

"Yes. He's very passionate. Skillful, in fact." Daniel lifted his glass to his lips, keenly aware of the way her eyes widened. "I'm a very lucky person." Daniel turned away and let Rachel stew on that. Daniel hadn't told a lie, exactly. Daniel had a good idea that James was passionate...and he was skillful in certain ways. He'd simply left his answer nonspecific and let Rachel draw her own conclusions.

"I see." Rachel's voice grew a little deeper as the music ended. She reached for her glass and downed the rest of the wine, heading off toward the bar. Daniel turned back to the entertainer, who had by now stripped down to a small pair of briefs and was making his way into the crowd. Daniel snickered to himself and smiled as the ladies shoved their dollar bills into the man's underwear.

"Why are you staying back here?" Daniel jumped at Weston's voice. What the hell was he doing here?

"Are you following us?" Daniel challenged. This was creepy as all hell. Though nothing surprised him about Weston. He had the Hannibal Lecter award sewn up for this wedding.

"No. I was feeling better…" He flashed a dull smile, and Daniel lifted his glass.

"Would you like some wine to go with the cheesy line that's about to spew forth from thy lips?" Daniel was making fun of Weston, but he didn't care. All he really wanted was for the guy to take a hike.

"You think you're really clever, don't you?" Weston's tone was light, but his eyes were dark and hard. Daniel refused to be intimidated for a second, but he did wish James was here as backup. For a second, it struck Daniel as odd how he wished a cop were here. Maybe he needed to adjust his position on that particular breed of the species, but now was not the time.

"I know I am, honey, and you need to learn some manners. When a lady tells you she isn't interested, that means no. There's no middle ground or 'playing hard to get' crap. No means no. Understood?" Daniel had had more than enough of this lech and wondered about how he had treated the other women in his life.

"All women play hard to get. It's part of their makeup." Daniel took the small step to Weston with a smile and a slight sway of the hips. "See, I knew you'd come around."

Daniel evaluated Weston and moved fast, a hand at his

throat, nails positioned tight at the air passage—just enough pressure to scare—the other at his crotch, long nails digging in. "I will never come around to your way of thinking, and your head needs an adjustment. So listen to me closely." Daniel pressed Weston back against the wall. "You move and you lose a nut. I'm tired of your attitude. Who taught you that shit? Was it your mama?" Weston's eyes grew dinner-plate wide and his breathing became shallow. He tried to squirm, and Daniel gripped harder on his balls. "Answer me or there will be no little Westons in your future."

"No..." he whimpered. "Jesus, you're crazy."

Daniel ignored the second part. "Was it your father? Did he treat women like they're nothing?" When Weston didn't answer, he added pressure on his throat. "It doesn't matter who you got it from, I'm doing the teaching now. So listen good. When you approach a lady—and all women are ladies...always—you be polite, and when she says no, you have two responses, thank you or have a nice day. Let's practice that. I'm saying no."

Weston stared at him and Daniel squeezed down below. "Thank you," he ground out. "Have a nice day."

"Much better. And I'll give you a hint, when you meet a lady that you like, you offer her a drink. And I'll let you in on a secret. You ask her about her day, and surprise, surprise, you listen to what she has to say. You may learn something, and for god's sake leave the cheese at home." Daniel kept his voice level and calm as sweat rolled down Weston's neck, his face as red as a tomato. "Now it's time for you to leave this party. The appropriate response is good night, and say it with a smile." Daniel pulled back, and Weston gripped his throat, huffing for air.

"You are one crazy bitch," Weston growled. Daniel had had quite enough of this man to last a lifetime. Plenty of guys like him came through the club, and Lala handled them with her usual aplomb and a healthy dose of embarrassment. This one was worse than most and refused to get the message. Daniel moved closer once again, bringing a knee up fast and hard. It was time to put Weston out of every woman's misery. With a grunt, Weston slid down the wall, clutching his groin.

"And you don't learn very well." He turned away as a bouncer wove through the crowd. "You can escort him out, please. He's had more than enough for tonight."

"I'd say so," the bouncer said, yanking a still-groaning Weston to his feet. "My sister tends bar here—would you show her those moves?" He flashed a grin and hustled a protesting Weston out of the room just as one of the stripper's songs finished.

Daniel turned back to the table, picking up the glass of wine, and watched the festivities. Thankfully, the ladies were all engrossed by the jerky-looking stripper. This guy really needed dance lessons. He had one move, and it was so unoriginal.

As the stripper got close to Holly, Daniel drew nearer, standing between them. Holly seemed a little out of it, and with the way some of the other women were snapping pictures, he didn't want anything to surface that she would regret later. "Come on, let's get you some water." Daniel guided Holly to the bar and ordered some coffee as well as a little food. "I think you've had more than enough to drink." Holly was going to have one hell of a hangover in the morning. "Remember, you have dance class in the morning and the rehearsal dinner tomorrow night." At this rate, Holly was going to be one hell of a mess and would never make it through either one.

"How come you're so nicccce?" Holly wrapped her hand around the glass and tried to chuck the water the way she would a shot. Man, she was out of it.

"Drink a little coffee and have some of the pretzels. They'll soak up the booze." Daniel brought over bar snacks, and thankfully Holly ate a few of them.

"Why are you so nicccccce?" she asked again, this time eating a little more. "You fixed my wedding dress and everything." Holly stared at Daniel through bleary, half-lidded eyes.

"And you need to be able to stand up in the morning so I can fit it on you. Eat a little more and drink some of the coffee." Daniel caught the bartender's eye. "No more for her, and don't let any of the ladies buy her drinks." It looked like it was going to fall to him to get Holly home in one piece.

"My mother is such a pain in the ass." Holly patted Daniel's cheek, eyes really bleary. "She messed up my dress and the programs." Tears began running down her cheeks. "She always has to interfere with everything." Daniel handed her a napkin, and Holly dabbed her eyes. She was starting to look like a raccoon, with her makeup blotching and running around her eyes. "You're really nicccccce," she added with a sigh.

"And I'm afraid that you had too much to drink." The stripper was done and had left the building. The rest of the women were getting down to some serious drinking. Daniel was more than ready to call it a night. This sort of thing was not what he was interested in.

"Hey, Daniella, are your boobs real?" one of the women asked and then broke into a fit of giggles.

"No more real than yours," Daniel shot back. There was no need to say anything further. It was going to be taken as an offhand, one-upmanship remark. Holly dissolved into a fit of giggles. Daniel shrugged and made sure she stayed on her stool. At least laughing was better than the tears.

"Howard and I tried to be good," Holly said as she drank some more coffee. "Mom wanted me to stay pure before I got married, but pffft." Holly swayed, but managed not to fall off. "That ship sailed a long time ago. And Mama has already asked me how long we're going to wait before having kids." She sipped some more coffee and Daniel half held her up. "Can you believe that? My own mother asked me, when I told her I was getting married..."

"What?" Daniel asked.

"She asked me if I was pregnant," Holly said, speaking louder as anger set in. "My mom was asking me if I *had* to get married." There was nothing like the drunken wheel of emotion. Spin and see what you get from second to second.

"You had to get married?" Rachel asked from behind them. "Really."

Holly shook her head. "No. My mama asked that. There are no buns in this oven." Holly rested her head on the bar, and Daniel realized a few seconds later that she was sobbing for no apparent reason.

"Holly, you're drunk," Rachel told her. "Come on out here and dance. It's a party."

Somehow Daniel figured the party was over for Holly. It was well after midnight. Daniel called James and explained where they were. "Can you come pick up Holly and me?"

"I'm on my way," he answered without hesitation and hung up. Daniel did his best to get Holly to drink some more coffee. It helped for a little while and the crying at least died away. The partying continued around them, and Rachel managed to pull Holly onto the dance floor again. How she remained upright, Daniel didn't know.

"Where's Holly?" James asked as he hurried into the room. Daniel pointed, and James retrieved her while Daniel got his handbag. Holly made a huge show of saying goodbye to everyone, hugging all of them and making a huge fuss like she was never going to see them again.

"Let's go," Daniel said gently, guiding Holly out of the bar and into James's car. He got into the back seat with her, hoping that as they rode along everything she'd had to drink wouldn't make a reappearance.

"Holly," James snapped lightly to get her attention. She lifted her gaze to him before bursting into tears.

"You hate me..." she cried, and Daniel rolled his eyes and held her as James drove. After about five minutes, she quieted and went to sleep, drooling on Daniel's shoulder.

"How was it...before Sleeping Beauty there drank herself stupid?" James asked.

"It was fun enough. But god, those women can party, and they're bitchy when they're drinking."

James chuckled and then laughed. "I think it's all the repression. It comes out when they drink. The guys were the same way." They drove awhile and eventually pulled into the driveway. Daniel pushed Holly upright, lightly tapping her cheek to wake her up.

"Come on, Holly. We need to get inside," Daniel told her,

and thankfully James got her out of the car, walking Holly to the door and inside, where their mother met them with stern looks.

"I'll get the bride to bed," she said with surprising gentleness, tinged with a slight undertone of disapproval, and took Holly down to her room.

"I feel like I ran a marathon," Daniel commented as he followed James into the kitchen. Thankfully their mother had set out some cake, and James sliced each of them a piece.

"Me too. I only had one beer because I knew I was going to have to drive, and I found out something. These parties are awful when you're the only one who's sober." He pulled out the next chair to sit, and they ate in silence.

"You didn't drink and drive, did you?" Grace asked as she barreled into the kitchen.

"No," Daniel answered. "He drank soda all night and put up with Howard and all of his drunk friends." He was getting a little pissed at her attitude. "Your son is a good police officer and a nice man." He finished the cake and pushed his chair back. "I'm going to bed." He needed to leave the room before he said something stupid. Daniel had had just enough to drink that his tongue was loose, and the best way to counter that was not to be in the room.

Daniel had never been so glad to be behind a closed door in his life. He slipped out of the skirt, leggings, and blouse, pulling on the pink robe before heading across the hall to the bathroom, where he got comfortable and took care of business, then returned to the bedroom. James was already inside, sitting on the bed, tugging off his clothes.

"I should have asked for more money," Daniel whispered.

"Your mother is a pain in the ass, and your sister is a perfectly normal woman until she gets too much to drink, and then she's wild, crying all over the place about her oven not working. Her friends are a threat to humanity when they drink." He stripped off the last of his clothes, spent some time removing his makeup, put on his PJs, and got under the covers. "I swear the poor stripper was lucky to get out of there in one piece."

"The guys were much better behaved. Howard stayed in the back, and I sat with him." James pulled off his shirt and slipped out of his pants. "I can say one thing. He certainly loves my sister. He didn't pay any attention to the stripper and seemed relieved when it was over. He didn't drink too much either. It was like he was trying really hard to be good."

"I'm sure he was. I think Howard is just as ready to have all this wedding stuff over and done with as Holly is." Daniel propped the pillows under his back. "The whole wedding process is really stressful. You're the center of attention, but that means all eyes are on you, and people comment on everything from your dress, the tuxes, to the centerpieces and the food. Every single thing you pick is under the microscope." Daniel tried to make himself comfortable. He waited while James left the room in his robe and turned the light out.

Daniel spread the pillows back out and rolled over, determined not to watch as James returned and got into bed. Not that it mattered. As soon as he slipped under the covers, James's warmth spread through the bed, and Daniel clenched his fists with tension, trying to ignore him and finding it impossible.

"I'm sorry you didn't have a great time tonight," James whispered.

"It wasn't bad, just stressful. It seems Rachel is still holding a candle for you." He snickered.

James chuckled. "She was always trying to get me to go out with her. Even if I was inclined that way, I was not going to go out with that shark. She's nice enough, but I don't think she's ever been a really good person." James rolled over, and Daniel felt his breath whisper over his skin. "There's nothing wrong with her, but she pursued me way too hard, and that wasn't what I wanted."

"Rachel is one of those people who knows what she wants and is willing to go after it," Daniel explained.

"I don't think so. She's the female version of Weston. I don't think she understands when to stop." A warm hand pressed to Daniel's shoulder. "I saw what he did to you tonight."

"Yeah, well, the guy is a real prick."

"He called you names as he walked away, and Howard sent him home. He was livid about the whole thing. I wonder what's gotten into him?"

Daniel slowly rolled over. "Some guys think they're god's gift to the world and don't understand why anyone would tell them no. I know how to handle stuff like that. I get it at the theater all the time. Six months ago, I had a patron send me flowers every Saturday night for a month, asking me out after the show. I turned him down nicely the first few times, but after that I had to bar him from the theater." Daniel sighed softly. "I don't even know if he was gay or just enthralled with me and the character." He rubbed his eyes from fatigue.

"I guess it's hard not knowing if someone is interested in you or the character you play," James said.

"Yeah. That's pretty observant of you. When my star was

on the rise, I used to be really flattered with the guys who wanted to take me out. Until I realized they wanted to date Lala and they expected me to put on a show all the damned time. That shit is exhausting! Lala is part of my personality, but she isn't who I am." Most of the time people didn't understand that Lala was a persona. Sure, the fabulousness was part of who he was, and Daniel would be bereft without Lala, but she wasn't all he was. "It's sometimes hard to explain."

James stroked Daniel's cheek. "You're a complicated person. Lala is part of you, but not all of you. You're Daniel, and Lala is just a part of that."

He slipped closer. "You do understand."

"I think so." James slipped his arm around Daniel's waist, tugging him closer. "We all have various parts of our personality. When I'm at work, I'm a real hard-ass. I have to be sometimes." Daniel tensed automatically, and James pulled his hand away. "I didn't mean to be too forward." He pulled away, and Daniel closed his eyes, missing the warmth.

"It's not you. I don't like to talk about it, but I was arrested two years ago."

"What for?" James asked. Now it was his turn to tense.

"My manager had talked me into doing a tour. With the popularity of RuPaul, he thought a drag tour would be great. But the stupid promoter booked us into St. Louis. Not that there's anything wrong with the city itself—it should have been fine—but he didn't research the venue properly, and things got out of hand. The police had to be called, and they went after the performers rather than the patrons who were causing the trouble. They hit some of the girls and forcibly carried us out and into the street. We were treated badly just because of who we were and how we looked, and because

I was the leader of the troupe, I was singled out." He didn't go into the fact that he hadn't been able to perform for days because makeup could only cover so much. "The organizer and even the club owner were trying to explain, but they didn't listen. They should have but they didn't. Those officers didn't use facts, just their own hatred and prejudice. It seems that one of the troublemakers was the mayor's kid or something. The charges got dropped, but we were all processed and humiliated before those assholes let us go." The memory made him angry. "After that, we went on with the tour, but none of us got any joy from it. They stole that from us."

James rolled back over. "Jesus." His arm returned. "I'm sorry you were treated that way. You didn't deserve it." James seemed to know the courage and trust it took for Daniel to share this.

"No one does," Daniel whispered, and James's weight shifted. He didn't move quickly, and Daniel could have moved away, but he found himself drawn closer, his lips parting as James's lips met his in a kiss that sent a wave of molten heat running through him. James enfolded him in his strong arms, pulling him close.

James tugged the top of his pajamas upward, his warm hands sliding over Daniel's skin, sending goose bumps rippling wherever they went. Daniel groaned softly, returning James's kisses with ever-increasing fervor. He wanted this man, and loved the way he touched him. Daniel had never been one to lie still, and he pressed forward, sucking on James's lower lip as his control wavered. This was a bad idea, and yet he wanted it, hands exploring James's hard, hot body, sliding down a strong back as James rolled him, climbing on top, weight pressing him into the mattress.

"Is this okay?" James whispered, his breath tickling over Daniel's lips. "I know I can be forceful. I need to hear the words."

"Yes…" he heard himself say, as the last of his willpower crumbled to dust.

# Chapter Eleven

James had been waiting for this moment. Daniel was his, and James took advantage of the opportunity. He had lain awake listening to Daniel breathe for nights, wishing he was his to take and make love to. And now he was. All the drama and excitement of the day slipped from his mind, James's attention narrowing to just the two of them.

Squeak… They shifted together, and the bed frame made the slightest noise. When he moved again, it did the same. James was beyond caring. He had slept next to Daniel for days, listening to him snore, inhaling his scent every single minute. The stuff was like nasal Viagra, racing through him the entire damned time. He didn't intend to let a little squeak get the better of him. He shifted slightly, moving fluidly, holding Daniel tighter, luxuriating in the feel of him in his arms.

"You've driven me crazy for days," James whispered into Daniel's ear, then sucked it between his lips, nibbling on the lobe, shaking slightly at Daniel's barely uttered moan.

"James…" Daniel shook under him, sliding his hands

down James's back, under his boxers and over the curves of James's butt. He growled and kissed Daniel once again, silencing both of them out of sheer need and necessity. James wanted this more than he had wanted anything in his life.

Squeak… James stilled, breathing like he had just won a race. The house was quiet, his parents long asleep. There was no need to worry about a little sound. Squeak… Maybe they should simply move to the floor. James growled and backed away. There was no way he was going to make love to Daniel for the first time on the damned floor. He deserved better than that.

"We're in your mother's house," Daniel said, and James huffed. James was ready to chuck that out the window. His desire had grown to the point where he needed Daniel. His taste, the feel of his soft skin, the flex of his muscles under his hand, and the way Daniel breathed deeply and his hands quivered all told him Daniel felt the same way. His parents were likely long asleep, James was about to explode, and… "We can't…" Daniel added.

James paused, closing his eyes, trying to put the genie back into the bottle before it could completely escape. "Daniel… I…"

Daniel hugged him close, head against his shoulder. "I know, but we can't. Your mom and dad are on the other side of that damned wall." He put his hands against James's chest, their gazes locking in the near darkness. "I'm sorry."

James slowly rolled off Daniel, staring up at the ceiling, his blood racing in his ears. "No, it's the right thing to do." He hated actually saying the words, and he hated doing the right thing.

Daniel shifted in the bed next to him. "Maybe I should

grab a pillow and blanket and sleep on the floor." He pushed back the covers.

James kept the frustration out of his voice as best he could. "Of course not." He rolled over. "I'm not going to jump you in your sleep or something." James placed his hand on Daniel's shoulder, stilling them both while reestablishing the connection. He didn't want Daniel to leave.

Daniel lay back down, both of them staring up at the ceiling, and then he began to laugh. "Can you imagine how many of your mother's commandments we almost broke?"

James rolled his eyes. "You really think this is funny?"

Daniel began to cough. "Of course it is. You need to keep your fly zipped and yourself pure as the driven snow for marriage." He snickered again. "Though your mom and dad already know you've blown that little commandment big-time."

James snickered. "Yeah, well, it's the commandments that aren't on the list that I'm worried about." He leaned close. "You know the ones."

Daniel settled down. "You mean the eleventh one, though shalt not be gay, and number twelve, though shall not take a drag queen to your sister's wedding?"

"Exactly." James was well aware of those particular unwritten rules. "Those two pretty much trump the other ten." He hated thinking about them at all. "Just a few more days and then we can go home and go back to our real lives." It was easy to say that, but James wasn't sure what the hell he wanted any longer. Yeah, he'd go back to Chicago, but his family would know no more about his life and the person he really was than they did now. He and Daniella would break up a short while later, and everything would be the same. It was what he wanted—what he'd said he wanted all along. But what he didn't understand was why that left him completely empty.

That notion alone was enough to cool his remaining ardor, and James closed his eyes. It was time to just go to sleep.

"Oh god," Holly groaned at the kitchen table the following morning, holding her head as James came in search of coffee. "Why do you look like shit?" she whispered and then groaned. "I know why I look terrible. Didn't you sleep?"

"I did a little."

"But you didn't drink much. I remember you driving me home…barely. Who put me in bed?"

James chuckled.

"Oh shit."

"Yup. Mom took pity on you." He smiled. "So get ready to pay for it. You know how she is." James handed her a mug of coffee and poured one for himself just as his mother tooled into the kitchen, pulling out pans to make breakfast.

"Jesus, Mom," Holly groaned.

"Don't you dare talk like that, and I'm not the one who drank so much she had to be put to bed by her mother. What were you thinking?" She banged the pan on the stove, and Holly groaned.

"Then be nice. I'm trying to get my head to stop pounding and you aren't helping. I have to be on for the rehearsal dinner."

"And you and Howard have your dance session in two hours," James reminded her. "Daniella and I promised to go with you." He sipped the coffee. "Daniella is trying to finish up your dress." He met her gaze. "You need to get yourself together, because things aren't going to stop." Yeah, he was grumpy and short with her, but he hadn't slept well, and he was still at odds over Daniel and last night. "I'm going to check how preparations are coming." He patted Holly on the shoulder, silently apologizing. Then he got another mug and headed back to the bedroom.

Daniel was at the sewing machine, still in the pink pajamas, working feverishly. "I'm almost done." James gave him the mug, and Daniel stopped long enough to take a couple of sips before returning to work. "Go get cleaned up, and I'll take my turn when you're done." Daniel didn't look up from the machine.

James shaved and showered, returning to the bedroom, where Daniel had made the bed and laid the dress on it. "Is it done?"

"Yes. I need to hang it up and steam it. Holly can try it on once we get back from the dance session." He yawned. "Look, James, I need to talk to you about last night. I got carried away, and I think you did too." He sighed and stepped back. "We need to keep this professional. I'm here to do a job, and we need to keep our feelings out of it. Otherwise we aren't going to make it through this. Like you said, in a few days we'll go home and return to our own lives. It's best if we don't get things all tangled up before that happens." Daniel gathered his clothes and makeup case, heading quickly across the hall like he needed to escape.

James sat on the edge of the bed, smarting from the way Daniel had used his own words against him. Maybe he was right and the two of them had nearly made a mistake last night. When he listened to his head, he knew he and Daniel should simply stick with their professional arrangement and keep their hands to themselves. But as he sat and stewed on it, he grew angry and more determined. No one had ever captured his attention the way Daniel did, and it didn't matter if he was dressed as a man, as he had been on the flight and in the airport, or as a woman, as he had been the last few days. The clothes didn't make the person—it was who was in them, and James only saw Daniel, no matter what he was wearing.

The idea rather shocked him in some ways. James had always seen himself as a man's man. Sure, he liked other men, but he'd always gone for manly men, and Daniel certainly didn't have that appearance. James liked guys who were strong, sure of themselves, and knew what they wanted. Over the last few days, however, he'd learned that his views of people and what made someone strong and confident had changed. Daniel had those characteristics in spades. James hadn't anticipated that...and it pissed him off. He was learning things about himself that weren't pretty, and Daniel was stepping away because of it.

"Aren't you going to get ready?" Daniel asked as he returned dressed and with his makeup in place.

James jumped to his feet, closed the door, then folded his arms over his chest. "You had your say, and now I want to have mine. If you want to keep things between us professional, then there's nothing I can do. That's your decision."

"I'm glad you think so." He knew Daniel well enough now to know when he was being sarcastic. Daniel crossed his own arms and glared back at him.

"But I never pictured you as a coward. I've seen you as many things, intense and protective, determined, and god knows as a woman who turned my head and I had no fucking idea why. When that curtain first parted on that stage and I saw you come out." James stepped closer. "Do you know what I thought?"

"That you had been played?" Daniel deadpanned.

"Well, maybe." He had to admit that. "But I also thought that I would never have the guts to do what you do. You have the internal fortitude to play my girlfriend for my sister's wedding, and yet when there's the chance that things might get more serious and that we might have the chance at something more, no matter how crazy or unrealistic that may be…you're the one to chicken out." James stared into Daniel's eyes and saw only resistance and the hardness of stone. "Fine." He turned away and found a pair of light tan slacks in the closet. He pulled them on along with a blue button-down shirt, and put on his shoes, not looking at Daniel. "Let's go."

"The first dance at your wedding is one of those moments when all eyes will be on you," Beverly, the dance instructor, said and then positioned Holly and Howard in the center of the wood parquet dance floor, surrounded by mirrors.

"I'm going to hurt someone. I'm a menace on the dance floor."

"I've taught many reluctant grooms. Just relax." Beverly talked them through the simple dance steps, breaking them down, and then started the music. Howard took two steps, promptly stepped on Holly's foot, and managed to kick her in the shin.

Holly yelped, and Howard apologized, looking about ready to bolt for the door.

"Your twenty bucks from the other day says he makes a run for it," James whispered to Daniel, who nodded and smiled as Beverly coaxed Howard back, and then they started again.

The second time, he lasted longer. "I can't do this. I have never been able to dance." Howard released Holly and backed away.

"Howard," Holly said gently, coaxingly, and they tried again and again.

"Safe money," James said with a grin. Howard gazed at the door longingly, the look in his eyes remarkably similar to that of a panicked deer. Maybe five more minutes and Howard would be out of there.

"You're mean sometimes, you know that?" Daniel snickered.

"Just calling them as I see them," James retorted as Howard stepped on Holly's foot once again.

"Anyone can dance," Daniel proclaimed and stepped forward, flashing James a wicked smile. Holly's poor feet had probably had enough by this point. "Let me try." He stood right in front of Howard. "Now take my hand and my waist just like you held Holly's." James was just close enough to hear what Daniel was saying.

Holly limped over, standing next to him. "Thank god. My poor feet. We're both going to owe her big-time. At least my feet sure as hell will."

"But I can't do this," Howard protested.

"Bullshit," Daniel growled, and the dance instructor inhaled sharply. Daniel seemed to ignore her and continued. "Have you ever seen one of those old movies with Fred Astaire and Ginger Rogers?" Howard nodded and shrugged, probably confused. "Well, think about it. You have the easy part. Your job is to make Holly look like an angel. Ginger

Rogers did everything Fred Astaire did, only backwards and in heels. Please start the music." The instructor turned it on, and James watched, enthralled, as Daniel started with Howard. If he was honest, he might have been a little jealous.

"Look at me. Not your feet. For now, I'm Holly, and you watch her when you dance. She is your entire focus. Look into her eyes, feel the movement of her body, make her as beautiful to everyone else as she is to you." Daniel pointed. "Your feet are uninteresting anyway. Watch my eyes and my expression." Daniel slowly guided Howard through some simple steps. "There you go," he said when Howard didn't smash his feet. James was grateful for that, because he had plans for Daniel and his feet. "Now do it again. Don't pay any attention to your feet—they'll follow the rest of you. Just look at me." Daniel touched Howard's chin to move his gaze upward. "Dancing is like sex, standing up," Daniel commented, and Howard nearly tripped. James stifled a snicker, and Holly snorted from next to him. "It's about two people communicating with their bodies. When you're dancing, just watch Holly and you'll be fine." They continued moving, and Daniel guided Howard through more and more steps. They were all simple, and yet they looked good together. "Just relax and have fun. This isn't torture. You're going to be taking the woman you love most in the world and giving her a taste of what's to come when the two of you are alone." Finally, Howard stopped moving like a robot and their dancing improved greatly.

James watched Daniel and occasionally glanced at Holly, who shifted her weight from foot to foot.

When James could stand it no more, he nodded to Holly.

"Go get your man." She retrieved her husband-to-be, and James tugged Daniel into his arms.

"But..."

"You cheated...and you were amazing." James smiled, locked gazes with Daniel, and glided him around the floor. "You're a stubborn pain in the ass, and you look gorgeous when you dance, absolutely breathtaking." He smiled, and Daniel stopped trying to lead. James pressed Daniel even closer. "I see your attraction and I felt it last night," he breathed. "You can say what you want, but your eyes and body give you away."

Daniel stopped in his tracks, and James tugged him close once again and then spun him out and back, taking Daniel around the waist.

"I told you..." Daniel stiffened in his arms.

"I know what you said." He gazed into stormy deep blue eyes and propelled Daniel around the floor, keeping him close, never faltering in his gaze, determined to communicate with his body where words seemed to fall short. "This is your punishment for cheating. You have to dance with me."

Daniel chuckled. "Do you always make your punishments so pleasurable?" His deep blue eyes actually sparkled with excitement.

"I try." James made sure Daniel could feel his breath. "Believe me. The more pleasure and the longer I can delay it, the more delicious it becomes." He swung Daniel around more athletically, letting his soul take both of them on their dance-floor journey.

The song ended and another started, the beat slightly different. James moved accordingly, spinning Daniel and recalling him, keeping a tight hold when he was near, watching his expressive eyes, the occasional flare of his nostrils. Daniel's gaze shifted, his expression becoming less stormy, but still intense. He loved that Daniel threw himself into everything he did, and at least while they were on the dance floor, that energy was all his. And damn, it was excitement personified. James twirled Daniel as they circled the floor, movements fluid, languid and easy, yet intense. Daniel felt right in his arms, like he was made for him. He'd had multiple dance partners, but he hadn't danced like this in quite some time. The movements came right back, and as the music shifted, so did James, keeping Daniel on his toes, changing direction and tempo right along with the music, carrying Daniel along. There were missteps, but they quickly became fewer and fewer as the two of them became one along with the music. "I had no idea you could dance like this," Daniel said, a little breathlessly.

"I'm a man of many hidden talents," James tossed back. "It's up to you to try to determine what they are…if you have the guts." He dipped Daniel at the end of the song, grinning from ear to ear. "So how about it? Do you have the courage or not?"

"That was lovely," Beverly said, and it took James a second to realize she was talking to Howard and Holly. Not that he minded. James held Daniel's hand, escorting Daniel off to the side as Howard moved Holly around the floor. He hadn't become proficient in a matter of seconds, but he and Holly were smiling, and it seemed his sister's feet were safe for the time being.

When yet another song began, James held out his hand, a silent question. Daniel took it, and they took the floor once more. "Remember what you told Howard," James teased and swung Daniel into a dramatic spin, catching him when he returned and gliding him across the floor.

James knew he was dancing with a man—the muscles under Daniel's clothes were unmistakable—but he also made sure to show him off, displaying Daniel's grace and poise with each turn. "What?" Daniel asked, his gaze searing into James.

"That dancing was like sex." James held Daniel firmly. "I can feel you quivering in my arms and I know exactly what I'm doing. This is making love standing up, and you know it." He spun him once more as the song ended. Then he hugged a flushed Daniel tightly, deciding that they had probably had enough excitement for the time being. James sat in one of the chairs by the wall and relaxed, stretching out his feet, pleased with himself.

Daniel was still breathing hard, and James could almost feel each time he glanced his way. The next steps were up to Daniel, but James had definitely given him something to think about while Howard and Holly continued the rest of their lesson.

"One last song," Beverly told the bride and groom a little while later.

"Are you up for it?" James asked, holding out his hand. He held Daniel's gaze until he accepted the invitation, and James once again reminded Daniel of exactly what he was offering.

"The real question is, are you?"

"Can we look into Reverend Creepy now?" Margot asked in a whisper as soon as James and Daniel walked in the door. "Mom is out doing some last-minute shopping. She wasn't happy with the dress she was going to wear tonight so she decided to try to find something else." Howard had dropped them off and needed to return home for a few hours.

"Daniella and Holly need to check that the wedding dress fits, but you and I can do some work to see if there's anything going on." James had figured this little exercise would give him and Margot something to do together. If Margot wanted to be a police officer like him, then she needed to learn that a lot of investigations came to nothing, especially fishing expeditions like this one.

"We can go to my room while they use yours. Mom will have a fit if she finds out we're doing this."

"Yes, she will," their father said as he glared at both of them, shaking his head. "What do you think you're up to, young lady?"

"Dad…" She huffed and disappeared into her room, closing the door harder than was necessary.

"Son?" Now James was in the hot seat.

"Let's go check on that dress," Daniel said quietly and hurried past him and down to the other room.

"Cowards," James called as they disappeared behind a closed door, leaving him to face his father's glaring indignation.

"Spill it," his dad growled.

"The girls don't like the minister. Holly doesn't, and neither does Margot." He motioned down toward the living room. His dad sat in his chair and James on the sofa. "Margot calls him Reverend Creepy, and I have to tell you there's something off about the guy. Have you been in his office?"

"Can't say as I have."

"The floor is raised behind his desk to make him seem taller and more imposing. It's weird, Pop, and that lectern, like he needs to seem closer to god. That's downright bizarre. I took some pictures while I was in his office, and since Margot says she wants to be a cop, I figured we could look into a few things, make her see that the guy is a little weird but harmless, and then she can move on." He shrugged.

"And if there's something to what the girls feel?" his dad asked, carefully.

"Then you need to listen to them. They deserve to be comfortable. He may be creepy, but that isn't illegal. Is the guy dipping into the communion wine?"

His dad chuckled, but didn't relax for a second, leaning forward. "You know I'm on the board of elders. Your mother put me up to it last year." He paused a few seconds as though he were thinking. "I can keep my eye on things, but you know your mother when it comes to the church."

"Okay, like I said, I promised Margot that I would look into him with her. If we come up with anything, I promise to tell you." He really didn't expect anything to come of any of this. "Let me find Margot." James stood just as Daniel hurried into the room.

"She's ready." Daniel grinned from ear to ear as fabric rustled, Holly gliding down the hall. James barely registered his father standing up as he stared at the vision his sister had become. Without makeup, her hair just combed…none of it mattered.

"Holly…" James breathed as she stopped in front of the full-length mirror on the linen closet door. She paused, tears running down her cheeks, and Daniel hurried over.

"God, I'm sorry, I…" Daniel began, and Holly held his hands.

"You turned me into a princess," Holly whispered as Daniel smiled. "This is how I always wanted to look on my wedding day." She took the few remaining steps out of the hallway, slowly turning, the dress flowing around her, hugging her hips, and the bodice now accentuating Holly's figure rather than covering it up.

"Sweetheart," his dad said, looking at Holly with what James could only describe as astonishment. "My little girl is all grown up," Dad croaked and turned away. "It's gorgeous," he told Daniel with a sniff.

Daniel stepped away, and James wrapped his arm around his waist. "Thank you. You're a magician."

Daniel leaned really close, resting his head on James's shoulder. It didn't take much intuition for James to know exactly what Daniel was thinking. *And the best damned drag queen in Chicago…and don't you fucking forget it.*

"Thank you," Holly said again, hurrying over to hug Daniel. "If I had room in the bridal party, I'd add you as a bridesmaid for this alone. You deserve a damned round of applause." She sniffed once more, still hugging Daniel.

"Go take the dress off so I can make sure it's pressed and steamed for tomorrow," Daniel explained.

"And whatever you do, don't let your mother see it until it's too late for her to try to overrule you," Dad added. "I'll deny I said that, and having even seen the dress at all beforehand, to my dying day." He sat back down as Holly disappeared into James's bedroom, now a changing room, with Daniel right behind.

"Son, that girl is a keeper. You need to hold on to her with both hands." His dad turned on the television, and James wondered just what his father would think if he knew that the girl he thought so highly of was really the man who was quickly stealing his heart.

# Chapter Twelve

"You really like my brother, don't you?" Holly asked as Daniel unfastened the hooks on Holly's wedding dress.

"Of course I do," he answered as calmly as possible. Since last night he'd been in an emotional tug-of-war. Not that it mattered. Once the wedding was over, the games would end and Daniel would go back to his normal life, one that involved returning to the theater, nightly shows, and not having to tuck his balls every minute of the damned day. And it wouldn't involve James. That part of the equation was what caused him both pain and relief.

"But the two of you are arguing about something," Holly observed, pulling her arms out of the gown and sliding it down her hips. "I love that dress, but I can tell you I'm a lot more comfortable in jeans than I am clothes like this." She set the dress on the bed and pulled on a T-shirt and dark denim pants. "What?" Holly asked, turning around.

Daniel shrugged. "Everything is fine."

"And I'm a mountain goat." Holly jabbed her hands to her hips. "I have eyes. I saw the two of you. That was love/hate dance fucking if I ever saw it." She tucked in her T-shirt and sat on the side of the bed, pulling on her shoes.

"It's complicated," Daniel said softly.

Holly stood and went to the door. "When people say that, it usually means it isn't." She left the room, shutting the door behind her. Damn, she knew how to make an exit.

"Sister, you have no idea," Daniel whispered out loud to himself. This situation was becoming more and more complicated by the second. There was little to do about it now, though. He stood and left the room as well, finding James and Margot at the kitchen table.

"Where do we start?" Margot asked.

"Usually with what we know," James answered. Daniel sat next to him, looking over the things on the table, including notebooks and Margot's laptop.

"Okay. The guy is creepy," Margot said. Both he and James chuckled.

"That isn't enough. In an investigation, we deal with facts and things that are provable. Documentation and witnesses. You use them to build a picture and try to get it as clear as possible," James explained. "So, what do we know?"

Margot shrugged. "He's been here about five years. He has a wife and two kids, a boy and a girl."

James began making notes, but Daniel took the pad, figuring it would give him something to do.

"Where was he before that? Do we know if the congregation and board vetted him before giving him the job?" James asked. Daniel wrote it down with a question mark behind it because it was an unknown. "I seem to remember it happened pretty fast."

"It seemed that way to me too," James's dad said from the

doorway. "But I wasn't on board then." Daniel added that to the notes.

"Okay. What if they didn't? What if the congregation was taken in by his charm and personality? That's what we're trying to look into, then, and unfortunately, we can't just go asking around. What else do we do?" James turned to Margot. "What do you think?"

"Okay. If everyone was taken in by Reverend Creepy, then we need to look into his background. But how do we do that?" She thought a minute. "We could break into the church office and try to find the records." God, she was adorable and had good instincts. He could really see a lot of himself in her.

Daniel chuckled. "The police don't do things like that."

"Well, not as a habit, no." James bumped his shoulder. "Have you done an internet search on him? Publicly available records are always a good place to start."

Margot began typing and turned the computer to show the results. "It's all about the church here. Their website comes up, as does his bio and stuff." Margot began clicking around. "What about where he came from?" She continued searching, and James glanced over. That seemed strange to Daniel. He would have thought there would be a history. "Here's something," Margot said. "It says in this old bio from Facebook that he was at the Carthage Community Church in Middleton, Texas." She smiled.

"Bring up their website and see if there's anything on him," Daniel suggested. This was getting a little interesting. He leaned over James's shoulder to see the screen better, momentarily getting lost in James's woodsy scent. Daniel shook his head to bring himself back to the here and now.

"Nothing," she said, deflating like a balloon, her excitement fading away. She needed to be more resilient, but Daniel kept that to himself.

"No. Look. They have a history page. Check there," Daniel suggested.

"I did," Margot groused.

"No, that chart over there." Daniel pointed. "It looks like a ministerial history of some sort." He leaned closer as Margot brought up the chart. "There he is, but it's an active link." Margot clicked on it and a brief history page appeared along with a picture. "That isn't Reverend Dick."

Margot snickered. "No, it's not. I'm bookmarking the page." She was getting excited and the way she looked at James was different now. Daniel loved that the two of them seemed to be bonding.

James leaned closer. "Look, this bio has a lot of the stuff that's in Reverend Dick's bio. It could almost have been copied." Daniel took down notes from the page. "So his background might be sketchy." James turned to where his dad still leaned against the door frame and then he met Daniel's gaze with a "holy shit" look. "What else do we know?"

"Not much," Margot said. "There isn't a lot of information here. But isn't that suspicious in itself? Most people leave huge footprints on the web. Reverend Creepy has very little." She seemed pleased with herself.

"True, but that's intuition, not facts. As an investigator, you deal in facts. Intuition might lead you in one direction, but it has to be backed up with facts or it's meaningless."

Margot snickered. "Like the time you snuck out of the house, got drunk, and tried to climb in my window instead of yours?" Daniel definitely wanted to hear more about this story. Dang, Margot could be wicked.

James gaped at her for a split second. "See. That's what I mean. Facts. Yes, I did sneak out. You assumed that I was drunk, but my window was locked and yours wasn't. I had actually gone to a concert in town that Mom would have had a fit about. I know you understand that."

Margot sighed dramatically.

"And there was no drinking involved."

Daniel wasn't so sure he believed that was true, and he bumped James's arm slightly just to let him know he wasn't buying it.

"What's all this about sneaking out?" Phillip asked from the doorway.

"Nothing," James sang, and all three of them collapsed into a fit of giggles.

"What about the pictures you took in his office?" Daniel asked, changing the subject.

"You took pictures?" Margot smacked James on the shoulder. "Good job. That was really smart of you. What made you think of it?"

"Very funny. What is it, pick on James day?" He tried to look hurt and failed.

"I don't want to know about any of this…unless you find something," Phillip said, returning to the living room.

"Where's Holly?" James asked his dad.

"Howard picked her up for a little alone time," Phillip answered, turning on the television.

"Let's see those pictures." Margot rubbed her hands together impatiently while James emailed her the pictures.

Daniel was curious too, and intrigued by seeing James in action...so to speak.

Margot shifted her chair closer so they could all see the images as she brought them up. "Get your laptop as well," Daniel suggested to James, who retrieved it from the bedroom.

"He didn't think there was anything to be found, did he?" Margot asked quietly. "Everyone treats me like I'm a kid and don't know anything. 'Go to your room!'" She did a pretty good imitation of her mother.

Daniel hedged. "I think your brother is more cautious than you think he is. But he's also a man of action when it's warranted." He leaned closer to view the images, copying down places and dates from the various framed diplomas and certificates. "I also think that if you want to be taken seriously, then you need to act serious." He smiled. "Emotional outbursts won't get you accepted. But acting grown up will get you treated like a grown-up." Daniel leaned closer. "Though my real advice would be to enjoy being young while you can. Life has a way of ripping it away soon enough." By the time James returned, Daniel and Margot had a list of points of research.

"How do we check these out?" Margot asked. "I doubt we can just go online and get lists of graduates and degrees. I could try to hack into their systems."

James looked like he was going to swallow his teeth. "There's no need for that."

"Why not?"

"We don't have to." James picked up his phone and made a call. "I have a friend who can. Ronny and I went through the academy together." As James made the call, Daniel stood to stretch his legs. He stepped out back, taking in the mountains and fresh air while giving himself a chance to think. Emotionally he was a mess, with his head spinning, and to add to it, this little mystery seemed to have grown into something more than just a diversion.

"He's got something," Margot said, poking her head out the patio door. Daniel returned inside.

"Thanks, Ronny. I sent you copies of the diplomas as well as a list of what they represent. I just need to know if Richard Peterson ever attended any of these schools?... I hate to ask, but the sooner the better. I'm heading home in a few days." He listened some more. "You're the best. I'll talk to you soon." James hung up and sighed. "Ronny is going to check into this for me and call us back."

"How can he have information like this?" Margot asked.

"As I said, Ronny and I went to the academy together. Afterwards, Ronny went into cybercrime analysis. The man is a wizard at tracking people. You might have met him at my graduation, remember?" James bumped his sister's shoulder. "He's the guy you told Mom you wanted to have his babies." Daniel snickered and wondered just what this guy looked like. Not that he could hold a candle to James—Daniel was pretty sure of that.

Margot snickered. "I did that to get Mom going, which was fun. But yeah, he was something."

Daniel laughed. He could see Grace having a fit at that declaration. "What do we do now?"

James smiled at both of them. "What other leads do we have? Is there anything else in the pictures that raises questions?" Daniel looked closer at each one, and Margot did the same.

"There isn't much visible," Margot observed. "The desk

and the shelves are all perfect." She turned to James. "It's like everything is there to be looked at. The room is for show and not for work."

James nodded slowly.

"I don't see anything more," Margot said.

"Okay. Now we have to wait. It's one of the hardest things an investigator has to do sometimes," James declared, to Margot's chagrin. Daniel remembered being her age when everything was "now, why not now?"

"Let's have lunch?" Daniel offered. When things got tough, you ate. "We can go out."

"Yes." Margot grabbed her computer and was out of the room like a shot.

"You don't mind, do you?" James asked. "I think she's been kind of forgotten in all these preparations." He shut down his computer and gathered their notes.

"That's why I suggested it. Let me check my face and grab my bag, and we can go." Daniel got his things and met the others in the living room, where Phillip and James were talking.

"I told you before, you need to hang on to that girl. She's something else." Daniel's lips quirked and he stifled a chuckle, once again wondering what Phillip would think if he knew the truth. One thing was for sure: Daniel really wasn't interested in being around when he found out.

By and large, Daniel didn't want to disappoint James's family. They were good people, and he was growing to like them. Daniel hadn't really thought a great deal about them when he had agreed to do this. Holly was a solid person and she cared for her brother a great deal. Even at a time like this where she was under a lot of stress, she still looked out for him. Margot was a cool younger sister, and Phillip…well, he wouldn't mind having Phillip as a father…or a father-in-law. Grace was a different matter, but she had her good qualities. She only wanted what she thought best for her family, even if she did take things to extremes. He thought James would be much better off if he came clean with them and just explained who he was, let them see the real person inside. But he also agreed with James that now wasn't the time, so he would go along until it was time to go home and let James come out to them in his own time. After all, it wasn't his secret to tell, and outing someone was bad form.

"Are you ready to go?" James asked, pulling Daniel out of his thoughts, and all he could do was nod.


"This entire wedding thing is just more than I thought it would be," Margot said as they sat in a small pub downtown. "It's been nonstop for days, and Mom is all worked up about Holly and the arrangements. I was in the house most of the day yesterday, and other than getting me for meals, she didn't even know I was there." She snagged a fry, and Daniel patted her hand. "I'm supposed to be a bridesmaid and I don't want to do it at all. Except then I'd leave Holly high and dry." She sat back. "It isn't like anyone is going to be looking for me anyhow."

"This is Holly's day. It isn't yours or mine. We're here to support and help her…and not let Mom drive her out of her mind." James smiled, and Daniel loved how he gentled her. "That doesn't mean you shouldn't have a good time."

"But…" She crossed her arms over her chest and sat back, shutting down.

"When you get married, everything will be about you.

That will be your day. This one is for Holly." Not that the family couldn't have made sure that Margot was more involved in the planning. "But…" Daniel smirked and leaned over the table. "What are your plans for the wedding getaway car? Condoms, balloons, a goat…?" He grinned. "I think the decorations for the car are the little sister's purview."

James nodded. "That sounds right to me." Margot immediately perked up, and Daniel wondered what her teenage mind was going to come up with. "Get a few of your friends to help." Daniel loved how James got on the bandwagon.

"Do you have older sisters?"

"Biological ones, no. I was an only child, and the only family I have left is a grandmother. But I have lots of girlfriends, some of them older, though if I were to mention it, they would probably roast my behind in two seconds flat." He shared a grin with James. "Bella would go through the roof if I were to spill her little secret." Daniel put his hand over his mouth in mock horror. Thankfully, James got the joke.

"I'll have to give her grief about it the next time I see her," James added.

"I always wished I had sisters, either older or younger, but it was only me growing up."

Margot ate a little more and then pushed the remnants of her burger aside. "Sometimes I wish I were an only child. Mom is always talking about Holly because she's the oldest and James because he's the only boy, and I just got stuck on the end."

"Soon enough you'll be the only one home, and then you'll get all the attention you could possibly want," James said with a sigh. "Just remember that Holly and I wore Mom down for you."

Daniel shook his head. "Guys are clueless. You need to be yourself and let that come through. You aren't your sister or your brother. You're Margot, so fight your own battles and do what it is you want to do in life." Daniel leaned over the table. "Just don't get in your own way. I know your mom and even your dad can be a pain sometimes, but take it from me, I'd give just about anything to have my mom and dad back again. You get to hug them good-night." Daniel hadn't intended to bring all that up, and the intensity of the loss struck him unexpectedly. James patted his leg under the table, and Daniel was grateful for the care and the comfort.

"Have you thought about what you want to say tonight?" James asked Margot. "Holly is having an open mic sort of thing. She thought it would be nice for people to say a few things, maybe share some funny stories. I think it would be cool if you were the one of us to say something."

Daniel squeezed James's hand under the table. He seemed to understand what Margot needed.

"Really?"

"Yeah. I think it would be great," James added. "I was going to say something, but I think it's better if you do."

Margot smiled brightly. "I should think about it." James finished his burger, and Daniel picked at the last of his salad before James requested the check.

"That was pretty awesome," Daniel said once Margot excused herself to go to the bathroom. "You actually gave her something to do."

James shrugged. "You gave me the idea." He leaned closer. "This wedding would be a disaster if you weren't here. You have to know that. Holly's dress would be a wreck and cobbled together, she'd be pissed at Mom because of the music, Margot would be sullen, and I'd be in the middle of it all, trying to stay the hell out of it."

It was Daniel's turn to shrug. "Speaking of your mother, at least you get props for keeping the 'not fighting with your sisters' commandment." He snorted, and James dropped his fork with a clang.

"Great, one out of ten. That's a real fucking accomplishment." Thankfully he seemed to find the idea funny as well. "Mom's expectations…"

"They're so thick you could trip over them sometimes." Daniel was really coming to understand her in a way, the good and the less good. Daniel didn't doubt that she wanted what *she thought* was best for her family. "Though it is hard to stay mad at her."

James ground his teeth. "That's the real pain in the ass. But trying to change her mind is like pulling teeth. She's stubborn." He checked his phone when it vibrated. "It's Ronny. He says he's still digging." James set the phone aside.

Daniel squirmed under James's intense gaze. "What?"

"I'm glad you came here with me." The words were simple, but the sentiment and the implication went much deeper. Daniel swallowed hard, trying to work out for himself what he thought of the whole situation. "Somehow I know that things aren't going to be the same once I get home."

Daniel was intrigued. "What do you mean?"

James glanced in the direction of the restrooms. "I think I had these conceptions of what it meant to be a guy…a man… I'm not sure. But I can see they're meaningless." He leaned closer. "You're more of a man…wearing a dress…than I think I've ever met in my life."

A lump formed in Daniel's throat. That little declaration was more affirming than just about anything he had ever heard in his life. James had changed quite a bit—at least his outlook had—and yet he was still the same person who made Daniel's heart beat a little faster with just a glance.

"I don't know what to say…"

James smiled and sat back. "Now, there's a first." The mirth in his eyes was adorable. "Not that I want you to change for anything." And just like that, Daniel had some of the acceptance he had gotten remarkably little of for much of his life. Oh, he put on a show when he had to because you should never let them see you cry or bleed, no matter how much they hurt you. That was how the bastards won. But Daniel had lived his entire life fighting the bigots and the shortsighted, and it felt good to be appreciated for who he was.

"Are we ready to go?" Margot asked when she returned to the table, breaking the moment of intimacy. Daniel sat back in his chair, wondering what would truly happen when they returned home, and hoping it was something other than what he feared.

# Chapter Thirteen

James sat at the kitchen table back at his parents' house with Holly, Daniel, and his mother once they arrived home from the restaurant. Margot had gone right to her room, apparently to put together what she wanted to say that evening and to make arrangements for decorating the car. Lord help Holly and Howard.

"You have to be kidding me," Holly said, aghast. "You told Margot she could decorate the car? If there's some animal inside, so help me I will never forgive you."

"Holly," his mother cautioned.

"You didn't give her a real role in the ceremony other than bridesmaid, and she felt left out. So I gave her one." He leaned closer. "And she's going to talk tonight, so hold on to your garter." He grinned, because it was funny seeing Holly so on edge. Okay, he was taking perverse pleasure in the situation, but so what?

His phone chimed. Call me now, the message from Ronny said, and James excused himself, meeting Daniel's gaze.

Thankfully, he understood and followed him down to their room. James made the call as soon as Daniel closed the door.

"What did you find?" He put the phone on speaker and turned down the volume.

"Nothing…" Ronny said. "Absolutely nothing at all. No records of any of the degrees, no record of graduation from a divinity school of any type…nada. I wish we had something else to trace, but Reverend Richard Peterson in Missoula, Montana, is a complete and total falsification. The man does not exist in any of the forms he has stated. Did the church do a background check at all?"

"I have no idea, but obviously not," James answered, as a chill raced up his spine. "My sister's wedding is tomorrow."

"For goodness' sake, don't let him perform it. Who knows if it will be legal, or if anything he's done is legal." James turned to Daniel, at a loss.

"I'm Daniella, a friend of James's, and I think you shocked him completely. Do you know who Reverend Dickhead Imposter really is?"

All James could do was worry for Holly and her wedding. He had to get himself together, and fast.

Ronny cleared his throat and chuckled. "No idea. He took the name of a real person and seems to have spun his identity from there. I checked the church's website and pulled down pictures, but they aren't telling me much. If he has a record, I might be able to find something out, but it's a wide world and a huge search. I've been able to do this much in my spare time, but that kind of search is going to take a lot more resources than I have right now."

"I understand," James said, finding his voice again. "I thought something might be wrong, but this…" He gasped.

"My sister…her wedding…my parents…the guests…this is a disaster." James wanted to sink into himself, but he couldn't. This had to be handled, and he had to be strong for the rest of the family, who were in for one hell of a shock.

"Okay. I get that," Ronny said.

"Can you send him any proof that you have? This is going to send his entire family reeling, and it could resonate a lot further than that." Thankfully Daniel took over while James quickly digested all this and slipped into cop mode.

"Sure. I already gathered everything and will send it over now. James, I'm sorry about this." James jumped slightly when Daniel squeezed his hand, he was so keyed up, then relaxed, knowing he had support.

"Don't be," he said, once he had himself a little more together. "I asked you to help, and I can't complain about the answer I get. I appreciate you looking into this." His phone chimed softly to indicate an email.

"Let me know if I can do anything more, and good luck."

James sat on the side of the bed as Ronny hung up. "What the hell am I going to do?"

"Is there a choice?" Daniel asked. "What happens if you say nothing and then your sister's wedding is invalid?"

"What about all the other people he's married? My god, this could get really ugly…fast." He took a deep breath. "The wedding is tomorrow. If I said nothing to anyone except Holly and Howard, they could go through with the ceremony and then get legally married at the courthouse to cover their tracks."

Daniel stepped in front of him, between his legs, hugging him tightly. "You need to do what you think is right. But let me ask you this: Shouldn't Holly and Howard be the ones to make this decision? This isn't up to you. Holly hates the minister anyway."

He rested his head on Daniel's shoulder, inhaling the scent that had driven him crazy for days, but now it seemed comfortable and steady, which he needed. "You're right."

Daniel hugged him tighter. "Of course I am. I want you to write that in a diary and remember the date."

"You're an ass," James retorted and couldn't help smiling.

"I know. But for a second you felt better." Daniel didn't move, and James soaked in the support.

"I guess we have to tell Holly. And Margot. She deserves to hear what we found too. But what do we do if we don't use Reverend Creepy?"

"You tell them, and we'll figure it out from there. Once a decision is made, we can figure things out." Daniel breathed steadily, and that calmed James's racing heart.

"I can do just about anything when I'm on the job, but this…"

Daniel nodded against him. "It's a different skill set. You don't have to have all the answers. That's my job." James snickered and appreciated Daniel's lightening of the mood a little. "You need to be strong and steady for the family." Daniel released him, and James grabbed his phone, messaging both of his sisters that he needed to talk to them right away. Then he checked his watch. It was two in the afternoon, which left them with some options, but they were limited to a few hours before the rehearsal.

"Howard and I are on our way," Holly messaged, and James went to Margot's room, knocking and cracking the door open to find his sister on the bed, listening to music on her computer.

"Yeah?"

James nodded and put his finger to his lips. "Meet you outside in the yard in five." He closed the door and returned to Daniel, heading out of the house.

Holly and Howard returned in Howard's car, and once Margot came out, the five of them took a walk around the block. "Okay." James wasn't sure how to break this news. "We have a problem, but before I tell you, all of you are sworn to secrecy until we figure out what to do. Got it?"

"Yes," Holly and Howard answered.

"Margot…?" James questioned. "A nod isn't good enough."

"Yes," she answered snappily.

"Margot and I did a little investigating of Reverend Nutcase."

Holly stopped. "And you found something? Is he a pedophile? Or does he beat his wife? I never liked that guy."

"He's a fake. He used someone else's name, and all those diplomas and certificates on the wall are forgeries."

"Ha," Margot said, smiling for a second, and then her face fell and she grew quiet.

Howard hugged Holly as she gasped. "Everything is set, and we… Wow do we… What…?" She buried her face in Howard's neck.

"What do we do?" Howard asked levelly. James hated that his sister was coming apart right there on the street and wished he had thought of a better place to have this discussion, but he didn't want his mom and dad to overhear anything. Not now. James would have to tell his dad, but only once they had a plan.

"That's up to you. We can stay quiet and let the wedding happen. You would need to prevent the reverend from signing the marriage license and have it signed by a JP on Monday. That would handle the legal issues for you."

Holly pulled away. "I am not getting married by Reverend Creepy McFraud Face. No way in hell. I don't know what I'm going to do, but it certainly isn't that." She stood tall, wiped her eyes, and glared at all four of them. "We will fix this somehow, and so help me god, I want to hang him by his nuts until he screams bloody murder."

"You can go as feral on him as you want once we figure this out, and after you're married," Daniel said. "But I like it."

James chuckled. "Then we need to figure out what to do about the wedding. We already have people coming and it's too late to send out a change of venue. That would confuse everyone. I don't know if we can use the church without the reverend." He tried to think of alternatives.

"Let's keep our attention on step one," Daniel said. "First, think about it: Are you sure you don't just want to move forward? This drama doesn't have to affect your wedding."

"I'm sure. I never wanted him in the first place."

"Okay. Then let's assume that the wedding can still take place at the church." Daniel huffed, clearly thinking. "Did you sign an agreement for the venue or make a donation to the church to secure it?"

Holly glanced up at Howard. "Did we?"

"Yes. I made out a check."

Daniel smiled and James understood where this was heading. "Perfect, then. We can argue that we rented the sanctuary for the service," James said, and Daniel nodded. "But that means we need to find someone else to perform the actual service. Worst case, we let the wedding itself just go ahead." One hurdle down, and another rose up right behind it.

"We can try to find someone," Howard said, looking tired. "It's going to be nearly impossible, though." James wished he could argue, but Howard had a point. "Maybe we just have someone who can lead the service, and go to the courthouse quietly on Monday to make it legal. I don't know. Holly and I will work on it."

"Good. Then I think we have the rehearsal so everyone is familiar with the church. James will go to the police and turn this guy in, and they can take it from there. The wedding can go on as planned and the police can handle Reverend Creepy." Daniel seemed really pleased about that, and James had to admit, he would be relieved to see the end of all this. "Is that acceptable?"

Holly and Howard both nodded.

"So none of you say anything to anyone." James looked right at Margot. "Not a word to anyone."

"What about Mom and Dad?" Margot asked.

"We'll talk to them at the right time. Are we all agreed?" James asked, and the four others nodded. "We have a plan." James sighed.

"But…" Margot said. "I don't think it's fair to keep the parental units out of this. They will have to know."

She was right. "Okay. Let me handle it. Holly and Howard, you go on as though nothing is happening. Other than trying to find an officiant, leave the rest to us. You have more than enough to deal with." He took Daniel's hand, grateful for the support, because trying to do this alone would be a nightmare. "The rehearsal is in less than two hours, so you should go get ready and try not to think about all this."

"Like we can somehow *not* think about our wedding completely self-destructing," Holly deadpanned.

"It isn't that bad. We'll try to find someone to officiate, and the rest will go on as planned. Try not to worry about it too much." James hugged his sister tightly. "I mean it. I'll say the words if I have to, and we'll make sure everything is legal. You'll have a wonderful wedding. I promise." The last thing he wanted was for Holly to be disappointed. "It will be better than with Reverend Creepy."

Holly quivered in his arms, and he thought she was crying, but it turned out just the opposite. "I think anything is better than that. I just hope the 'reverend' pays for what he's done." She returned to Howard, and they walked to his car, then pulled out of the drive.

"Why don't you go back to your room, and be sure to say nothing, okay?" Daniel asked Margot, and she hurried off after promising to keep quiet.

James stood in the yard in front of Daniel. "What the heck are we going to do now?" He could scare the reverend half to death, but he had no idea what to do to try to fix this.

Daniel put his hands on his hips, and James knew that was never good. He wondered what he'd done wrong. "Let me guess… I've fixed the program." He held up his hand. "Resurrected that awful dress and turned it into a thing of beauty." He ticked those off his fingers. "Let's not forget I'm here because you needed a date, and now what?" He shook his head. "Save the entire wedding so your sister doesn't walk down the aisle to nowhere?"

James stepped closer. "I guess so…yeah." He cocked his eyebrows.

"You know, there are limits to my SDQ powers." James was coming to treasure that whip-smart look in Daniel's eyes.

"SDQ, that's a new one."

"Super Drag Queen. Maybe I'll embroider it on my shirt so you can remember it. Now, sewing I can do, and I'm incredibly organized, as I'm sure you know. But pulling an officiant out of my ass, well, that takes a miracle." Daniel opened his bag. "Nope, not one in there."

James smiled. "I knew you'd come up with something."

Daniel smacked him lightly on the shoulder. "You really are an ass sometimes."

"Yup. It takes one to know one." James flashed a wide grin. "Come on. Let's go inside and figure out how to resurrect a wedding. Or at least keep this one from going down the tubes."

"James, it isn't that bad."

That stopped him in his tracks. "Now *you're* the master of understatement. I have to tell my father that the minister at his church is a fraud, and since he's on the board, he's going to have to be the one to break it to the congregation." James's hands went to his hips. "What do you think is going to happen? Dad will tell them, and everyone in the church will be so grateful they'll give him a ribbon and throw a party in his honor?"

Daniel snickered. "I suppose not. Though frustrated smart-ass is a good look for you."

"I'm trying to be serious." James just glared.

"Then you're failing. I know what's going to happen. I've seen it before, on one of my first jobs. One-third of the people will think the reverend was so great that the church should just overlook this little transgression. His pastoral skills or directorial skills are just perfect." Daniel rolled his gorgeously blue-shadowed eyes, filled with mischief and sass. "One-third will want him booted out of there and would pay for the pleasure of kicking his sorry ass all the way down the main street of the city…or town, as the case may be, making sure he never pastors or directs in this town again."

"I see… You've got a few issues."

"Issues… Issues… Mack Silverton," Daniel spat, like he tasted something awful, "was the damned director of my first big break…or he was supposed to be. He told everyone that he had tons of experience and knew everyone who was everyone. We were going to be on TV, and our careers were going to take off. All the hyperbole in spades." At first James thought the agitation was put on, but Daniel's eyes darkened, and James realized it was very real. "Turned out his mother paid someone to get him the job, and the entire thing was a disaster of epic proportions. Which brings us to the last third: they'll jump the sinking ship like rats racing to fill the last lifeboat on the *Titanic*."

He took Daniel into his arms, holding him tightly.

"I'm sorry that happened to you. I'd have joined you in kicking that guy's ass down Halstead if it would have helped." He inhaled slowly, excitement rising in seconds just from the proximity and from Daniel's scent. Standing at the edge of the neighbor's front lawn was so not the place to be popping wood, but Daniel just did that to him.

"I know you would," Daniel said, and James held him just a little tighter, arms encircling his waist. "I don't want to go in there."

"Me either, but I think we have to tell my father. I promised him." This was going to be a shit show of epic proportions, and there was little James could do to stop it. "I hate that my parents are going to be really hurt by this."

Daniel sighed. "There's going to be a whole hell of a lot

of hurt to go around. We have to tell your parents eventually, and we have to make sure Reverend Asshole, the cause of all of this, feels as much of that hurt as possible."

Amen to that.

## Chapter Fourteen

"Do you want me to be with you when you talk to your father?" Daniel asked James once they had escaped to their room and the door was closed. He used the makeup mirror to check his makeup and his wig, then did a few touch-ups. James sat on the side of the bed, his gaze intense enough that Daniel felt him watching.

"I never thought putting on makeup could be so sexy." The bed creaked a little as James stood, and then he was closer, his heat reaching Daniel's back.

Damn, he felt sinful. "Do you want a little? I could line your eyes, make them seem bigger."

"No thanks. You look great like that, but it isn't for me."

Daniel set the lipstick on top of the dresser. "Is that part of the 'men don't wear makeup' stuff? Does the thought make you seem less like a man?"

James stilled. "I don't know. It's something I'm not comfortable with."

And just like that, honesty. Daniel's heart sped up. He

tried to remember the number of times he had been with someone and had a moment of unmasked, laid-bare honesty.

"Okay." He stroked James's rough cheek. "I can accept that." He turned back to the mirror. "You didn't answer my questions, though."

"I think so. You've made me look at things differently, but makeup isn't for me." James sighed, pressed to Daniel's back, as he returned his attention to the mirror. "We look good together."

"With the makeup and all…?" Daniel whispered.

"With or without the makeup, you always look good." James turned and kissed his cheek, then lightly touched Daniel's chin, and when he turned in to the enticement of those fingers, James kissed him. "I don't have any illusions about you. I see the person under all of it…and I like him…a lot." Daniel felt his eyes widen. "See, that's it right there. Your eyes are so expressive, and they always show the man, the real you, no matter what you're wearing."

Daniel was struck dumb, and he blinked rapidly. "I think that's the nicest thing anyone has ever said to me."

"Then the people you've been seeing are fools." James kissed him again as the door opened. Daniel stepped back and turned away.

"Sorry," Margot said. "Are you going to tell Dad? Mom is dressing and she's going to be a while. I'm trying to help her."

"Thanks. Yes, we'll do it in a minute," James told her softly, and she closed the door once more. Daniel used the few seconds to get hold of himself again. He had gotten carried away on James's words. Daniel had been so determined to keep the relationship between them professional, but his heart clearly had other ideas.

★ ★ ★

"Dad," James said gently. "We need to talk." Tension rolled off James like a tsunami.

"O-kay," Phillip said defensively. "I'm supposed to get dressed for the rehearsal and dinner soon."

"We know," Daniel said gently, touching James's shoulder just to let him know he was there.

"Then let's go on out to the shop," Phillip said and got up from his chair. He led the way out of the house and through the garage to a small extension off the back filled with wood-working tools and half-completed projects.

"This is nice," Daniel said, picking up a piece of smooth, lathe-turned wood.

"I got an idea to make some Christmas things for your mother. They're going to be holiday figures that she can put up on the porch near the door. With the wedding, I haven't had a chance to finish them." Phillip leaned on the work-bench, and Daniel gently set the piece of wood back where he found it. "Just tell me, how bad is it?"

"Dad, the reverend is a fake. None of his credentials check out, and he seems to have stolen someone else's identity. It's pretty cut-and-dried. None of the degrees on his office wall are real. I had them checked out. His bio is largely stolen from someone else. That has been confirmed. I suspect his driver's license and other ID are fakes as well. I have friends working to determine his real identity." James spoke as clearly and nonemotionally as possible.

Phillip seemed to lose his footing and pulled out a stool, managing to sit without falling. "What are we going to do about the wedding? Everything is set and…"

"We're working it out, Dad. The rehearsal is going to go

on as planned. The church is going to have to figure out a way forward without him, but I'm sure you all can plot a future."

"What about tomorrow?" Phillip grew paler by the second.

"Holly and Howard already know and they're working to get someone else. The biggest thing is for you to breathe and take it easy." Daniel stood on one side of Phillip, and James on the other. "In and out, deep and slow. That's it."

Phillip remained silent, just sitting, and slowly his color returned. "How did we miss this?"

"Because no one looked, is my guess. They were taken in by his personality, and he had all those plans that everyone fell in love with. He simply carried everyone along with him. It's what people like this do. They're very good at taking people in and covering their tracks."

"After all this time, he felt secure and didn't think anyone would follow up. But your son is no fool, and neither is your daughter." Daniel met Phillip's quizzical gaze.

"Looking into him was Margot's idea," James explained. It hadn't been totally, but Daniel liked that James was giving her the credit.

"The rehearsal will happen?"

"Yes. So that everyone knows what they need to do tomorrow. We will find someone to step in for Reverend Nutcase if we can, and the reception will go on as planned. That's how we envision things now." James did a good job of keeping his father calm. "We haven't told Mom, and I don't know if we should until it's absolutely necessary."

"But I should..." Phillip stammered.

"You don't need to do anything other than get through the rehearsal as though nothing has happened. Let me handle

this. I know what I'm doing. I'm going to call the local police and have him arrested for fraud, embezzlement, taking
money under false pretenses, and anything else I can think
of. I know there's a chance that the church could decide not
to press charges, but how many people has he married ille-
gally? He isn't a minister, so all the things he has done are
now suspect. I'm sure there will be enough people clamor-
ing after his head that he isn't going to stay around." James
hugged his dad. "I'm also doing this to try to take this out
of everyone else's hands. That way the church can hopefully
move on."

Phillip nodded. "I pray we can."

Daniel hoped the same. But there was going to be pain.
"I have a friend who is contacting the person whose identity
he's been using as cover to create his fictional background,
and I suspect he'll press charges." James was a rock, support-
ing his father in this. "Just trust me on this." He winked, and
Daniel rolled his eyes.

"Very funny, son," Phillip said. "Okay. I'll go along with
this."

"And if it goes wrong, you know nothing and had nothing to do with anything. It was all me, and I'll take the fall
so you can hold your head high." James was a good son.

Daniel leaned in to Phillip. "This man, the reverend, isn't
normal. He's a sociopath. I had a director who was the same
way years ago. He isn't concerned with anyone but himself.
No one else matters, and he's taken the entire congregation down the garden path because it was what he wanted.
Nothing more. The pulpit, the church building, the weird
office, all of it was done for his aggrandizement and self-
importance. He wasn't trying to help anyone or do any good

work at all. Everything was about him. It's that simple, and you don't need that kind of person leading the congregation. You need someone who actually wants the best for everyone, not himself." There were so many more things he could have told James about his experience with the director, but he didn't need to hear all the ugly details or how stupid Daniel had been. He didn't want something like that to happen to James's family.

"Can you do that, Dad?" James asked.

"It's hard keeping things from your mother, and she's nervous enough as it is. I won't say anything, but you'll have to tell her this evening. She deserves to know, and not tomorrow when there's no minister at her daughter's wedding."

"I'll take care of it," James agreed, and Daniel could almost feel more weight falling on James's already encumbered shoulders. "Besides, you have bigger things to worry about. Margot is going to be speaking at the dinner tonight."

Phillip gasped. "Are you nuts?"

"Your daughter is a young lady now," Daniel said. "She needs her moment to shine, and I think she'll surprise you." Margot had promised to show him what she wanted to say so Daniel could help her with it. He really wasn't worried. Though there were bound to be a few jokes at her sister's expense, Daniel actually expected Margot to do a good job.

"I'd better go back in the house and get dressed for the rehearsal," Phillip said. "You all should do the same. It's going to be an interesting night."

Now, *that* was an understatement.

Daniel checked himself in the mirror one last time. "You look really good," he told James, doing his best not to rake his gaze over James's midnight blue shirt and light pants. "If I didn't know better, I'd say you had a great stylist."

James's eyes twinkled when he turned around. "I'd say so too if I hadn't done it all myself." He adjusted his collar. "Ready to go?"

"Yes." Daniel had picked out a blue cocktail dress that hugged his accentuated figure in all the right places. He knew he looked amazing. What he really liked was how James kept looking him in the eyes, like he was watching him rather than the couture.

"Are you? There's a lot you need to do tonight."

"I'm as ready as I'll ever be." He smiled. "The truth is, while I hate that this is going to hurt, my mom especially, I like this sort of thing. I went into law enforcement to be able to take out the bad guys and keep folks safe. That part isn't going to be too hard. It's holding myself off until after we're done with the rehearsal—that's going to be hard, but I'll manage." He opened the door and held it for Daniel. James's parents had already left, but they stopped by Margot's room and knocked.

James stopped dead when his sister emerged from her room in a fitted silvery dress that shimmered in the light. "Is that what you were doing earlier?"

"Just giving her a few makeup tips," Daniel explained as he took James's arm. "Close your mouth. She's your sister."

Margot chuckled, and James did as he was told before the three of them left for the church.

Daniel hated the building, and at night, with all the exterior lighting on the stark white outer walls, it seemed even more imposing. They went inside and into the sanctuary, where

Daniel took a seat close to the front across from Grace and Phillip to watch the proceedings, while the others gathered in front for initial instructions. Daniel watched as everyone took their places, shaking his head when he realized Reverend Sociopath had installed himself at the top of a set of risers just in front of the altar. He spoke, and then everyone moved to the back of the church to process in, going through all the motions, until Howard and Holly stood together in front of the minister.

Daniel figured this was a good time to use the restroom and quietly left the sanctuary, finding the bathroom out front. He wasn't sure how long this would last, so he hurried and returned to find Weston sitting in his pew. Daniel took his place once again while Holly and Howard spoke with the minister, doing his best to ignore Weston, but it was difficult with the way he kept staring at him.

"You still can't take no for an answer?" he finally whispered and motioned. "Go sit somewhere else, please. Your attention is not appreciated." He almost got up to sit with James's parents, but Weston stood and joined the rest of the wedding party when they were called forward.

It took another fifteen minutes to run through the reading and the final vows before they were dismissed. "I have a few things to ask the reverend," James said as he approached his parents. "Would you please take Margot with you to the restaurant? The two of us will be along shortly."

Grace grinned from ear to ear, and Daniel had to wonder if she was hearing round two of the "Wedding March" in her head. Daniel hated to disappoint her, but he and James weren't getting married, and if he did ever walk down the

aisle, it would be to something much more meaningful…
like "Dancing Queen."

"We'll see you at the dinner," Holly said to them both,
hugging James and then Daniel.

He and James purposely avoided the reverend before following Holly and Howard out into the parking lot. "Have
they been able to find an officiant?" Daniel asked quietly,
standing near the car.

"Howard was still working on it," James said. "But I'm
wondering what I should do. I don't want to mess up Holly's
wedding and yet I know I have to do what's right."

Daniel nodded. "They know the plan. Stick with it. Howard will find an officiant and Holly doesn't really want to
be married by him anyway." He tilted his head toward the
church building. Daniel got in the car and James did the
same, then he made the call on Daniel's phone so he could
have his free for incoming calls. Daniel sat next to him with
a hand on his leg, just to show his support.

"I know this is out of the ordinary, but I'm James Petika,
a police officer visiting from the Chicago area, and I have
something I need to report." James sounded so confident,
and it occurred to Daniel in a passing moment that he wished
that confidence would extend to him being honest with his
family about who he was. It was shame that he didn't let
them see the impressive man that Daniel saw.

Daniel pulled his attention back to James as he explained
what he'd found out and what evidence he had been able to
collect. James laid out his case right there over the phone and
as he spoke he sent various messages and images through text.

The strength he displayed as he relayed information, the
organization, and the sheer confidence in his voice were

sexy as all hell. James really knew what he was doing. Seeing him in action had been awesome, and hearing him lay out his case was almost thrilling. Which was a bit of a surprise.

"Yes," James said as he wrapped up what he was saying. "My sister is supposed to be getting married tomorrow and he's going to do it...yes... Thank you." He listened some more and then, after thanking the person on the line once again, ended the call.

"Is everything okay?"

James nodded and sighed. "Yes. They said they'll look into everything I gave them. They were impressed at what I sent."

"They should be," Daniel told him. "You and Margot did good work."

James sighed softly once again. "Anyway, they'll look into it, but things aren't going to happen all that fast. So tomorrow should be fine. Holly will get married tomorrow, and everything will be okay. It isn't the best solution, but at least the show will go on."

"You were amazing," Daniel said as he leaned over to him, throwing his arms around James's neck. "You did what was right and safeguarded the wedding so your sister could have the big day she deserves." James was a good man, there was no doubt of that. Daniel kissed James hard, moaning as James's strong hands wrapped around his back.

James held him tighter, kissing harder, pressing him back against the seat. "Hell, I want you," James growled. "I have for days." Daniel found himself caught in James's intense gaze. "Do you have any fucking idea? I've gone to bed every night with a permanent hard-on, smelling your aromatic Viagra. I haven't gotten more than a few hours' sleep, and my imagination has been running on overdrive with you right next to me and off-limits."

James didn't give Daniel a chance to respond before he kissed him again, reaching over to put the seat back. "You need to stop me now, or..." James's eyes were as dark as night and his breathing shallow. "Say you want this too."

"James," Daniel gasped as James slid his hand up under his clothes. Daniel had never been so happy in his life to be wearing multiple layers to keep his manhood hidden instead of tucking, because damn, his heart pounded as excitement raced through him like wildfire. "I want you, but..." He gasped for breath before James tugged at his lips. Daniel held him tighter, sucking on James's tongue, his control slipping. "We're in the church parking lot." He didn't want to think about it.

James paused a second, lifting his heated gaze. "Damn..." He sat back in his seat, breathing hard. "This is too open, and I don't intend to share you with anyone." He swiped his hand down his face. "I must be crazy."

"What?" Daniel whispered.

James took a deep breath, held it, and released it slowly. "I'm not going to do this here."

"Because it's a church?" Daniel was seconds from jumping James. Daniel had been going out of his mind for days and was tired of this waiting. He wanted to get his hands on James and feel what all of those incredible muscles and hot skin next to him were like. He wanted to know what it was like to have James all to himself in the most intimate way.

"No..." James closed his eyes. "I can't believe I'm doing this...but no. Not here. I don't want to do this here." He seemed to steady himself once more. "When I get you all to myself…alone and open to me, I want it to be more mean-ingfully than fucking hurriedly in the damned car. I want it to be in a bed with you naked, laid out for me, wanting, begging, looking at me like I'm the center of the universe. I want to take my time and show you everything you de-serve." He swallowed hard, and Daniel put his seat back up.

Daniel did his best to catch his own breath and tamp down the disappointment that welled inside. "I…" He sighed.

James stopped. "You deserve more than this. You deserve the biggest, most comfortable bed…hours of exploration… days…maybe even weeks. You should be treated as though you're worth every second we spend together and not just a quickie somewhere." James drew closer. "Because when I have you, I want all of you, every single inch, and every bit of your attention. I'm a selfish man, and I only want the best." James held his hand, the energy between them filling the car. "We'd better get to the rehearsal dinner."

"Or your mother will start wondering if we're flouting her damned commandments again." Daniel had to do some-thing to cut the tension between them otherwise he was going to explode.

Thankfully James snickered. "You know, if that's what she's thinking, then it will be one of the few things that Mom might have gotten right with this wedding."

Daniel rolled down the window, thankful for the crisp mountain air to help clear his head. It seemed that the last of his defenses had been smashed to the ground. Daniel breathed slowly, grateful that one of them had come to their senses. Or was he? Daniel wanted James, and he could repeat oth-erwise in his head until the cows came home, but that sure as hell didn't mean that his heart was listening. And holy hell, James's reasons for waiting... Daniel had been waiting to hear those words forever. He knew he was good in bed, and most guys were only interested in that...however they could get it. This seemed different, and...dare he think... maybe exactly what he'd been looking for. He stuck his head out the window and looked up at the stars, wondering if he actually dared to let himself hope that there was even the remotest possibility that the fantasy, the fairy tale, could come true for him.

# Chapter Fifteen

"Where have you been?" Holly whispered forcefully as he and Daniel entered the restaurant.

"Sorry. I had to make a phone call." James held her gaze until she nodded slowly. "Everything should be okay for tomorrow."

"Good. Now take your seats so the dinner can start." She led the way through the crowded restaurant to the private room in back.

"Bossy, isn't she?" Daniel asked.

"Hangry," James retorted. "This is what you get when she hasn't eaten." He pulled out Daniel's chair and then took his own.

"Thank you all for coming and being part of our wedding," Howard said after standing at his place at the head table. "Please enjoy the dinner and have a wonderful evening." Everyone clapped as servers fanned out, taking orders and bringing drinks.

"Good evening," Weston said as he took a place across from them at the table. Smug, smarmy bastard. "I thought

I'd come over to say hello." He leaned over the table, looking at Daniel.

"I suggest you go back to your table or you'll be drinking your dinner through a straw," James growled.

"It's okay," Daniel told him with a gentle pat on the hand. "Actually, I have a few questions I'm hoping Weston can answer." Daniel smiled seductively. "Do you mind?"

"Of course not." He leaned back in the chair as though he were content and had won something. All James wanted to do was beat the shit out of him.

"Awesome. So I was wondering what barn you grew up in? You obviously have the manners of a goat and the behavior of a pig in heat. I was wondering if acting this way really gets you what you want?"

Now it was James's turn to sit back.

The woman seated next to Weston snorted. "I thought I was the only one he treated that way." She hit Weston with a glare that could have frozen fire in its tracks. "I wish I'd have put him in his place that easily." She extended her hand to Daniel. "Margie Bell. I went to school with Howard. And unfortunately for me, this loser."

"Margie, I…"

"Unfortunately, I married him and then figured out what an ass he really was…and divorced him two months later." She turned to Weston. "Go on. I'm looking forward to this evening, and that means not sitting anywhere near you."

"Despite that lapse in judgment, you remedied that little walk down the path of bad taste." Daniel glared at Weston. "You heard the lady. Get lost."

James stood as Weston scraped his chair back, glaring hard

at Daniel, and left the table. "Has he been bothering you a lot?" Margie asked before James could.

"Yes. Though he never had a chance. James is wonderful, and Weston has more lines of cheese than Kraft."

Margie chuckled. "I wish I'd had your mouth when I was dating him. He was always crude. But be careful. Weston is vindictive. He believes in exacting a hurt for a hurt." The server came to their table. James ordered the prime rib, and Daniel the glazed salmon.

"Do you mind if I have a taste of yours?" Daniel asked.

"Of course not." James put an arm around Daniel, squeezing lightly and sharing a smile. It finally felt like the two of them were on the same page, and that not only added excitement and anticipation of what was to come, but also happiness and contentment. He still needed to check to see if an officiant had been found, but if necessary, James would figure out how to get ordained on the internet and perform the ceremony himself. One way or another, this wedding was going to come off, with hopefully a minimum of additional drama. "Thank you for everything you've done." He leaned close enough that only Daniel could hear. "This wedding is going to be wonderful, and Holly will look amazing because of you."

Daniel smiled, and even though they were in a room full of people, that smile was only for him.

"James," his mother said from behind him, and James immediately tensed. He knew that tone. "Something is going on and your father won't tell me what it is. Holly is avoiding me, and so is Margot, which can only mean that they are hiding something. Every time I ask, they look toward you." She folded her arms just under her bosom.

"They're serving the drinks and will be bringing out dinner soon. I'll explain everything after we've eaten. I promise." James smiled, and she seemed satisfied, returning to where his father waited for her.

"All right," James said after he hung up the phone, unable to eat the last of his dinner. Pushing his chair back, he motioned to his father, who got his mother and joined him before they all left the room and went out into the main restaurant. James led them through to the large wooden front doors and outside. "I'm going to make this brief and as truthful as I can."

"I'm waiting," his mother said, her gaze hard.

"Before I begin, there is nothing you can do or could have done, and the problem has been handled." He took a deep breath. "The man you know as Reverend Peterson isn't a reverend at all. He's a fraud. The local police have contacted the church, and now the good reverend is apparently nowhere to be found." That had been one hell of a call to receive during dinner. "He was a fraud and took someone else's identity in order to lead this congregation."

"But... Those accolades..."

"All fake. Everything about him was a lie. He has left the church and the police are looking for him."

"How could you?" his mother demanded. "He's the best minister we've ever had."

"Mother," James snapped. "He isn't a minister at all. He's a fake, someone who stepped in off the street...a nobody." Part of him knew this was why they had never told her, but it still hurt that she took the reverend's side over his, and ignored the fact that he had uncovered someone who was only going to hurt everyone badly in the end.

"Let me get this straight. Reverend Peterson is gone?" his mother said levelly, and James nodded. "The night before your sister's wedding?" James nodded again. "You couldn't have waited?" The fire in her eyes and the way her hand clenched and opened again told him she was about to explode and things were going to get really ugly, like mama tiger ugly.

"Grace, it's going to be fine. Think about it. If he wasn't a minister, then would the marriage have been real in the eyes of god?" his dad asked, and that seemed to give his mom pause. "Sure, the ceremony could have happened, but would it have meant anything?"

And that was when she turned on him. "You knew, didn't you?"

"Now, Grace. You need to calm down and remember that we have to go back in there and face the wedding party and Holly and Howard's friends, as well as Howard's parents. There is nothing that you can do about this. It's done. Getting angry isn't going to help." Somehow Dad kept his cool, and Mom calmed down. "This isn't your fault."

"No." Her stare clearly communicated that she thought the fault rested with James.

"It's not his either, so don't do or say something you'll regret. He didn't bring this about—the reverend did when he lied." His dad took his mom into his arms, holding her tightly. It was one of the most tender things he had seen his father do in years. James turned away to give his parents a moment of privacy. "We all know what hurt a lie can wrought. It can tear everything apart, and the reverend was lying to all of us. He lied to the church, and everyone is going to be just as hurt as you are." James couldn't help drawing a comparison between the reverend's lie and how he wasn't being truthful with his family about who he was.

People came and went from the restaurant, pretty much ignoring his mom and dad, thank goodness. "Phillip, I really don't understand all of this."

"None of us do. And everyone at the church is going to have to deal with it eventually." He broke the hug, but held her hand. "We need to be strong so we can get through this, all of it. The church and everyone who is part of it are going to need our strength."

"But the wedding…?" she said, her shoulders slumping, though she didn't seem as fragile as she had.

James used his most gentle tone. "We're working on it. One way or another, the wedding will go forward. Holly, Howard, Daniella, and I are all figuring it out." James motioned toward the door. "Everything is going to be beautiful, and Holly is going to be married. Things will work out." James only wished he knew exactly how that was going to happen. "There's nothing you can do at the moment, but we thought you should know what was going on."

She sniffed and dabbed her eyes with a tissue she always seemed to be able to produce from somewhere. "You never liked the reverend, none of you kids did."

James nodded. "True. It was the girls who thought there was something wrong, and it turned out they were right. Mom, I'm a cop, and I see this all the time. Don't misplace the blame for this. It belongs with the reverend and no one else. All the hurt feelings and inconvenience and worry should be placed at his doorstep and no one else's. He's the one who did something wrong, not Holly or Margot, and not me. Just remember that."

She shook her head as though she were going to argue. "So help me..." Anger welled up again.

"Don't worry, Holly has already threatened to rip his nuts off if she sees him again." For the first time his mom smiled.

"That's my daughter."

"Come, Grace. We can go back to the party and leave the details to the young people." His father led his mom back inside, and James took a deep breath of the crisp night air before rejoining Daniel inside.

"How did it go?"

James put an arm around Daniel's waist. "Better than I expected it to. Mom wasn't happy, but she calmed down. What's happening here?"

"Margot is just about to give her talk." Daniel held his hand tightly as she made her way to the front and cleared her throat.

"I'm Margot, Holly's younger sister, and I thought I'd share a few memories with you tonight. See, growing up with Holly wasn't easy. I was always the disappointment, or it felt that way. Holly was the perfect one. Mom and Dad told me more times than I could count that they wished I could be more like her. That really sucked." James turned to Daniel, wondering where this was going. Daniel patted his hand.

"Until I realized that Holly was someone I should look up to. She's kind and warm, and always made time for me. Even when I was a little brat being a pain in the butt." A chuckle wound through the room, and James squeezed Daniel's fingers. "When Holly went away to college, she invited me to come visit her for a weekend, and all her friends were nice to me." She quirked her eyebrow. "One of them even gave me my first taste of beer. Don't worry, Mom, I didn't like it…much." Another laugh, and James relaxed.

"I was lucky to have a big sister like Holly, mainly because she paved the way and wore Mom down." She slipped Holly a thumbs-up. James rolled his eyes as his smile grew bigger. "And now she's found Howard. I hope the two of them will be happy together as they go out into the world to build their own lives." She moved closer to the table. "And, Howard, I want you to know that if you don't make Holly happy, you'll have to answer to me."

"I promise," Howard said, holding Holly a little closer.

"Now let's raise our glasses to Holly and Howard." She lifted her glass of ginger ale, and everyone in the room joined her in the toast. "May they know happiness and joy, may they have a dream wedding tomorrow, and may their life be filled with the pitter-patter of little feet doing the same things we did." Her expression grew devilish, and Holly laughed as everyone drank.

"You had me right up until the end, little sister," she shot back, still smiling.

"Was that your doing?" James whispered to Daniel, who shrugged and tried to seem completely innocent. "That isn't going to work."

"She wanted to be able to end with something humorous," Daniel said, "and it worked. Everyone is smiling and Margot is happy—even your mother. This was all your idea, remember?" James was more than well aware of that. "Maybe now that dinner is over, you and I can leave and have an hour or two alone." James's eyes grew wide, and heat spread through him within seconds. James nodded without saying a word and got to his feet, but a hand on his shoulder stopped him.

He closed his eyes, swallowing the curse that bubbled upward. He wanted Daniel with every cell of his being, and this up and down, push and pull was becoming more than he could bear.

He turned to where Howard waited and stood. "Excuse me, I'll just be a minute." James held Daniel's gaze for longer than was necessary; he didn't want to leave. Daniel nodded slowly, and James followed Howard just outside the room.

"We didn't find anyone. I made a few calls and came up empty." He seemed extremely on edge. "Holly is growing more nervous and determined. She doesn't want to have to get remarried at the courthouse. You know how your sister can be once she sets her mind to something." Howard seemed pale, and James understood exactly how he felt. Holly was their mother's daughter, and she could be as stubborn as any mule.

"It's all right. I told Holly I'd make sure the wedding was a success and I will." More of the burden of this wedding settled onto his shoulders. James was even more determined that Holly got married on schedule and that the ceremony went off without a hitch. "I'll see about ordination on the internet if I have to." He patted Howard on the shoulder. "Everything is going to be fine, one way or another." James hoped to hell that was true. "Go on back in to your guests."

"And your parents know?" James confirmed it with a nod. "I haven't told mine yet, but I will once the dinner is over." He took a deep breath. "Thank you for being such a good brother to both Holly and me." He turned and went back into the room, with James following and intent on excusing himself with Daniel so they could get back to where they'd left things earlier.

★ ★ ★

"Ladies and gentlemen." Weston seemed to have found a microphone and the lights had been dimmed. "Here he is. We've been waiting for the groom to return. Holly and Howard asked me to give you all a little presentation. I've known Howard since we were kids in high school together. I played football; he played chess. I lettered in track; he was president of the computer club."

"And even then, you still couldn't get the girls to notice you," Howard interjected. Everyone in the room laughed, especially Margie, who seemed to be getting a perverse pleasure out of how red Weston blushed.

"No matter what, we were friends. I got him through gym class, and he got me through math and English." James quietly took his seat next to Daniel, figuring that once this speech was over, the two of them would excuse themselves and go. James placed his hand at the base of Daniel's neck, running his finger lightly above the collar of the silk blouse, Daniel's skin softer than the fabric and ten times more tempting to touch. Daniel shivered and leaned closer, and they shared a heated gaze that only made James more impatient.

"Howard and I both went to college, where he studied, and I partied." The pictures on the screen shifted to the two of them—Howard in a collared shirt, Weston holding a pitcher of beer. "After we graduated, he worked hard, built an amazing career…but don't ask me what he does because I don't understand it. Nobody gets it. I just say that my friend Howard is a rocket scientist because his actual work is impossible for us laypeople to understand. But…the truly important thing is that he met Holly, and the quiet, self-reflective person I'd always known suddenly went to parties and smiled…a lot. He was happy and excited…about some-thing other than math, computers, and science." Weston paused, and the two guys shared a fist bump. The image on the screen changed again, this time to a gorgeous picture of Howard and Holly standing together on the beach with the sun setting behind them. It was stunning, and both of them were smiling brightly.

Daniel patted his leg under the table, and then that hand grew bolder in the darkness, slowly making its way higher. James swallowed and held his breath. He didn't dare move, though he wanted to shift desperately because things down south were constrained and really uncomfortable. "Soon…" Daniel whispered, his breathing growing shallower, and James was worried he was about to go off like some teenager.

"But all isn't as it seems," Weston continued. "I love my best friend. He's always been there for me no matter what stupid shit I do. That's why it really hurts me to say that someone here tonight is not as they appear, and I feel as though I have a duty to keep them from hurting my friends." James glanced around the room briefly before returning his attention to Weston, who was focused solely on him and Daniel.

His blood turned to ice water in an instant.

## Chapter Sixteen

James might have seen what was coming, but Daniel was taken by complete surprise. Weston had been rambling on with the usual pre-wedding sort of slide show of people Daniel didn't know, containing jokes he wasn't privy to. So there wasn't much to hold his attention, other than the way James lightly stroked the back of his neck and how his firm thigh muscles quivered under his touch. Daniel hadn't dared go too far, but the rising color in James's cheeks and his shallow breathing told Daniel that he was having the desired effect.

"This Daniella person," Weston said, yanking Daniel's attention away from James and back to the present. "Though that isn't her real name, given the fact that Daniella isn't actually a woman."

A gasp and few stray snickers went through the crowd. Weston gloated and stayed quiet for effect. James launched himself across the dining room, landing right near Weston, who ended up on the floor. The microphone rang loudly, and then silence reigned until James got back to his feet. "You son of a bitch." He pulled Weston to his feet.

"I saw his driver's license," Weston said.

"And how did you do that?" James glared at Weston, and Daniel knew the only possible way was if Weston had gotten into his bag. "Spying, snooping, going through bags. Did you steal anything?" James asked. Daniel had to give James a whole hell of a lot of credit for keeping the attention, at least for the moment, on Weston. "Maybe all the ladies in the room should check their purses just to make sure you haven't been stealing from them."

It was a brilliant ploy, and sure enough all the women pulled out their bags. "You need to go," Holly pronounced as she stood up. "This is in poor taste and the weirdest stunt you've ever pulled."

Daniel stood. "Holly," he said softly. "It's all right." He saw the instant that Holly saw through the makeup and the clothing to the man he was underneath. Her hand went to her mouth, and she then sat back down. Daniel picked up his bag, turned, and left the dining room without another word. He sure as hell wasn't going to explain anything to a room full of strangers.

"Well, Weston, how much did you steal?" James snapped, and Daniel was able to get out of the room with most everyone's attention on James and Weston.

Another scuffle reached Daniel's ears as he stepped out of the private room and into the main restaurant dining area, which had largely cleared out. He found a seat near the front of the restaurant, slightly away from the door, and wondered what he should do. This hadn't been in any of their plans, and Daniel had no idea if he should stay or simply try to disappear. He could go to a hotel for the next few days and then fly home. He had his ticket, and lord knew James was going to have enough trouble as it was.

"You!" Weston growled as he and two of Howard's other friends stomped their way out of the room and through the restaurant toward where he sat. "You've caused enough trouble already. Why are you still here?"

Daniel ignored Weston. "Where's James?" he asked one of the other guys.

"Still in there," he answered softly.

"What the hell is wrong with you? Are you some freak who likes playing with people?"

Daniel turned back to Weston. "I sure as hell got a laugh out of you. Making a pass at me every time you had the chance."

"I certainly didn't know," Weston answered, pulling himself upward. "I never…"

Daniel snorted softly. "Maybe thou doth protest too much." Weston paled. "Get out of here and watch who you're calling names, pig boy."

"Let's go," one of the other guys said and practically dragged a still-sputtering Weston out of the restaurant. Daniel slumped back in the chair, wondering what was going on. Had James thrown him under the bus and not told his family that he knew Daniella was really a guy? That seemed like the most obvious explanation, which meant Daniel needed to get the hell out of here before he found a pack of James's family members all gunning for him. Maybe if he was lucky, he could get back to the house, grab his things, and get a ride out of there before everyone else got home.

"Can I help you?" the hostess asked.

"No thanks. I'm just going to call a ride." Daniel brought

out his phone, ordered an Uber, and thankfully there was a car only a few minutes away. He didn't see James again by the time the car arrived, and he hurried out to meet it.

"Thank you," Daniel said and got out of the Uber, entering the house using the key that James had given him earlier. He placed it on the polished wood coffee table and hustled down to the bedroom he and James had shared.

The first thing he did was pull off his wig and then remove his makeup, cleaning his face, and stripping away the clothes, removing the last vestiges of Daniella, dressing himself in jeans and a T-shirt. It had been so long since he'd worn his boy clothes that they almost felt uncomfortable...almost.

He needed to pack. Daniel didn't know how much time he had, and he needed to get busy. After pulling his suitcases from under the bed, he slapped them onto the mattress and started the packing process. Haphazardly throwing things into suitcases wasn't usually his style, but Daniel figured he could repack everything once he got safely to the hotel.

With the suitcases all laid out, he began pulling outfits from the closet. Daniel got to the one he'd worn last night and his fingers glided over the fabric. He made it back to the bed intending to pack it, but instead sat on the edge, holding the hanger. "God damn it," Daniel swore out loud, flipping the dress onto the spread-out luggage with much more force than was necessary.

He'd been a fool, that was for damned sure, and Daniel hated being made to feel that way. He had actually thought that James had felt something for him, that the last few days hadn't been an illusion. But that was a joke, and the punch line was him. The guys with Weston had made it pretty clear that James had stayed with his family. Hell, he probably had them convinced that Daniel had pulled the wool over even James's eyes and that this was all his fault. He should have known. For all the talk about how James felt, when push came to shove, James hadn't had the guts to stand up and be himself. Instead, he'd taken the easy way out. Well, screw him.

Daniel deserved so much better than that. He hung his head. Why did he always go for the guys who could hurt him the most? He got back up and returned to packing. There wasn't time for this kind of soul-searching crap. He needed to get packed and get the fuck out of here, away from James and his family with their expectations, masks, and outward lies matched only by the ones they spun in private. Daniel shook his head hard to try to get James out of it so he could think.

Moving more quickly now, he emptied the closet and the drawers where he'd stowed his folded things. The shoes came next, and finally the wigs and other small items. Daniel checked the area over once more, closed the suitcases, and went to the bathroom.

"Fuck," Daniel groaned at the sight in the mirror. He looked like a damn raccoon had run hither and yon all over his face. Daniel grabbed a cloth, washing his face well to remove the last bits of makeup. His eyes were puffy and his cheeks red and blotchy—basically, he looked as bad as he felt. Well, at least there was no one to look good for, and he could rest at the hotel and wait for the flight back to Chicago and real life.

He dried his face with a towel, returning to the bedroom. Daniel closed all the suitcases, carrying them to the front door, before returning for a second load as light flashed across the living room walls from a car pulling into the drive. He moved faster, getting the last of his things together by the door, then bracing for whatever onslaught was about to come his way.

The front door banged open, hitting the stop like a gun-shot. "Thank god. I was wondering where you were and what happened to you." James raced inside. "They took Weston away."

"I suspected they would," Daniel said softly, arms crossed over his chest. "Did you get the message across that you wanted? Did everyone calm down once he was gone?"

"Yes. Most people settled back in their seats for the rest of the evening. I looked around for you, and the hostess said that you'd left. I hoped you had come back here." James rubbed the back of his neck with his hand. "I was worried sick and afraid that Weston might have hurt you or something."

Daniel stretched out his hands. "As you can see, I'm right here. At least for the moment. I was just about to call for a ride to a hotel. This little charade is obviously over, and I think it best that I leave so you can continue with whatever cover story you told everyone."

James stopped still. "What the hell are you talking about? My mom and dad are right behind me, and... You know, maybe a hotel isn't such a bad idea. The fallout from this is going to rain down for hours like some nuclear blast."

Daniel cleared his throat. "I'm going to the hotel alone. Whatever story you told everyone so you could get out of there and mend things with your family is fine. I just don't want to be a part of it any longer. You do whatever you have to in order to keep things quiet within the family. Tell them whatever you want, make me the bad guy, it's just fine. But I don't want to be here when you do, and I don't need to hear it." Hell, the thought of hearing whatever James had to say was enough to knock his legs out from under him.

"Once again, what are you talking about? The guys pulled Weston away to keep me from beating him senseless. Holly calmed everyone down, and I got out of there so I could try to find you. I haven't told anyone any stories or even explained. I wasn't going to do that in front of a room full of people…some of them near strangers."

Daniel put up his hand. "Wait a minute…hold the fort… I think you'd better start at the beginning, because I'm confused."

Another set of headlights illuminated the walls, and James groaned. "That would be my parents." He seemed to deflate visibly. "I was hoping to have a little time before I had to face them."

This was going to get really ugly and the best thing was for Daniel to get the hell out of dodge. He didn't need to hear whatever sparkling words of phobic wisdom were about to burst forth around here. The best plan was the original one: he'd simply call a car and get to a hotel so James could do whatever he wanted. "I should get going."

"Wait…please…" James added softly. "This is going to be a mess, and I know that, but…"

"What are you still doing here?" Grace demanded as soon as she stepped through the front door, pausing a second, probably to see him as Daniel for the first time. "Haven't you done enough already?" The fire in her eyes had Daniel stepping back. "All of this is your fault, I'm sure of it." She turned to James. "Your father and I want to speak with you, and I want that person out of my house. I certainly don't want to see him…her…again." She rounded on Daniel as though he had just invited the devil himself to tea. Or maybe it was worse than that and she saw Daniel as Satan himself. Daniel wasn't sure, but getting out of here was a good idea.

"James Harden Petika, what do you have to say for yourself?" Phillip rounded hard on James.

"That's enough, both of you," James snapped back sharply. "If you want to talk, then both of you go into the kitchen and I'll be there in a few minutes." He seemed determined and tired at the same time.

"You heard me," Grace said as she stepped into Daniel's space. "I expect you to be gone." Daniel reached down for his luggage. He could wait out by the street for his ride.

"Then get used to disappointment, Mother," James countered, and Daniel stilled. "I said for both of you to go into the kitchen. I won't tolerate any more yelling at me or at Daniel. You are out of line. And if you insist on continuing down this path, then we will leave, and after the wedding tomorrow, neither of you will ever see me again. Do you understand? I've done a good job of staying away for years, I can easily make it permanent." The anger rolling off James seemed to darken the entire room.

"In my house…"

James pointed his finger at his mother. "Don't even finish that, old lady, or so help me I will never speak to you again."

Holy hell. This hadn't been the reaction he had expected at all.

"Just go," James added to his father, who took Grace by the hand and led her out of the room.

"I hope you know what you're doing, son," Phillip added more calmly.

"Nope, I'm winging it, but I won't take being treated like this anymore, and I will not allow mistreatment of my friends no matter what." James's high emotion seemed to lessen as soon as his parents left the room, James's mother still fuming. "Please don't go," he said to Daniel. "I don't mind if you stay here or go back to the bedroom, but I don't want you to go."

"James, this is your parents' home and they want me out. I don't think I can stay." Daniel wasn't comfortable here any longer.

"I know what it is, and I have to talk to them, but I don't want you to leave. I need a chance to make them understand." Daniel stayed where he was as James hugged him and then went into the kitchen, giving him a nervous smile before disappearing behind the half wall that divided the rooms.

"Is he still here?" Grace snapped.

"Yes, because I asked him to stay." A chair scraped the floor. Daniel imagined James sitting down. "None of this is Daniel's fault or has anything to do with him."

"Of course it's his fault. You weren't like this until you came here with him."

"Like what, Mom? Do you want to elaborate? Because I've known I was gay since I was fifteen years old. Just because you found out about it today doesn't mean that it hasn't always been that way. I just neglected to share that information with you."

This exact conversation, or at least one very close to it, had played out between so many gay kids and their parents for decades. Daniel remembered his own conversation with his grandmother and how hard it had been, but also how free he'd felt once it was over.

"But…why didn't you tell us? We could have helped you.

There are places you could go to fix this," Grace said, and Daniel cringed for James, knowing that attitude was exactly why he hadn't said anything. She was so very old-fashioned, set in her ways, and just plain wrong.

"Because there's nothing for me to be cured of. I am this way because I was born like this, and before you say anything more…this is part of who I am, and anyone trying to cure someone of being gay is a quack and deluding themselves and you. Part of the reason I didn't tell you was because I knew you would act this way."

Daniel slowly sat down, trying not to make any noise and sending James all the strength and care he possibly could. He would do just about anything to prevent James from having to go through this, but it was a gay rite of passage for most people.

There were stages to coming out. The first was that you had to accept yourself as gay, then you told a few people close to you, finally you told your family…and eventually you ran out of people to come out to when you decided to live a fully out and open life.

"But the reverend…"

"You mean the same one who lied to everyone in the church? The one who took you all for fools? Reverend Sociopathic Phony. Is that the one?" James wasn't giving an inch.

"James. We just want to try to understand," Phillip interjected.

"I don't think Mom wants to understand. All she wants is for things to be exactly the way she expects them to be, and I can't do that anymore. I won't try to live up to her ideals and what she thinks she wants." Man, James was on a roll. Daniel sat back and could only hope that the hard line he was taking didn't end up scorching the earth of his relationship with his parents to the point where there was no turning back.

"Both of you need to take a step back," Phillip said, playing what sounded like the voice of reason. "Grace, James is our son, an adult, and he can make his own choices."

"And I'm his mother."

"With no right to make decisions for any of our grown children." Phillip paused, and Daniel leaned forward. "You've pushed and prodded for years, and now it's coming back to haunt you. I sat by and watched as you insinuated yourself into this wedding. You worked around Holly to change her wedding service and you did the same with her dress. And who fixed both of those problems?" Phillip grew quiet.

"The person you want to kick out of the house," James pressed. "You don't understand, so you demand and fuss and expect things to be done your way." Frustration rang in his words. Daniel wished he could help him, but everyone had to find their own way through this, even though it could be difficult. "I'm gay, Mom. I will never fall in love with a woman or get married to one. That isn't going to happen."

"But it's a sin..."

"No, it's not, but cheating is, and so is changing the order for your daughter's wedding dress, Mom. Pride is a sin too. And just so you know, that old 'it's a sin' argument is a bunch of crap. I was made this way. I came down the birth canal gay. I didn't choose it, and I'm certainly not going to deny that part of myself because it makes you feel better. And yes, Daniella is really Daniel, and he came to this wedding as my date because of you and your expectations."

"You're blaming this whole thing on me," Grace pouted.

Daniel could almost see the high-and-mighty expression on Grace's face. He couldn't take any more and he stood, walking quietly across the carpet and into the kitchen. Grace looked up from where she'd been staring at the place mat in front of her.

"Your son loves you enough to ask me to be his date to make you happy," Daniel said. "He didn't want to disappoint you." Daniel placed his hand on James's shoulder. "You can be angry all you want at me, but all he wanted to do was please you." He turned to Phillip. "Both of you."

"I only want him to be happy."

"No, Mom. You wanted me to be happy as long as it made you happy." James pointed to the wall. "Those stupid commandments. That was your way of telling us what you expected, but what about us and what we expect? Most of your children are adults now, and that means that we expect things too. We expect to be loved unconditionally, whether we're gay or not. We expect you to listen to us and value our opinions. You want respect? Respect is earned, not given, and it doesn't come with some needlepoint sampler on a wall."

"James, I think that's quite enough," Phillip said firmly. "She is your mother."

"I know."

Grace lifted her gaze. "What I really want to understand is why?"

"Why what?" James asked. "Why am I this way?"

Daniel tapped James's shoulder. "I think what she wants to know is what she might have done to make you this way." Daniel swallowed. "Grace, you did nothing at all. You raised a good son. There's no doubt about that." She needed to be reassured.

"But… I heard…" She really seemed confused.

"Most of what you heard was probably misinformation spread by people who don't know anything anyway. There is nothing that either of you did to make James gay. You brought him up the best you knew how, and he turned out to be a kind, strong man." Daniel half expected Grace to get angry, but she simply nodded.

"But what do we do now?" Grace asked.

"Just love him and accept him for who he is." Daniel quietly excused himself and returned to the living room. James and his parents talked for a while more, their voices softer.

"I think we should go to bed. I'm talked out for tonight." James joined him in the living room. "It's after midnight. Do you want me to take you to a hotel? I can if you really want me to. Mom has calmed down a great deal, though." James hefted a suitcase.

"Let's just go on to bed." Daniel stifled a yawn. This day had been a lot more than he ever bargained for.

"Okay." James carried Daniel's suitcases back to their room, closing the door behind them. "Thank you. I was running out of ways to try to make them understand, and what you said was perfect."

"Actually, your mom and dad took it pretty well. They didn't kick you out, and you even threatened to never see them again and they didn't bite. That's one thing in your favor." Daniel sat on the edge of the bed, losing the battle with the next yawn. "On a bright note, you don't need to hide your life from your parents any longer."

James sat next to him. "I wish that were true. My mother may have seemed a little cowed tonight, but she never gives up anything that easily. I'm willing to bet that tomorrow she'll be back at it again. It's what she does. If the world doesn't go her way, retreat, gather your forces, and then attack again...and again."

"What does she think you're going to do, turn straight?" Daniel chuckled behind his hand. "That's the most ridiculous thing I've ever heard."

"She'll push every woman she can find at me in case I haven't met the right one yet. It's just a matter of her regrouping." James nodded. "But I think I can deal with it now. They know part of who I am that they didn't before."

"What about Holly and Margot?" Daniel asked.

James shook his head. "I expected Margot to come home with Mom and Dad, so I don't know where she is, probably at Holly's. They were shocked, and I didn't have a chance to talk to either of them." He lowered his head, and Daniel put an arm around him.

"I saw Weston when his friends took him out of the restaurant. He was pretty messed up." Daniel smiled and lifted James's chin. "Why did you do that?"

"He started in on you, and I saw red," James said. "He could have attacked me all he wanted and I wouldn't have cared, but the asshole went after you, and..."

Daniel closed the distance between them, sealing James's lips with his own. Daniel pressed James back onto the bed, rolling slowly until he straddled James, kissing him harder, not wanting to break the connection between them.

"James..." Grace said from the other side of the door.

"Not now..." Daniel growled and turned back to James, determined that he was going to get what had been denied to both of them for days. He backed away and pointed to the head of the bed. "Get comfortable," Daniel snapped as he pulled off his shirt. Then he toed off his shoes before dropping his pants and pulling off his socks. Daniel stood at the side of the bed in only a pair of white bikini briefs, staring down at a shocked James.

"You told her…"

"To mind her own business in the nicest way I possibly could right now." Daniel placed a knee on the mattress, prowling onto the bed and up James's body. He loved his wide eyes and the way his breath already came in shallow pants. "I'm going to give you two seconds to get those clothes off or I swear I'll rip them away with my damned teeth." Daniel wasn't kidding and felt ready to grab James's collar and rip the damn shirt away.

Daniel might have grinned when James leaned forward, pulling his shirt over his head and shimmying his pants off like he was doing some demented dance, but all he saw was honey-warm skin, and once James lay back down, Daniel straddled him once again, running his tongue slowly up from his navel, blazing a trail up his belly until he closed his lips around a nipple. James quivered under his ministrations, and damn, that was hot, as was the skin of James's throat as Daniel kissed and licked his way upward, under his jaw and over his chin before taking James's lips once again. This time he let James guide the kiss.

"God, how did I manage to resist you this entire time and what the hell were we waiting for?" James held him tighter, his strong, thick arms making him feel safe, like nothing could hurt him as long as James held him. It was a strange feeling. Daniel had only ever relied on himself, but this was different. James had seen him vulnerable and scared, yet he'd wanted him and stood up for him. Hell, tonight Daniel had been that damned rabbit who wanted to run and hide when danger got too close. James had stood between him and the threat, taking it head-on and beating the crap out of it. "What are you smiling at? You're supposed to be kissing."

"You," Daniel answered, pulling back slightly so he could look into James's eyes. He wanted him to see. "Why did you do that?"

"Do what?" James asked.

"See? You don't even think about what you did. Weston came after me, and you took him out. Your world had the potential to fall apart. I mean, your sisters and parents knew what we'd done, and that whole load of shit was going to come your way, and instead of taking the opportunity to try to explain or smooth things over, you leaped at that asshole and beat the crap out of him. You protected me because you knew the shit was going to end up on me, and instead you took it…all of it." Daniel swallowed around the watermelon in his throat because he couldn't talk any more.

James closed his eyes a second. "I don't know why. I just did it. The entire thing was a reaction and high emotion. All I know was that in that moment, I couldn't let him hurt you, and so help me god, if they hadn't pulled me off him, I wouldn't have stopped until the fucker was dead. I had no self-control; it was all 'protect and take out the threat.'" James stroked Daniel's cheek, heat spreading through him with every single touch.

"You know you shouldn't do that. I can take care of my-self," Daniel said. "I'm perfectly capable of keeping myself safe and watching my own back."

It was James's turn to swallow. "I know. But just because you can take care of yourself doesn't mean that you should have to." James drew him nearer, silencing both of them with a kiss that seared its way deep into Daniel's being. It took a few seconds for the real meaning of what James had said to begin to sink in, and by then his brain had been short-circuited completely.

James rolled him on the bed, positioning him until his head rested on the pillow. "What are you doing?" Daniel smiled.

"Exactly what I told you I wanted to do when we were in the minister's office a few hours ago. I hadn't expected to ever do this in my childhood bedroom, and I don't care. Mom and Dad are going to get the surprise of their lives, but I am going to take all the time in the world." Daniel shivered, wrapping his arms around James's neck to hold on for dear life.

# Chapter Seventeen

James knew his mom and dad were on the other side of the bedroom wall, and at the moment he didn't care. All that mattered was Daniel laid out on the bed...for him. This scenario had run through his mind for hours each and every night he'd spent in this bed next to Daniel and had promised to keep his hands to himself. He felt like a complete chickenshit for waiting so long, but Daniel deserved to be treated special. The words *like a queen* came to mind, and he actually smiled before gathering Daniel in his arms, pressing to him chest to chest. He wanted all of Daniel and he wanted it now. His hands roved up along Daniel's shoulders and down his arms, then back upward to his chest and sides. He needed to feel all of him to know how amazing it was to have Daniel in his bed, really in his bed.

"We need to be quiet," James teased, even though he had every intention of pushing Daniel's limits in the sound department.

"I won't say a word. It's you I'm really worried about," Daniel whispered.

"Why is that?" James asked, his lips hovering above Daniel's.

"Because I'm just that good."

James paused, his entire body shaking as he closed the distance between them, needing as many points of contact as possible, all that heated skin pressing to his. James had waited long enough, and sliding his hands down Daniel's sides, he took the last remaining scrap of fabric that separated the two of them right along for the ride down Daniel's legs.

James shed the last of his own clothes, sighing softly as he finally felt Daniel with nothing between them. James had always wanted to explore, and now he took the opportunity. Lifting Daniel's hips, he slid his hands under him, cradling Daniel's firm butt while Daniel wrapped his legs around James's waist.

"Damn, you're even more stunning than I imagined." James held Daniel's gaze.

"I am, huh?" Daniel retorted playfully. "You know, my own mind could conjure up plenty, and you leave most of what I came up with in the dust." Daniel clutched him, holding tightly, moaning softly for a second before cutting himself off as James sucked a gentle line down his neck. Daniel held him tighter, his entire body shaking under him. "Don't you dare stop. I don't care if this house falls to pieces around us, just…don't…stop."

Not that he had any intention to. It was too late now, and James was too far gone. Every fiber in his being wanted Daniel, and he couldn't pull away now if he wanted to. James tasted Daniel, his fingers exploring the most sensitive, private places, sending Daniel into quivering passion. James was well versed in the male body. He not only loved men, but he was one too, and he was determined to send Daniel into orbit. And James knew just how to do it.

He slid further down Daniel's body, slipping his hands from under him. "James…" Daniel whispered as their gazes locked.

"I'm going to make you scream, and you know you can't." That was the delicious part of this. He kissed Daniel. "I'll continue as long as you don't make a sound." This was really going to be fun. "Close your eyes for me."

Daniel glared at him, but he did it anyway. James sat back, straddling Daniel's legs. He wanted to take a second to feast his eyes on this gorgeous man. Where James was muscular, Daniel was lean and slender, sleek and stunning. His hair was the color of spun corn, his skin pale and perfect. James leaned forward, lightly sucking a pink, pert nipple, teasing the bud with his tongue before continuing down his belly. A slight saltiness tingled his taste buds, becoming more intense as he got closer to Daniel's smooth bikini area. Damn, the perfectly shaved skin was erotic as hell, and he inhaled the sharp scent of arousal before sliding his lips over Daniel's shaft, slowly taking in more and more of him.

The intense tang of desire burst into his mouth as James took Daniel deeper. Daniel wasn't small, and James wondered at his ability to tuck himself. Not that that was the most important thought right at the moment. In fact, the notion lasted but a split second and was gone as James reveled in having Daniel and his pleasure all to himself. "Are you okay?" James asked once he slid his lips away.

Daniel nodded, making a soft whimper in his throat as he clenched the bedding. That was just what James had hoped for: near out-of-control desire. This was about pleasure and giving Daniel something he would remember forever. When this was over and they returned to Chicago, no matter what happened then, James was determined that when Daniel was old and sitting in the old drag queens' home in a gilded and sequined rocking chair, he would look back at tonight as the greatest pleasure he had ever had.

James took Daniel once again, deep and hard, Daniel's legs shaking. Feeling his excitement was almost more than James could take. Daniel throbbed between his lips, and James backed away, sensing that things were about to progress beyond his control, and he didn't want this to be over.

"You're incredible like this," James whispered in Daniel's ear.

Daniel sat up and grabbed him, pulling him down before rolling them on the bed. "So are you, and now it's my turn." He clicked his tongue. "You're a mean, cruel man, and so help me I intend to make you pay for that."

"Willingly," James whispered with a smile. "As long as I'm with you, I'll do just about anything to make you happy." Daniel closed the distance between them, tugging at James's lower lip, grinding their hips together in a slow, circular rhythm.

James noticed for the first time that the bed wasn't creaking, even though Daniel was getting more and more energetic. "Daniel..."

"It's your turn to stay silent." He placed his finger over James's lips.

"But the bed..."

Daniel chuckled and sucked on his ear before whispering. "WD-40. I love that stuff." He shimmied his hips, and James groaned softly, a jolt of intense excitement running through him. "I also put something special in the nightstand." He reached over, pulling out a line of condoms and some lube.

"Damn, I love that you think ahead."

"You do, huh? Well, I have to ask, are you a pitcher or a catcher?"

James figured that Daniel thought he knew the answer and was just playing with him. "I'm a switch hitter. How about you, hot stuff?"

Daniel paused. "Are you kidding me? I figured..."

James nodded. "I know what you thought. That I was a big old top and that was the end of it. I will say that I have taken that role more often than not, but I think I should make my partner happy. So, if you want to do the driving, I'm more than happy to go along for the ride." He grinned, and Daniel hissed, the heat in the room notching up by a good ten degrees. Daniel obviously loved that idea, and James snatched the condoms from where Daniel had dropped them on the bed, tore off a packet, and ripped it open, stroking Daniel's length as he rolled down the latex.

"You're almost too good to be true."

"Just remember that when something gets screwed up." James held Daniel's cheeks. "I will always try to make you happy, because you've done that for me every single day I've known you." James pulled Daniel down, opening himself to him. "Just take it slow. It's been a while."

Daniel nodded slowly, his eyes swimming. "Are you sure?"

"Oh yeah, sweetheart. I want all of you." He arched his back as Daniel prepared him and then pressed to his entrance, slowly entering him.

The filling sensation took James's breath away. He hadn't been kidding that it had been a while, and Daniel was not small. He bore down, breathed steadily, and relished every single sensation as Daniel and he connected. This wasn't just physical—James felt it deep down, his spirit reaching out to Daniel and receiving an amazing response in return.

"Am I hurting you?" Daniel asked quietly, stilling all movement. James breathed deeply through the heady burn and then began to move.

"You're amazing," James whispered, and Daniel leaned over him. James loved kissing, and apparently so did Daniel. He held Daniel, refusing to break either connection as each motion sent James closer to nirvana. The crisp, fresh sheets soothed his back, the bed rocking slightly under him. Daniel radiated heat as his muscles worked, driving deeply into him, and James treasured every second, each sensation of it. Fucking was one thing, but this was so very much more.

They clung to each other, the two of them moving together, breathing each other's air, joining in every way possible. "Don't stop."

"I won't," Daniel breathed to him, rocking more slowly, building the energy between them. "You're in good hands, and I don't intend to let you fall."

James nodded, knowing that was true as pleasure and energy slowly built until his control hung on by a thread. Daniel seemed to understand exactly what James needed and wanted. It was uncanny. "Can you read my mind?"

"No," Daniel whispered. "Your breathing. It tells me everything I could possibly need to know. Your breath hitches when I hit just the right spot, and it quickens when anticipation is high, smoothing out when you need a chance to recover. I know exactly what you're feeling and what you want." Daniel held him tighter. "You're an open book to me."

James wasn't sure if that was good or not. In bed, definitely good; at other times not so much.

"Don't worry, I can't read your mind, just your passion," Daniel added, straightening up, giving James a close look at his sleek upper body, slick with a sheen of sweat that glistened in the street light shining in the window from outside. It was enough to send James's head spiraling nearly out of control, and a sight he swore he would never get tired of.

"Then don't stop, and I'll tell you anything," James groaned, and snapped his eyes closed as Daniel glided long and slow over that spot inside him. He loved that, his head clouding and ears ringing a little. It was almost like he had lost control of himself and given it to Daniel. And damn it all if he wasn't in good hands.

"Are you ready?"

James nodded once.

"Good. I can tell you're so keyed up your head is about to spin. I want you to come for me. Don't touch yourself, just think of me and your pleasure, how I make you feel what you want. Give yourself permission to fly, and I guarantee you'll take off like a rocket."

James panted softly. "I don't know…"

"Yes, you do. Just let go and you'll fly." James clamped his eyes tighter. "Just give yourself to me. Don't worry about anything and don't try to control it. Just let go. I'll take good care of you." Daniel did that thing again, stealing his breath, and then James did as Daniel asked, giving himself over to him, and holy hell, his release barreled into him without warning, like a runaway train. James let it come, holding on to Daniel, riding out the storm his own body intended to unleash.

James tingled all over, every nerve firing from head to toe at the same time. His mind took off for the clouds, hanging there until the tempest passed. Then he floated, alone with Daniel, breathing deeply as contentment spread all through him. Finally, he returned to himself, blinking and wondering if he was still in one piece.

"Wow," James whispered into the quiet room, only the sound of their breathing breaking the silence.

Daniel moved slowly, James quivering when their bodies separated. He didn't dare move in case the spell around him broke, so he didn't see Daniel take care of things, but he heard it and felt Daniel wipe down his belly before settling on the bed. James gathered Daniel to him, holding him tightly, his body still tingling from the intensity of what the two of them had experienced. "It's been a long day and it's going to be very busy tomorrow," Daniel said.

James couldn't help chuckling. "You know, you have a real interesting postcoital chatter. No kind words or sweet nothings—just wham, bam, go to sleep."

Daniel groaned softly. "I'm right here holding you. I know it's not the most romantic notion, but..." Daniel slowly rolled to the side of the bed. "It's after midnight, and who knows what time your sister is going to show up in the morning, raring to go and full of nervous energy. So you and I need to get some rest." He snuggled closer, head on the pillow, arm across James's chest. "My head is still spinning with everything that happened today."

"Your head?" James sighed. "I feel like I have whiplash. It's been one damned thing after another these last few days, and now... I was trying to avoid all this drama."

Daniel stroked his chest and over his shoulder. "Relax

and let it go for a while. There's nothing that you or any of us can do about what's in the past. All we can do is handle what comes next, and you can't do that if you're wide awake all night. Whatever argument your mom puts up or however she decides to act, that's on her now. She knows the truth and who you really are. If she can't deal with that, then it's her problem."

"But she's my mother," James whispered as a sense of dread came over him.

"Yes, she is. And I heard what you told her, and you were right. She should love you unconditionally and accept you for the incredible man you are. Maybe we shouldn't have pretended that I was a woman, but she needs to accept that you're a gay man and love you for that. It's that simple. You deserve that sort of love. We all do." Daniel gently patted his chest. "As much as I hate to say it, we don't always get that kind of support. But I've spent time with Grace, and I think she really does love all of you. She may not understand being gay, and I'm sure that she's heard her entire life that it's wrong…" Daniel's hand grew still.

"What are you saying?" James asked.

"That maybe there's a fight going on inside her. That she's going to struggle, but most likely, if you help her understand, the love she has for you will win out." Daniel shifted, and James turned to see him peering into his eyes. "Your mom has heard all her life that homosexuality is a sin and that it's wrong, and today she found out that her only son is gay. It's going to be really hard for her."

"Yeah…and she's going to expect me to change to fit her beliefs," James groused.

"Of course she is." Daniel lay back down. "You changing

the way you are eliminates the conflict. Her world is set to rights, and she didn't have to do a damned thing. It's all on you, and she doesn't have to search her own soul to figure out if she's right or not. There's no effort on her part." Daniel chuckled. "Most people will take the easy way out, and if they can get someone else to do the work, then all the better." He patted James's chest. "Do your best to go to sleep. If you rest, you'll be in a better position to go to battle with her."

"I'm glad you think this is funny."

Daniel stared seriously. "I don't. Tomorrow you'll have to have some of the most difficult conversations of your life. You'll have to explain who you are to your family. That's frightening." Daniel slid closer. "It isn't funny at all. I was only laughing because I'm glad it's not me."

James lay still a second and then rolled over, running his fingers along Daniel's ribs. "I swear I'll tickle you into submission."

"Your mother," Daniel gasped, and James pulled back. "That was really mean."

"Not as bad as you picking on me." James fake pouted, and Daniel snorted, clearly not buying it. "Come on, let's try to get some sleep." James held Daniel and closed his eyes, sleep coming to him much quicker than he'd thought it would.

Daniel was still asleep when James woke and carefully got out of bed. He needed the bathroom, and his mouth was desert dry. After dressing quickly and taking care of business, he padded barefoot to the kitchen for some coffee, where he found his mother already up, sitting at the kitchen table. James said nothing and went to the coffeepot to pour a mug. It was too early for an argument or to discuss the things they needed to talk about. "Holly's wedding is today," he began. "Let's just concentrate on that."

His mother didn't reply, and James took her silence for agreement, leaving the kitchen to sit in the living room alone. Everything was a mess, but he had to concentrate on what had to happen today, and one of those things was to figure out an officiant. James set down his mug and quietly returned to the bedroom where he couldn't help himself and watched Daniel sleep for a few minutes, then got his laptop and exited the room, closing the door as silently as he could.

When James returned to the living room, he found his mother sitting on the sofa, apparently waiting for him. "I think we need to clear the air now." Her lips were thin and her eyes hard. "Was that little display last night for my benefit? It was clear enough what the two of you were doing."

"Oh please, Mother. Are you upset about what we were doing or the fact that you obviously weren't?" James regretted the comment as soon as it crossed his lips. "Sorry. That was uncalled for." He still had to stifle his smile.

"I'll say it was." She pursed her lips. "I won't have that kind of behavior in my house. I want..."

James groaned. "For god's sake, Mother. I'm twenty-eight years old, not twelve. Give it a rest. I'm tired of fighting with you about things that are none of your business. You don't get to run my life or Holly's any longer. Margot is going to be attending college soon and then she's going to be gone. All of your children are adults, or very nearly so, and we'll decide the course of our lives without you or your interference. Holly will be married today, and she and Howard will build their own lives together. I'm going back to Chicago tomorrow, and I'll return to the life I have there." He lowered his voice. "Do you want to be part of our lives going forward or not?"

She sat back and gasped. "Of course I do. I love my children and I want them to lead good, productive, happy lives. And I fail to see how you being…with Daniel…the way you obviously are…is going to make you happy. That lifestyle isn't healthy and is only going to lead to misery. I know it in my heart. You have to fight this. Just because you were born gay…which I don't believe… Well, even if it is true, you don't have to act on those feelings. You should pray to God to give you strength and keep you from temptation."

"No," James said flatly.

His mother clearly hadn't been expecting that response. "What do you mean no?" She set down her mug, glaring at James as though he had just crapped on the sofa.

"Just what I said. No. I'm going to live my life the way I see fit. And just so you know, Mother, you're the one who's wrong. Why should I deny who I am because it makes you feel better? I am who I am, and I'm going to celebrate that and live my life in order to be happy. I'm not going to pretend to be someone I'm not. I've done that for years, and it sucks. I can't do it any longer. Part of me was ready to curl up and die, and I won't go back there."

"But…"

James leaned forward and took both her hands in his. "You're my mother, and I love you, and your only job is to love me back and accept me for who I am. That's all there is. Don't judge me, don't try to change me, just show me the loving mother you've always been."

She pulled a hand away and dabbed her eyes. "Of course

I love you. But you were never like this before this Daniel person."

"Yes, I was. I just didn't tell you. I have a different life in Chicago, one where I can be the person I really am. And Daniel is the best person I've ever met. He's kind, thoughtful, and selfless, but also funny with a great sense of humor." James sighed. "Daniel makes me laugh and he makes me happy."

"That's false happiness, just like all of this is. You can only be truly happy if you live a normal life. Not this." She pointed down toward the hall with her hand. "That will only lead you down the wrong path."

James stood. "It's my path to choose, and I will take the one I want. You don't get to choose it for me, not anymore. Your expectations are a fiction, your own illusion so you can try to dictate what is out of your control. My life is my own, and if you can't understand that I'm gay and that I will never marry a woman, then so be it. I won't do that to myself or to someone else. My parents taught me to be honest and to live a good life. For me, it means being true to who I am, regardless of whether you agree or not."

"Daniel needs to go," she countered, her eyes as dark as night.

"Fine. But if he goes, then I do too. We'll pack up and go to a hotel. But understand, there won't be any more visits on holidays or any other time. I'll see and talk to Holly and Margot, but not you. If they wish, they will be part of my life, but you won't. Not anymore." It was James's turn to be harsh, to explain to her the way things were going to have to be.

His mother stood, stepping closer to him. "You'd give up

your family, your parents, for this lifestyle, this Daniel person?"

James nodded. "I love him, Mother. It's that simple. I love Daniel Bonafonte, and if he'll have me with all the stupid things I've done, by god, I will follow him to the ends of the earth. I'll stand beside him, proudly, and introduce him as my boyfriend."

"But he dresses as a woman!"

"Those are just clothes, the trappings on the outside. I don't care if Daniel wears men's jeans and a T-shirt, a cocktail dress, or one of his theatrical gowns with enough sequins to blind half of Chicago. I love the man under the glitz, gowns, glamour, makeup, and fake tits. I will be proud of who he is because Daniel is the most wonderful person I know. But you don't know him at all, and yet you're willing to pass judgment." It hit James hard that he had done the same thing.

"But a person like that…isn't a real man. How can you…?" Her mouth was moving, but no more words came out.

"Daniel is more of a man than most of the guys I have ever met. He knows who he is, and the rest of us can be damned if we can't accept that." He sat back down and waited for his mom to do the same. Maybe it was time to really talk to one another instead of talking at each other. "I didn't see that at first either. I just needed a date for the wedding to make you happy. But Daniel is so much more than I expected. My world has shifted, and it's because of him. Mom, he showed me the path to myself. I know that's hard to understand, but he did."

She leaned forward. "I don't know what's real."

James chuckled. "Sometimes I didn't either, but all I have to do is look into Daniel's eyes and I know what's real, what's solid. The person I fell in love with is the one under all the clothes. He's the one who saved Holly's wedding dress, and the one who made Holly happy with the service." James glossed over the fact that his mother had been the cause of those problems in the first place. "He was the one who helped Howard comfort Holly when we found out about Reverend Fake." James sighed. "I still don't know what we're going to do about an officiant, but I'm sure Daniel will be there to try to help. That's the kind of person he is."

His mom swallowed hard and her entire expression had grown softer. "What kind of life can you have?" She dabbed her eyes again.

"A good one, if he'll have me. I don't know if I'm what he wants or if this is just some sort of illusion brought on by close proximity. I'll find out in time, I'm sure. That's for me to figure out, and I will eventually. I don't know what the future is going to hold, but I know that it will be a lot easier if my mom and dad try to understand." James thought he might be getting through. "I don't expect you to just change on a dime and suddenly have everything figured out. But at least I ask that you love me enough to believe me when I say that I'm not going to change and I can't, not this. I have to be true to myself just like anyone else." He sat still and waited for some sort of verdict from his mother. She dabbed her eyes again and nodded. James got up and hugged her tightly. "You don't have to have all the answers, any more than I do. All you have to do is try." James let her go and stepped back, intending to leave the room.

His mother lifted her gaze from the top of the coffee table. "As a mother, what we all want is for our children to be happy." She wiped her eyes. "Sometimes I guess we don't understand how our kids can do that. With my mother it was bell-bottom jeans." She smiled. "I wanted a pair more than anything else, and your grandmother hated the idea. She thought it foolish, stupid, and a hippie waste of money. Her exact words. She hated your father for years after we got married because she'd wanted me to marry her best friend's son, Kyle." Mom shivered. "I never liked him. He was always mean and self-entitled. So was his mother, come to think of it."

James didn't say anything at all. He didn't want to interrupt whatever thought flow she was having. Even when she grew quiet, he didn't speak.

"How do you know that this is going to make you happy? Because as far as I can see all you're opening yourself up for is a lot of hurt." She tried to smile and failed.

"Mama, this isn't something I just decided. I have lived with knowing I was gay for almost thirteen years. I've lived with hurt and experienced hate firsthand both in my personal life and at work. I'm well aware of what's coming my way. But you need to know that there are good parts too. I have wonderful friends and I work with good people." He wanted to make her feel better.

"They know?" she asked, and James nodded. "But I didn't. I'm your mother, I should have been told. I may not understand, but you didn't even give me the chance to try. You kept that from me and your father. I think that's what hurts the most."

"Mom," James growled. He was about to call bullshit on that. "You know you want things the way that you want them. How long have you tried to fix me up with the daughters of your friends? Would you have tried to fix me up with their sons instead? Or tried to sweep that I was gay under the carpet? Be honest, if you had known when I was seventeen that I was gay, what would you have done?" He hit her with a level stare and saw the answer in the way she bit her lip. James knew she and his father would have tried to fix him, and that would have been a fate worse than hell.

"Still, finding out you're gay on the eve of Holly's wedding and that your date is a transvestite wasn't exactly a barrel of monkeys." She actually smiled, and James knew in that instant that things were going to be all right. His mom may not understand, but she would try, and that was all he could ask for.

"I'll give you that." He smirked, and she smacked his arm.

"Don't be smart," she snapped lightly.

"And just so you know, Daniel isn't a transvestite, he's a drag queen, and the best in Chicago. Daniel didn't lie about his background; he is a performer. He does cabaret and is breathtaking. He sings, dances, and acts…all of it in front of a live audience, and Daniel does it with style and in the highest heels you have ever seen." And a grace that blew James away. "When I saw the show, I didn't know what to make of it at first."

"Is that the sort of thing that you like?" his mother asked hesitantly, probably realizing where this was going and unsure how to stop herself.

James's eyes widened. "Do you really want to talk about the kind of guys I like? Because I don't think that's a subject you're really up for right now. I sure as hell know that I'm not." That was definitely more detail than his mother needed.

"Yeah, okay. I agree." She waved her hands in front of her

face. "And Daniel…what are you going to do with him?" she asked.

"I don't know. All I know is that I love him, Mom, and I haven't even said so to him yet. That's probably kind of backwards to tell you first, but I do. I've fallen in love with him. I need to tell him, and find out if there's a chance that he might want to see where this could go between us." James wrung his hands, just like he always had whenever he seemed to be stepping into an argument with his mother.

"Yes, we need to talk," Daniel said from behind him. James turned, not knowing how Daniel would react. "And you're right, things are definitely backward if you're telling your mother that you love me first." Those incredible hands made their way to Daniel's hips, a sure sign that James had messed up again.

His mother got up and left the room, still dabbing her eyes, but she seemed calmer. James knew he'd have to have a similar conversation with his father eventually, but right now, he had a much more important one to have with Daniel.

"Did you mean it?" Daniel demanded.

"How long were you standing there?" James asked.

Daniel didn't move. "Long enough. What I want to know is if you meant what you said about me and the clothes and all of that. Was that something you used to get a point across with your mother?"

James shook his head. "I meant every word."

"Even the glitz, glamour, and tits part?" Daniel actually smiled, slowly lowering his arms.

"Yes. I meant all of it. Remember, I fell in love with you while you were wearing a dress most of the time. But I was always aware of the person underneath." James drew closer.

"So yes, I need to say the words to you, so you know exactly how I feel. I love you, Daniel. I'm not sure I know or understand when it happened, but it did. I don't have any answers as to what will occur when we go home and return to our lives. But I do know that I want you to be part of mine, and I want to be included in yours."

Daniel shifted his weight from foot to foot. "Chicago is a long way from here, and things are very different there. I have commitments and a life that I don't want to give up." He cleared his throat and did something James hadn't seen before: fidgeted and prevaricated. Daniel wasn't the nervous type, at least as far as James knew. "It's easy enough for you to think that everything is going to be just like it was here when we return, but it isn't. Are you really prepared to be seen by not just your friends, but the people at work, with Lala on your arm?"

James opened his mouth and snapped it shut as he tried to answer the question. Honestly, it wasn't something he had thought about before. Not that he was ashamed of Daniel in any way, but the notion hadn't crossed his mind thus far. Probably like many things when it came to Daniel.

"That's what I thought."

"Now, hold it…" James interjected.

Daniel took another step back. "You don't need to make any commitments now. What you said is sweet, and you don't know how much I appreciated hearing it." Daniel stroked his cheek. "But let's not take things too far too fast." His breath skittered, and James felt Daniel's jitters roll off him in waves. "You just told your parents, and you're going to have to deal with your sisters, and then the wedding and the reception, where you're going to be the talk of the evening. Everything has changed for you." He pulled his hand back. "That's a lot to take in all at once, and it's natural for you to want to hold on to anyone who might seem safe or known." Daniel blinked. "You're an amazing man, James, but you've been through a lot. You don't need to make commitments in the heat of emotion that you may regret."

James drew nearer, not ready to let Daniel just walk away. "Are you saying you don't feel the same way? That you aren't interested in even seeing if we're a possibility?"

Now it was Daniel's turn to hesitate, and James thanked god for it. He had half expected Daniel to tell him no immediately.

"I don't know," Daniel answered, and James had never known those words to feel so final and so harsh. He suddenly and clearly understood his own feelings, and to have Daniel hesitate hurt more than he'd thought it would.

"I need to dress and check some things on the internet about officiating today," James explained as he passed Daniel on his way back to the bedroom.

Daniel followed, which wasn't exactly ideal, since James had been hoping for a few minutes alone to try to deal with his disappointment.

# *Chapter Eighteen*

*Damn it all*, Daniel thought as the bedroom door closed behind him. He knew he had hurt James, but what he'd said was the truth. With all the upheaval of the last few hours, it wasn't fair for Daniel to hold James to some words said in haste and high emotion. He didn't doubt that James was feeling some, maybe all, of what he'd said, but he had just come out to his family. That was a moment of real vulnerability, and Daniel wouldn't take advantage of that. He didn't know what he was going to do or what was going to happen when they got back to Chicago. It was just too soon. "I did some looking on the internet and a couple of 'churches' will ordain you right away."

"Okay," James answered quietly, sitting on the edge of the bed. "I need to get my laptop so I can make that happen."

Daniel sat down next to James. "It's not that easy, though. The sites all say that before performing any service, you need to contact the local county clerk for instructions and to notify them that you are ordained and planning to perform marriages. There are registration forms that need to be completed." He hated being the bearer of bad news.

"So you're saying that I can't do it. The clerk's office isn't open on a Saturday." James hung his head a little lower. "Not that it would have made a difference, but I should have checked all that yesterday. I might…" He seemed so defeated. "What am I going to do? I promised Holly I would see that this worked out for her. I want this wedding to be the best possible, and instead I wrecked everything." He hiccupped and groaned softly. "I should call her and see what she wants to do."

"No," Daniel said, taking a play from James's book. He shifted on the bed. "We need to talk and we need to do it privately."

James stood, reaching for the door. "I think you made yourself perfectly clear."

Daniel smacked James on the ass, harder than he'd intended, but it got his attention. "Gran was on a farm when she was a girl. She told me once that the way to get a mule's attention was to kick it. So, consider yourself kicked in the ass."

"Excuse me? I heard what you said."

"No, you heard what you thought I said." He stood once again, hands on his hips. "I heard what you told your mother, and I know you believe it. And by the way, I will always, always remember hearing those words from you until the day I die." He tapped his foot, growing agitated. "I don't know what is going to happen once we're back in Chicago. You said the same thing to your mother. Are you angry that I didn't say that I loved you in return, so you and I could have one of those television commercial moments where we run across a field in flowing clothes and into each other's arms?"

"I don't want you to say anything that you don't feel," James countered.

Daniel sighed. "James, I don't know what I feel right now. Everything has been so up and down. I love the time we spent alone together, and the person you've shown me is pretty awesome." He closed the distance between them. "I think you've been through damned near hell in the last twenty-four hours." Daniel wound his arms around James's neck, glad he didn't pull away. "Let's just give this some time. That way you and I can have some distance."

Daniel really wanted to tell James that he loved him too, but he couldn't. Not right now. Daniel was pretty sure that the cop he had fooled in the theater with a dress and a figure had somehow wormed his way into his heart. The thought of going home and not seeing James again made his blood run cold. But he knew enough about James to know that if he told him how he felt, then James would feel obligated to him, even if all of this was just some emotional roller coaster that led to nowhere.

"I know my own mind," James told him.

"But do you know your own emotions?" He pressed closer to James, resting his head on his shoulder. "We have to listen to our hearts. So rather than getting worked up right now, let's give each other some time. That's all I'm asking for." He caught James's gaze. "If you got anything from last night, it should have told you pretty clearly how I feel about you."

"Okay. I think that's fair," James whispered, and Daniel held him close once again.

"Right now, we have to figure out how we're going to get your sister married."

The bedroom door burst open, with Holly standing in

the doorway, glaring at both of them. "Why didn't you tell me?" she demanded, stepping inside and kicking the door closed. "I'm so angry at both of you I could spit quarters."

"Oh, for god's sake, knock it off, Holly. I've already had a talk with Mom and Dad last night, and another one with Mom this morning." James sighed, but didn't step away. Daniel liked that he wasn't ashamed. "Suffice it to say that I'm gay, and this is Daniel."

"But…"

James rolled his eyes, which was adorable. "Fine, you get the quick version. I've known since I was fifteen. I didn't tell anyone here because you know how Mom can be and I thought it would be easier. I thought about saying something before the wedding, but didn't want the drama. And yeah, I see how that worked out. I told Mom that I loved Daniel, and he heard it. The two of us are trying to figure shit out, and when we know, I'll tell you. I promise." James took a deep breath. "Right now, we have to figure out who is going to officiate at your wedding, because I can't. There isn't time for me to become legal. You're all up-to-date now, so let's move forward."

Holly shook her head. "You sure know how to give a girl whiplash." Daniel found himself edged out, and Holly gave James a hug. "Nothing has changed as far as I'm concerned. Margot feels the same way." Holly stepped back. "Now, you get me married, because I'm not going to go through all this shit again. What are our options?"

James nodded and wiped his eyes, clearly relieved. "I can perform the ceremony, and then you and Howard can make the marriage legal on Monday. That way all the plans can go on."

"Except Howard and I are supposed to leave Monday morning for our honeymoon." A tear ran down her cheek. "He wanted to surprise me, but because of all this, he told me about the trip to Europe last night. Ummm, that means that…" Holly held her hand over her face. "I have to go on my honeymoon and not be married."

James sat next to her, holding Holly's hand while she cried.

"There is another option," Daniel said softly. "But…it's a little unorthodox." He hadn't brought this up because before yesterday it hadn't been a possibility. But with them both being outed…

"What is it?" James asked.

Daniel sighed. "Holly." He sat on the other side of her. "This has to be your and Howard's decision, not your mother's or anyone else's. James has seen me onstage in full drag, and my professional name is Lala Traviata. The thing is, Lala has been doing Pride weddings for years, all over the country, and I did a fly-in wedding three years ago at a Pride event in Helena."

Holly sniffed. "So you can perform the ceremony?" She blinked, and Daniel met James's gaze.

"Why didn't you say anything?" James asked. "This solves everything."

"Not exactly. Lala is the one who performs the weddings. Not Daniel. When I sign the license, it will be as Lala."

"But that's okay. I don't care how the license is signed," Holly explained as she perked up.

James patted her hand. "You don't understand. Lala only performs in full drag. That means that Lala can perform the wedding, but it will be in theatrical drag. Granted, from what I've seen it will be gorgeous, but it will also be Lala."

Damn it all. Daniel had been trying to keep his distance so he could think, but James got it. He understood, and Daniel's heart rejoiced at that. Daniel had thought that James might have been giving his mother lip service earlier, but he was wrong. James got it.

Holly turned to Daniel, and then looked back to James before her gaze shifted to Daniel once again. "Okay. I'll call Howard and we'll talk and decide. You two need to stop eye fucking each other, because this place is starting to smell like a locker room." Holly skittered out of the room, shutting the door after her.

"Oh god," James groaned.

"Look, if this is going to cause even more problems, then you can forget it." He didn't want to cause trouble. "I can do the wedding as Daniel and then sign the certificate and…"

James whirled around. "Don't you dare. Lala does weddings, and if Holly and Howard agree, then Lala is doing it, and they are going to get all her fabulousness and over-the-topness. This will be a wedding that everyone is going to be talking about for years."

"But your mother…" Daniel said, swallowing.

"I know. She's going to blow the top of her head off and steam is going to come out of her ears if Holly and Howard go forward with this idea." James grinned devilishly. "Wanna watch when I tell her?"

"Is that what you were choking up over? I thought you were upset." Daniel put his hands on his hips, and James took a step back. God, he loved that reaction. "You are one evil son. Of course I want to watch." Daniel lowered his hands. "But you need to give your mom a break too. Yeah, she can be pushy."

"More like dictatorial."

Daniel rolled his eyes. "Let's go with pushy—it sounds better, and I like your mom, I really do. She's fierce. I bet she stood up for you in school when shit happened, and nobody hurt any of her kids without paying the price." Daniel could respect that a great deal.

"Yup!" James agreed.

"I understand fierce. It takes a good dose of that to do what I do. I stand onstage in all my finery and put part of myself out there each and every night. Yes, I'm a performer. But it's still me under all the glitz. So give your mom a break."

"And how do I do that?" James asked, his hands on his hips.

Daniel shook his head. "You're doing it wrong. If you want to do the hip thing effectively, put your one foot forward, cock your hip slightly, and project attitude. It isn't just the stance, but the whole picture." James tried, bless his heart, but he couldn't quite get there. "Maybe you have to picture your balls pushed up into your body, your dick taped back, multiple layers of underthings, layers of padding, and a gown worthy of Cher on Oscar night to be able to do it right."

James quivered and put his hands up in surrender. "Fine, oh sage one. What do you suggest?"

"Have Holly there, to start with. It's her wedding, and this is her and Howard's choice. Lead off with the fact that you found a minister and that the service is going to go on as planned. Then ease into how Lala is going to officiate. Don't start with 'Mom, Holly is going to have a drag wedding.' She'll probably go running from the house looking for the men in their clean white coats to take all of us away."

James hooted, laughing so hard he had tears running down his cheeks. "I suppose we need to wait for Holly's answer."

Daniel leaned closer. "Yes…and what do you want to do until we hear from her?" He leaned close enough that James's heady scent filled his nose. Daniel closed his eyes, his nose riding the olfactory amazingness like a surfer rides a wave.

"I know I'd like to take you back to bed and spend a few hours reviewing what I learned last night. But we have a wedding to attend, so we'd better shower and be ready for whatever this afternoon will bring. Rain check?"

Daniel smiled. "You better believe it."

"Are you sure you can do this?" Holly asked. Holly, Howard, Daniel, and James sat around the old picnic table under the tree in the backyard. Daniel hoped to hell he didn't get ass splinters from the old wood and did his best not to actually move too much.

"If you are both in agreement, then we need to go over some things," Daniel said, pulling out the order of service that he had helped Holly with earlier in the week. "Thankfully, we didn't specify the readings in the program. So what we'll do is chuck the Wedding in Cana stuff out and bring in some wonderful marriage poetry." Daniel used his laptop to show them some of the texts he'd used in the past. "Glance through these files and see if there's something you like. We can still use the music. That isn't a problem, because the few hymns you chose will work and that way, we won't piss off the organist." Daniel let them take a look at the files, leaning a little closer to James. He really hadn't been expecting to do this, and now at the last minute he was practically throwing a wedding ceremony together like it was improv night. He'd spent much of his life on the stage and for him this was just another performance.

Except it wasn't. Mostly when Lala did weddings, it was at Pride Fest celebrations for sometimes dozens of couples at a time. That felt more like a performance. This was much more intimate because it was only for one couple, and he liked Howard and Holly. They were wonderful together.

"You okay?" James whispered while the other two talked softly.

Daniel nodded. He would have to be. "I always get nervous before I have to go onstage." And this was going to be a performance, he had no illusions about it. Daniel was well aware that the invitees to the wedding were expecting a traditional church service, not a cabaret performance.

"You do?" Holly asked. "How long have you been performing?"

"Five years professionally. Doesn't matter though; the nerves are always there. I think it's just something that keeps you on your toes and stops you from getting cocky, because the first time you do anything onstage and think you have it nailed, everything will fall on its tits and you'll look like a fool." It was the first lesson his drag mother, Tulane Highway, had taught him.

Holly turned to Howard, and the two of them did this silent communication thing, which would have been kind of creepy if it didn't demonstrate how much the two of them knew each other. "Is this what you really want to do?" Howard asked Holly, who nodded, then the both of them turned to Daniel. "If Lala is going to do this service, then we want you to go for it all the way." Howard smirked. "I went to

New York for two weeks between my junior and senior years at MU."

Daniel gasped. "Did you see a drag show while you were there?"

Howard smirked and blushed. "I was there with a couple of friends, and they thought it would be fun. I was really straitlaced back then, even more than I am now, but I went along, expecting to be uncomfortable. It was hilarious. I never laughed so hard in my life. And that's what I want. Doing this straight…is going to seem dumb. So, go for it. There will be children there, so we have to keep it clean, but otherwise give them hell." Howard knocked on the top of the table and then stood up, extending his hand to Holly, helping her up. "You need to stay here to get dressed, and I'm going back to my place to make sure the guys are ready." He kissed her on the cheek. "I'll see you at the church. I'll be the one down front waiting for my princess to save me." He squeezed her hand, and Daniel sighed. He wanted that someday and was man enough to admit it.

Howard left the yard with all eyes on him. "You found yourself a good one," Daniel told Holly. "Once you have your hands on him, never let that boy go. He'll make you happy forever."

Holly smiled and checked her watch. "I need to get dressed and call my matron of honor to make sure there are no issues. The limousines will be here at one."

"What about Mom and Dad?" James asked. "We need to explain what's going on."

Holly stopped in her tracks, and Daniel excused himself, getting out of the line of fire.

# Chapter Nineteen

"I can't believe you were trying to skip out and leave me with telling the folks," James scolded Holly, once Daniel had gone inside. "It's your wedding. I can explain what will happen, but you at least have to say that you and Howard made the decision."

She sighed. "Okay. Let's get this over with." Holly strode off toward the house, pulling open the sliding glass doors. "Mom, we found someone to do the service," Holly said as soon as she stepped inside. "Howard and I have decided what we want to do. I have to go get my hair done, so James is going to explain what's going on." Holly grabbed her purse and was out of the house in two seconds flat.

"Damn her," James swore.

"Your sister was always good at sticking you with things she didn't want to deal with," his mother said as she set a mug of coffee in front of him. "What is it this time? I take it she and Howard have made some decision that they don't think I'm going to be happy with, and she figured you could be the one to tell me." She sat down, and James thought his mom was being pretty calm after all the drama and surprises of the last few days.

Daniel pulled out the chair next to him, and they shared a quick glance. Clearly Daniel was curious to see if this was what pushed her completely over the edge. At least that was what he thought, until Daniel's hand slipped into his, squeezing lightly. Daniel wasn't going to let him face this alone.

"Grace," Daniel said softly.

"What does all of this have to do with you?" she asked snappily, turning on Daniel.

"Knock it off, Mother," James growled. "We need to tell you and Dad what's going to happen today as far as the officiant at your daughter's wedding goes. Dad, can you come in here?" They may as well get this over with all at once.

The living room chair creaked, and his dad came in, sitting next to his mother, both looking concerned.

"As you know, the reverend is gone."

His mother nodded. "My phone and the church gossip network have been buzzing about it all morning. All my friends have called to ask if the wedding is still on and what we're going to do." She gulped her coffee, and James narrowed his gaze, taking her cup and sniffing.

"What did you put in this?" James curled his lip.

"Whiskey. It's medicinal. I need something to get me through this. My daughter is getting married, we have no minister, your sister blames me for problems with her dress and everything else that has gone wrong. I swear if it rains, she'll blame me for that." She snatched back the mug and downed what was left. James didn't point out that some of that was indeed her fault. No point pouring gasoline on a raging fire.

"Grace, dear," his dad tried soothing.

"Hell no. Don't try that with me." She got up from the table, refilled her mug, and returned, plopping the bottle onto the table. "Want some? You may as well get ready, because Holly skipped out, leaving James to hold the bag, which means we're going to need some fortification."

"James," his father said plaintively.

He lifted the bottle, pouring a glug of whiskey into his father's mug.

"You may as well." James waited while they both took a couple of sips and then began. "This is what's going to happen. We have an officiant and the wedding will be legal."

"Who's going to do the wedding?" his dad asked. "Rip the bandage off and get this over with."

"Lala Traviata," James answered.

His mother paused with the mug halfway to her lips. "Who?"

"I've performed weddings in many states, but only as my drag persona, Lala Traviata. That's how the license will be signed and how my weddings are performed." Daniel remained calm, while James's insides felt like they had been thrown into a blender.

"Mom, Dad, like to or not, Holly and Howard are going to have a drag wedding. Or at least a wedding officiated by a drag queen. Daniel is available and he will perform the ceremony as Lala. It's how he does them, and Holly and Howard have agreed." Both his parents remained silent, each reaching for the whiskey bottle at the same time. Dad added a splash more whiskey to both mugs and set the bottle down within easy reach.

"I'd ask if you were kidding, but I can see this is serious.

So I'm going to ask how this is going to work. Will you be dressed as a nun or something?"

"Dad!" James interjected.

"No," Daniel answered calmly. "The service has already been reworked to remove the biblical readings, and they'll be replaced with literature and poetry about the meaning of love, which is what we're really here to celebrate. I've done this before, granted not in a setting like this, but we'll make do. And your daughter and son-in-law will be married and they can go forward with their lives together."

His mom and dad turned to each other, saying nothing. His dad was stunned. There was no denying that for a second. James waited for his mother to react. She sat back in her chair, placing her mug on the table. Finally, she pushed her chair back, stood, and slowly went over to the sink. Was there going to be an explosion, tears, maybe some of both?

"Really, I don't know what to say at all." She turned around. "If I'm honest, and I've had enough whiskey to loosen my tongue, I don't give a fuck who wears what at this wedding." She wove slightly as she approached Daniel. "At this point I could care less if you marry them wearing nothing but a thong, a corset, high heels, and a feather boa. Just get them married and on that damned honeymoon before I have an ulcer or drink myself into oblivion." She snatched up her mug, drank the last of the now coffee-flavored liquor, and started for the hallway. "Come on, Phillip, we need to get dressed."

"Okay, but am I supposed to wear a dress now?" he asked as he left the table.

"No, Dad. You wear your tux. Just leave the rest of it to us." Good lord, James was going to need that whiskey too.

★ ★ ★

"Are you done in the bathroom?" James asked Daniel as he grabbed his things.

"Not yet."

"Did you shower?" James watched as Daniel wandered the bedroom in a pink robe. He was just trying to figure out where they were in the dressing process.

"Yes. You go ahead and shower, then return here. There are things we need to do before dressing." He pulled out a ton of makeup, brushes, lipsticks, laying it all out on the dresser. James didn't ask what was going on, just grabbed his things and raced across to the bathroom. He showered quickly, returning to the bedroom, where Daniel had added creams and lotions to the myriad of product already on display. "I got this out for you. It's a moisturizer—rub a little into the skin of your face and neck. It will soothe and moisturize, making your skin really soft."

James went right up behind Daniel, arms sliding around his waist. "Honey, you use whatever you want on your face. I have my shaving cream and soap and water. That's all I need, except a little cologne." He glanced around the room. "Doesn't Lala need to get dressed? What are you going to wear? Did you bring anything?" James didn't remember seeing any clothes that he thought Lala would necessarily wear, especially not on the stage.

Daniel crouched down, that cute little butt waving seductively in the air. He was tempted to grab it and let nature take its course, because...damn. Daniel pulled out the biggest suitcase and set it on the bed, opening it almost reverently. "I always take a little Lala wherever I go."

A firm knock on the door interrupted their moment. Holly

barely paused before bursting into the room. "Can you help me with my makeup?" She seemed flustered and looked like hell.

"What happened?" Daniel fluttered, settling Holly in the chair.

"My hands keep shaking," Holly explained, and Daniel quietly took over, fussing over Holly before standing back.

"There, honey. You look beautiful. Now go put on your robe and try to relax. Once I've got my makeup and hair on, I'll come over and help you into your dress before I finish getting ready, okay?" Daniel seemed to take all of this in stride, and James felt completely useless. He mostly stayed out of the way, sitting on the edge of the bed, fascinated as Daniel put on the makeup that slowly transformed him into Lala.

"Why use that color?"

"It will work with the eye color I'm going to put on afterwards," Daniel answered as he continued working. "It can take hours for me to do this. I usually try to perfect a different look for each performance. Today, though, to save time, I'm re-creating a look I've done before." He painted lines from his eyes, creating exaggerated curves that he filled in with shades of blue that made his eyes look enormous. "Okay, what do you think?"

"Stunning," James breathed, unable to move as Daniel finished his makeup. It was indeed over the top, with incredibly exaggerated cheekbones and luscious lips. Once he seemed satisfied, Daniel pulled a nylon cap over his head, then attached a tall platinum wig with tape, clips, and even adhesive at the hairline.

"That's…" James didn't quite know what to say.

"The higher the hair, the closer to god, and we *are* going

to church…" He cocked his incredibly prominent eyebrows, and James groaned. "You loved it." He did another look from all sides before standing. "I need to help Holly. You finish getting dressed and then keep your parents and sister calm until the limousine gets here to take them to the church. You will drive me, and we'll go in the side door so we don't cause too much of an early stir."

James rolled his entire head. "You want to make an entrance."

"If this is going to be theater, then it's going to be as dramatic as hell." Daniel's hand shook a little, the only sign that he was nervous, and no one else would pick up on it, but James did. "I've got to help Holly." He flashed a brilliant smile and then left the room.

James dressed in his black tuxedo with a light gray vest and royal ascot tie. He liked the way he looked, and once he had his cuff links and shoes on, went in search of his parents. Mom was already in the living room, dressed and sitting carefully on the sofa. "Where's Dad?"

"He's almost ready. I helped him with his cuff links and tie." She bobbed her leg slightly, clearly nervous. "What about Holly?"

"Daniel is helping her into the dress. The limousine will be here in half an hour. Her makeup is done and her hair is beautiful. She's going to be a stunning bride, Mom." The door to Holly's old room opened and, in a shimmer of white with a jeweled hairpiece tucked into her hair, Holly floated down the hallway toward the living room.

Mom inhaled sharply as she got her first look at the restyled gown.

"You look incredible," James breathed as Dad came down the hall behind her.

"Honey, you look like the princess I always knew you were," their dad said.

Margot joined them as well and even she told Holly how gorgeous she looked. All that praise kept anything Mom might have said to herself.

"Daniel did it," Holly said, twirling slowly, the dress the perfect length so it seemed to float around her. James saw Daniel sneak back into their room and close the door. He hugged Holly carefully and kissed her cheek, then did the same with Margot, who was stunning in royal blue. It really was her color.

His phone vibrated in his pocket with a message from Daniel to come to the bedroom. He went down and knocked. The door cracked open. "This is for Margot." Daniel handed him a jeweled necklace. "It's the mate to Holly's hairpiece." He smiled and closed the door once again.

He helped Margot with the necklace, and Mom insisted she get a picture of the three of them together. James also wanted one of his sisters. "Do you have everything?" James asked once he'd snapped an amazing image. "Something old…"

"Mom gave me grandma's necklace." She placed her hand at her neck, the diamond sparkling when it caught the light.

"Something new…"

"The tiara from Daniel. It's new and borrowed, so all I need is something blue, and there are sapphire stones in it." The tiara really set off Holly's eyes.

"The limo is here," Margot announced, then turned away from the window. "I want to see Daniel before we leave."

"I'm sure you'll see everything possible when we get to the church. We need to go so we aren't late." It seemed Mom still had some snide left over, or maybe the whiskey had worked off and she just needed another buzz. Either way, James shot her a look before herding the four of them out the door.

"Daniel, we need to leave," he called once they were gone. James was getting nervous and waited in the living room. His attention shifted in an instant when he heard the door open. Lala stepped out in the hall, a red flowing dress trimmed in ermine and sparkling jewels. "Should I bring the cape, or is that too much?"

James couldn't seem to get his mouth to work. Lala was incredible, but for a second, James didn't see any of Daniel. It was like a stranger was walking toward him, and he stepped back. The reaction caught him off guard until Lala drew closer and James looked into his eyes. Then Daniel was there and he smiled. "Nope. I think you should go for it. A queen can never have too much ermine." James draped the cape over his arm and escorted Daniel to the door. It was funny, but even dressed this way, in all the finery and with god knew how many layers of fabric, not to mention a completely different look, it was still Daniel next to him. He smelled the same, the eyes and mouth were the same, even if the rest was hidden and colored—this was still his Daniel.

The thought about Daniel being his startled him a little, given their earlier conversations. But Daniel *was* his—James was coming to realize that. He simply needed to be sure Daniel understood that as well. "Let's go. We don't want to be late, and I have to verify that all the changes we needed to make have been understood and are ready."

"There's nothing to be nervous about," Daniel said.

"Are you kidding, or have you been dipping into Mom's whiskey bottle?" James couldn't help teasing as he followed Daniel out of the house, locking the door and somehow getting Daniel and the dress into the car.

James joined Howard and the groomsmen once Daniel was inside, using the reverend's office while they waited for the service to start. "Does everyone know what they need to do?" James asked. "You all know there's been a change of program due to the fact that the minister is no longer with us." Yeah, he wasn't actually dead, just gone, but that was fine.

"We're good," one of the guys said, and then the others nodded. Weston sat off to the side, his fellow groomsmen ignoring him. James was a little surprised he was still there, but that had been up to Howard, who had decided not to rock the boat, even though he was obviously upset with his most likely soon-to-be-former friend.

"I read him the riot act and told him if he so much as stepped out of line for a second, I'd personally kick his ass. I checked with the guys doing the readings, and they're all set." Howard checked his watch. "It's just about time," Howard explained quietly. James and the guys left the small room off the back of the church, where they paired off with their counterparts as they had in the rehearsal.

He was with Holly's friend Janice, and he took her arm as the organ music began. James knew the second Lala stepped out into the sanctuary, standing front and center, not a single set of eyes able to look away. A light murmur went through the crowd and a few of the bridesmaids tittered before growing silent.

"Damn, I want that dress," Janice whispered from next to him.

"Don't we all," Margot said from just behind them, and James relaxed. It was going to be all right. James and Janice followed right behind Weston and the matron of honor, slowly walking down the aisle toward the front of the church. He was unable to wipe the huge smile from his lips as he approached Daniel, a vision in red that James was never going to remove from his mind.

Once they had all taken their places, the music shifted, and everyone stood as Holly and their father came down the aisle. Holly was radiant, and Dad seemed as happy as James had ever seen him. Howard stepped out from the side, joining his bride right in front of Lala as the music drew to a close.

"Good afternoon," Lala said clearly, voice ringing through the cavernous space made more intimate by sprays of flowers and the guests clustered toward the center. "We are here to celebrate love. The all-consuming love that takes many forms, and joins two hearts together in a lifelong dance. Holly and Howard each stand before us, ready to make this commitment with all of us as witnesses." Lala stepped down and gently placed Holly's hand in Howard's. "When Holly and Howard asked me to step in as the officiant for this wedding, I asked them… 'Are you nuts?'" A chuckle went through the congregation, and James felt himself releasing the breath he hadn't known he'd been holding. The ice was broken. "They answered, 'No, but we want you to do it anyway.'"

Holly was married. With all the events leading up to the wedding, and the problems that had required solving, it felt like James had run a marathon. "I'm not sure what I should wear," Daniel said once they got back to the house. The after-service pictures were finished, and James had to give Holly a lot of credit. The photographer had been taking pictures throughout the ceremony, but he'd never gotten in the way, which was pretty rare as far as James had seen in his limited experience.

"Whatever you like," James said as he collapsed onto the sofa. The rest of the wedding party was already on their way to the botanical gardens for the reception, but Daniel needed to return and change. "How long will you be?"

Water ran in the bathroom, and James wandered down. A pile of makeup-covered tissues rested next to the sink. Lala's hair had already been packed away, and the dress lay across the bed. "I don't want to take any of the attention away from Holly. I had planned to wear a plum cocktail dress to the reception, or at least that was my original plan." Daniel finished washing his face, the last of the makeup gone.

James stepped up to Daniel, sliding his arms around his waist. "How do you want to go now?" Daniel was already adding a touch of liner to his eyes, and a small amount of lavender shadow.

"I have a deep purple shirt and a pair of slacks. I think I'll wear those. I don't want to take anything away from Holly, and while everyone seemed to accept Lala at the service, I don't know how they're going to feel about having dinner with me, or talking with me afterwards." He set down the brush with a sigh. "Would you be angry if I stayed here?"

James was a little taken aback. "No, but I will be disappointed." James hugged him closer, Daniel's scent sending his senses into overdrive. "You dress as Daniel, whatever that is, whoever you want to be. I'll wait for you in the living room, because if I stay, I'm going to tug off what you still have on and take you right here on the bathroom floor." Daniel shivered, and James was so damned tempted to make good on his threat...his promise? He wasn't sure which it was. He took a deep breath and backed away, returning to the living room.

Daniel joined him fifteen minutes later. He still wore the eye makeup and might have added a touch of color to his cheeks as well as some gloss to his lips. He wore flowing gray pants and a purple shirt that shimmered whenever he moved. "What do you think?"

"I think you look wonderful, and just so you know, your dance card is filled for the evening. If anyone asks, you're all mine." James tugged Daniel to him a little roughly, one hand around his waist, the other cupping his butt, taking his lips hard, desperately needing a taste of him.

"James..."

"I know. We have to go." James reluctantly pulled away, wanting to stay in this perfect moment, but wondering how much longer this was going to last once they got back to Chicago.

Drinks were being served by the time they arrived at the reception. Waiters in tuxedos carried trays of appetizers through the atrium of the large glasshouse facility. It was like stepping into another world. Howard and Holly mingled with their guests, talking and smiling with everyone. "Oh god," Holly called as she hurried over to Daniel. "Everyone is asking about you." Holly hugged him like he was her long-lost brother. "You did an amazing job. People haven't had that much fun at a wedding service in years."

"How much have you had to drink?" James asked. Holly smacked him on the shoulder.

"Be nice…and not that much." She stepped back, twirling once, the gown flowing beautifully around her. "I get to be happy. He saved my wedding and made me look like a princess." She zeroed in on James. "You need to keep him, okay?"

James hugged Daniel right there in front of everyone. "I intend to." He met Daniel's gaze, daring him to argue.

"Go get a drink," Holly instructed. "Dinner will be served in a little while, and then there will be dancing among all the flowers." She hurried off to talk to other guests, and James grabbed two glasses of sparkling wine and handed one to Daniel.

"Young man!" James knew that voice and slowly turned to face his father, but he was intent on Daniel. "You did a great job today. Holly is happy and she's married." Dad was a little tipsy, but he didn't seem to care, and James figured his dad had earned it over the last few days. "I think I lost your mother."

"She's over there. But you might want to sit down and maybe have something to eat." He got a server over and his dad dived into the shrimp puffs and stuffed mushrooms like they were going out of style.

"You're very talented, and I don't care if you are a guy, you look better in a dress than most women." He toddled away, and James didn't know quite what to make of it. In the end, he figured it was his dad's way of dealing with everything. Well, that and being well on his way to drunk.

"Come on," James said, taking Daniel by the hand, leading him through the gathering and into one of the garden rooms, which seemed quieter. "This is weird in a really good way."

"What were you expecting?" Daniel asked.

"I don't know. Maybe I should be grateful, but I guess that out of the drag, I was hoping to have you all to myself for a little while." He tugged Daniel into his arms. "But that's never going to happen, is it? You're always going to be surrounded by people and fans who want a piece of you." James was really beginning to get that now.

"Is that a problem?" Daniel asked.

"Nope, as long as you come home to me instead of them. They can have a tiny piece of you, but I get the whole thing." He grinned and kissed Daniel once again.

"God. Am I going to walk in on you two making out all the time?" Margot asked in that way that teenagers have. "Because it's kind of sad when my brother gets more action with guys than I do." She smirked, tipping her glass to her lips.

"Do Mom and Dad know you've got that?" James growled.

"It's grape juice." Once again, she played the put-upon teenager to the hilt. "I know you're a cop, but you don't need to be a fuddy-duddy." She came over and gave James a hug anyway. "Dating a drag queen is the coolest thing you've ever done in your life. Don't fuck it up." She giggled. "And don't worry about Mom and Dad. I'm going to get them to binge-watch *RuPaul*." She lifted her glass and then swept out of the room, with the two of them following into dinner.

James sat up at the head table, and it seemed a place had been prepared next to him for their officiant.

The bridesmaid sitting next to Daniel spent much of dinner doing her best to ignore him, and a few of the groomsmen went out of their way to avoid both Daniel and James, not that James cared. Weston was still an ass, and one of the other guys, someone he and Holly had known for years, gave James the cold shoulder, but all in all, the people he'd known most of his life seemed to accept him for who he was and didn't make a fuss.

"Do the two of you intend to dance?" Holly asked as she came up behind them once the meal was done.

Daniel hesitated. James didn't. "Yes."

"Good. That woman over there is Howard's aunt Sybil. She's a real uppity bitch. He made me invite her. Be sure to dance over her way. I'm sort of hoping the old bat has a stroke or something. She actually asked Howard if he *had* to marry me." Holly gaped. "She's been sitting at her table all evening, apparently complaining about everything from the food to where she's seated."

Daniel took Holly's hand. "Don't worry. James can dip me and then plant one on me right in front of her. Give the old 'phobe a real show."

Holly grinned. "Perfect. Maybe she'll leave and stop casting a pall over that side of the room." She swept away, and the head table cleared out for the introduction of the bridal party and the first dance, which Howard and Holly did before inviting the rest of the party to join in.

"Ready?" Daniel asked, taking James's hand.

"I've been looking forward to this since that lesson." He led Daniel to the floor, pulling him close, moving easily through the dance. "The wedding is nearly over, and tomorrow we go back to Chicago." The song changed, the music slowing, and they continued dancing, with James gazing into Daniel's eyes.

"I know, and I've been thinking…things are going to be different for both of us." Daniel smiled, and James wondered what he was up to. He leaned in a little closer. "Maybe you and I should have some rules…you know, a way to understand what's *expected*."

James moved them in a slow circle. "Oh, you think so, huh? What exactly crossed that devilish mind of yours?"

As if to prove his point, Daniel smiled evilly. "Well, I've had a chance to ponder it and I've come to the conclusion that your mother may have gotten a few things right."

James skipped a step and nearly stomped on Daniel's foot. Okay, maybe he did it on purpose, but he deserved it for that comment. Daniel did a little fancy footwork of his own to avoid catastrophe. "That's a frightening idea." James wasn't sure where Daniel was going with this line of thought, but he didn't like it one bit. "You know, we're dancing, the music is rather romantic, I have you in my arms, and you want to talk about my mother. Can you see what's wrong with this picture?"

Daniel nodded. "I happen to think we're on the right track at the moment."

"I'm going to step on your feet if you keep shocking me this way." God, James hoped Daniel was playing with him. At least that would explain this jump into the pool of insanity. "Did someone offer you some red Kool-Aid or something?" He was starting to think that Daniel's drinks had been spiked, though he danced perfectly and was steady on his feet.

"If you'll let me explain a minute," Daniel said as the song picked up tempo. James twirled Daniel away and then back into his arms, cradling him easily. "I was just thinking that when we return to Chicago, we should both know what to expect. I was thinking that we should develop a list."

James stopped them right there. "Oh no…" He shook his head. "Not Daniel's Ten Commandments?"

Daniel grinned. "*I never thought of that.*" James growled. "Let me think, Daniel's commandment number one: thou shall meet my grandmother and friends, and of course I'll meet your friends." He pretended to think. "Number two: thou shall take your boyfriend out at least once a week." James noted that Daniel had used the *B* word for the first time.

"And what else do you command?" Maybe this wasn't going to be so bad. "How do date nights end?"

"That's commandment number three. Dates shall end in the bedroom, behind a closed and locked door, without relatives anywhere nearby." Daniel fake glared.

"Amen to that. And commandment number four, thou shall go dancing with your boyfriend at least once a month, and afterwards…see commandment number three." James flashed a brilliant smile. "Do you think a theme might be forming?"

Daniel nodded. "I'm really liking where this is going."

"Me too."

"Number five, thou shall tell thy boyfriend that you love him at least once a day." Daniel slid his arms around James's neck. "I'll go first."

"Well, technically I went first…" James clarified.

"Then I'd say I'm one behind. But maybe we should see commandment number three once again for such an important conversation, one without other ears."

James leaned right into Daniel's ear. "You know, we're fulfilling commandment number four right now, and I got us a lovely hotel room within walking distance for the night in case we drank a little too much. We could go get started on commandment number three right away."

Daniel shivered against him. "And not a relative in sight."

James did something he had never done before, not caring who was watching: he leaned closer and kissed his boyfriend right there for all to see.

# Epilogue

James hated the Dan Ryan Expressway toward downtown. It was always jammed with traffic. "What has you giggling over there?" he asked as he slowed down. The rain seemed to be mixing with a little snow. It was forecast to switch over to all snow sometime after midnight, which was why James was driving Daniel down to the theater. Normally Daniel took the train in and out of the city, but tonight the reports of weather delays had come at a perfect time, James had offered to drive. Not that Daniel had a clue that this was the plan all along.

"Your mother," Daniel explained, still smiling.

"My mother is texting you?" James asked.

Daniel scoffed. "Sure. When I talked to her last week, she told me she wanted to redecorate the kitchen to look a little more modern and a little less grandma, especially since she's going to be one, with Holly already expecting." Apparently, Holly's fears had been unfounded, given the fact that she was starting to show. "I took the opportunity to mention that she might try ditching the sampler." Daniel snickered and

handed the phone over his shoulder to Margaret, his grandmother. "What do you think?"

Gran, as she insisted James call her, was wonderful. James
adored her completely, and when he'd explained what he
had planned, she'd arranged for the night out to come along.
He and Gran would have dinner and then see the show,
and then she'd spend the night and return in the morning.
Gran snorted. "The first time you told me about that thing
I thought you were joking. Now I think it's perfect." She
handed the phone back, and James wished he could see what
these two were cackling about.

"What gives?" James asked, slowing down yet again. He
had left plenty of time for them to get there. After all, it
would take Daniel some time to get into makeup once they
arrived.

"I suggested that your mom get a new table and chairs in a
lighter shade, change the wall color to brighten up the place,
and maybe replace the floors with a lighter wood laminate
and have the cabinets professionally cleaned to refresh the
finish. Apparently, she's started the process."

"Did she get rid of the commandments?" James asked.

"Not exactly," Daniel snickered as James pulled to a complete stop. They were only a few miles from their exit, and
James wished they'd been in a cruiser and he could simply
put on his lights and bypass this mess. Not that he would,
but a policeman could dream, after all. "Your mother added
to them."

"Oh god," James groaned, and Gran patted his shoulder.

Daniel cleared his throat. "Number eleven: thou shall
marry and love the person who makes you happy."

"You're making that up," James charged, and Daniel pulled the phone away as traffic started up again.

"Watch the road, and I am not. That's what it says. Number twelve: thou shall love thy brothers-in-law, no matter what they wear or how they dress. I think that's a reference to Howard's lime-green shoes from Halloween," Daniel quipped, probably to cover the hitch in his voice that James caught anyway. James patted his leg, damned proud of his mom. "Number thirteen: thou shall love thy entire family...one and all...without reservation." Daniel put down the phone, turning toward the window. "Dang it."

James understood exactly how Daniel was feeling. "Did she tell you she and Dad joined PFLAG? Apparently Margot took them to her Gay-Straight Alliance meeting at school, and they got them in touch."

"Yeah. She said she and your father are planning to come to Chicago this June for Pride. I thought she was putting me on. I guess not." Daniel put his hand on top of James's. "If you would have told me when I first met them that your family would welcome me, I would have thought you were crazy."

James had to agree with him. "I would have thought I'd taken the train to Looneyville myself."

"Folks surprise you," Gran said, and James nodded. His family certainly fit into that category.

The traffic ahead of them started to move just enough that James was able to slide over into the right lane and take the exit, weaving through city streets and down the alley to the theater door. "Is there anything you need?"

"Are you going to come in?"

James shook his head and reached behind his seat, handing Daniel a cooler bag. "She and I are going to have a quick dinner and then we'll be back. I made you something light to eat. I know they always have things there, but I tried to get some of your favorites." Daniel took the bag, leaning in to share a kiss, which James wished could go on for hours. Then Daniel got out, closed the door, and after waving, James pulled away.

"Have you got everything?" Gran asked.

"You better believe it. We'll eat and change clothes. Then come back closer to showtime so he doesn't see us." Now all he had to do was put his plan into action.

"How did you know what color tie to wear?" Gran asked as she stepped out of the restaurant's ladies' room, dressed in a vintage cream dress that went nearly to the floor. James was in a black tuxedo, white shirt, and royal blue bow tie. "I know you wanted to coordinate."

"Daniel said that tonight is the Ice-travaganza, which means Daniel will be the Ice Queen in blue trimmed with white." He had managed to extract all the information he needed without making Daniel suspicious. "Here's your coat." He held it for her and then put on his own, gathering their old clothes in the hanger bag he'd brought. "Let's go." James took Gran's arm and was sure to tip the hostess, who had allowed them to change in the restrooms, as they headed out into the evening.

James placed their clothes in the trunk, got Gran in the car for the return to the theater, and parked in the performers' lot, where a space had been saved for them. Candy met them at the theater door, beautiful in white and blue. "Get in here right away. Lala's still in her dressing room."

"Thanks for helping," James whispered.

Candy fanned her face. "Are you kidding? This is beautiful." She motioned them through the side of the stage.

"Tulane," James said quietly as a vision in light blue, blinged with enough crystal to blind half the audience, turned and smiled.

"Oh, honey. Are you ready?" Lala's drag mother, Tulane Highway, was appearing as a special guest for the week, and James had enlisted her help as well. "I'd kiss you both, but it would ruin the makeup. Don't worry about a thing. It's all set." She squeezed his hand, made air kisses, then did the same with Gran. "Go take your seats."

James offered his elbow, Gran accepted it, and they made their way out into the packed cabaret theater to their seats at one of the side tables in the front.

"Ladies, gentlemen, and everyone in between, Cabaret Candide is proud to present our bevy of talented ladies here to tickle your fancy—and anything else within finger distance," the announcer said as the curtain rose to reveal the company, on the stage in an ice palace setting, where they did a fabulous choreographed dance number that ended with all of them facing stage right. "Our star of the evening is our very own Ice Queen, the amazing, the operatic, Miss Lala Traviata." James stood along with Gran and half the audience as Daniel appeared, mesmerizing in ice blue that took James's breath away. She twirled onstage, gliding to front and center and singing a rather bawdy version of "Sleigh Ride" as the other ladies acted out the best parts. It brought tears to his eyes and left his belly sore from laughing.

"Darlings," Lala purred once the song was over. "I have a special guest tonight. She's my drag mother, which tells you just how old she is."

"Bitch…" a deep voice intoned from the wings.

"I love her to death, and she knows it. So please welcome, direct from New York, Brooklyn, the Bronx, and *Newark*, the one, the only, the well-traveled Miss Tulane Highway."

The music for Lala's signature number began, and James snapped out of his reverie. He had barely taken in the rest of the show, his attention on Lala the entire time. She sang her BDSM tribute to Doris Day and then thanked the audience. As expected, Tulane took the microphone.

"Sweetheart, we have one last bit of business this evening," she said. "There's a very special guest in the audience who has something he wants to say. He's making his cabaret stage debut tonight, so please give him a warm welcome." That was his cue, and James stood, walking to the side and up onto the stage.

The lights were nearly blinding, so he kept his eyes on Daniel as he accepted the microphone. Tulane moved downstage, as did all the other girls, leaving him and Lala at center. "I'm not as eloquent as our Ice Queen here, but for those of you who don't know, I'm James, Lala's boyfriend. At least for the next few seconds. Who knows, after this she might kill me." A titter went through the audience while Daniel blinked at him, the smallest signs of nerves visible around the eyes James knew so well. "But I think it's time that our own Miss Traviata become Mrs. Traviata." James reached into his pocket and then went down on one knee. Daniel gasped, hands fluttering. "Sweetheart, light of my life." He opened the box, displaying a white gold ring set with diamonds and sapphires. "Will you fill my life with excitement, joy, and a dose of unpredictability, and become my forever partner, taking my family as your own with all the insanity that entails?"

Lala choked out a yes, and the audience applauded as James slipped the ring onto Daniel's finger, then stood, taking the center of his life into his arms.

"I love you," Daniel breathed, his arms sliding around James's neck.

"I love you too, more than I can say," James said, kissing Daniel right there onstage. The audience applause grew deafening. Daniel's lips moved, but James couldn't hear him over the roar of the crowd. He kissed Daniel once again, holding his hand as the curtain lowered to the stage.

"Sweetheart, that was beautiful," Tulane said as she dabbed her eyes. "One question, though." She turned to Daniel. "Honey, what was that about later and commandment number three?"

They both smiled wickedly.

★ ★ ★ ★ ★

*A sexy Navy chief is looking for a rebound fling,
and his best friend's adorkable little brother
might just fit the bill...*

*Keep reading for an excerpt from*
Sailor Proof *by Annabeth Albert.*

# Chapter One

*Derrick*

It was going to happen. Today was finally the day I was going to deck an officer and thus end any hope I had of ever making chief of the boat, and probably earn myself a court-martial to boot. But Fernsby had it coming, and he knew it, the way he met my eyes as he gave a cocky laugh. He might be a junior-grade lieutenant who had to answer to the other officers, but he wasn't stupid. It didn't matter how much he had it coming, a chief fighting with an officer of any rank over a personal matter was going to be harshly punished.

But it might be worth it.

Fernsby had been goading me the entire long deployment, every chance he got, which considering the close quarters on a submarine was pretty damn often. And now here he was, joking with another officer about winning the first-kiss raffle for our homecoming, knowing full well that I was standing right there. And that he'd be kissing my ex.

Personal matter indeed.

And totally worth punching that smug smile away.

"I hope we go viral. Social media loves two hot dudes kissing." Fernsby smirked as he waggled his eyebrows at the big-eyed ensign who'd been hero-worshipping him all damn tour. And of course he was smirking. First kiss was a storied tradition for most navy deployments, and sailors loved vying for the honor of being first to disembark and greet their loved ones. Usually I was happy for whoever won, and over the years I'd seen more than one proposal as a result of that first kiss.

God, I hoped Fernsby wasn't planning *that*. Bad enough that he couldn't stop ribbing me that Steve chose him over me and that I'd been the last to know Steve was cheating. Watching them be all happy was going to suck.

"I'm gonna get so lucky." Fernsby's knowing gaze met mine over the ensign's head.

An angry noise escaped my throat. "And I hope—"

"Fox. A word. *Now*." My friend Calder appeared seemingly out of nowhere in the narrow corridor and hauled me backward, effectively cutting off my tirade along with a good deal of my circulation.

"Yeah, Fox. Go on with you." Fernsby made a dismissive gesture as I growled, but Calder kept moving, giving me little choice but to follow. He dragged me past various compartments through the mess, where two of our fellow chiefs were playing cards. He didn't stop until we were in the chief's section of the bunking with its rows of triple beds, steering me into the far corner by our bunks and about as close to privacy as we were going to get.

"What the fuck?" Calder wasted no time in unleashing on me.

"It's nothing." I looked down at my narrow bunk. I had the bottom bunk, another chief had the middle, and the top bunk was Calder's. And I was more than a little tempted to disappear into mine and pull the blue privacy curtain. "Fernsby was running his mouth again."

"You sure as hell looked like you were gearing up to slug him. I saw your clenched fist. I'm surprised smoke wasn't coming out of your ears."

Calder wasn't wrong, so I shrugged. "I need to stop letting him get to me. I know."

"Yeah, you do." He shoved my shoulder the way only a longtime best friend could get away with. We'd been lucky, meeting up in submarine school, both getting assigned to Bremerton, and then ending up on the same boat together as chiefs. Calder had a vested interest in me not fucking up, and my skin heated from how close I'd come to doing just that.

"I'm pissed because it looks like he won first kiss and now I have to watch that," I admitted in a low whisper.

"What you need is a kiss of your own," said the guy who probably had different dates scheduled for each of our first three days home.

"Ha. Would be nice, but not happening." It went without saying that I wouldn't have anyone in the throngs of family and friends waiting on me. Simply wasn't how my life was structured, and most of the time I was fine with it. Calder was the one who would have a big contingent of friends and family. And I was well-acquainted with his undying belief that the solution to one terrible relationship was to find another more casual arrangement. "I'm not exactly a rebound sort of guy."

"Everyone knows that about you." Calder rolled his eyes.

He was both taller and broader than me, which was saying something because I wasn't exactly tiny. However, his playful demeanor always made him seem younger. "But you should be. And I'm not even talking about getting laid. I'm saying you need to make Fernsby and Steve-the-lying-ex-from-hell jealous by having some hottie there to greet you."

"God. I wish." I let my head thump back against the panel where the bunks met the wall. Unlike Calder, I wasn't counting down the minutes until I could get lucky, but I had entertained more than fantasy about how to pay Steve back. A rebound held limited appeal from an emotional standpoint. But jealousy? Yeah, I wouldn't mind trotting out someone hotter than Steve, who always was a vain fucker. "But we're only a couple of weeks out from homecoming, and I'm not exactly in a position to meet someone while we're deployed."

Unlike some other deployments, the submarine force had very limited communication access. No cell phones, no swiping right, no mindless surfing of hookup sites. Hell, simply getting messages to friends and family could be challenging, let alone trying to conduct a revenge romance on the down-low.

"Call in a favor?" Calder quirked his mouth. He undoubtedly had multiple persons who would love nothing more than to pretend to be madly in lust with him.

"From who?" My back tensed and my nerves were still jangling from listening to Fernsby brag. "It's not like my contact list is awash in friends with benefits or even friends period."

"You need to work on that whole brooding-loner persona." Calder clapped me on the shoulder, nicer now. "It's not doing you any favors."

"Why be the life of the party when I have you?" I laughed, years of shared memories flowing between us. Any social life I did have, I owed almost entirely to Calder. He'd even introduced me to Steve.

"I do like to bring the party."

"You do." Closing my eyes, I took another deep breath, trying to steady myself. I truly did not want to fight Fernsby even if my fist tended to forget that. "You're right, though. Someone there, even pretend, would make me feel less like a fucking loser."

"Exactly," Calder agreed a little too readily, making my gut clench. Maybe I was that pathetic.

"But I'm not doing something stupid like an ad." I cracked an eye open in time to catch him laughing at me.

"Of course not. You save your stupidity for fighting with officers."

I groaned because he was right. "I'm not the personal-ads type. But who do you know? Surely there's a guy into guys who owes you a favor whom you could loan me?"

I wasn't too proud to borrow from Calder's vast social network.

"Hmm." Tilting his head, Calder narrowed his eyes, the same intense thinking he did when poring over the latest supply manifest. As a logistics specialist, Calder had a solution to almost every problem that could crop up, apparently my love life included. He muttered to himself for a few moments before straightening. "Arthur would do it."

"Ha. Very funny. Try again." I kept my voice down, but my laugh was a lot freer this time. *Arthur.* The nerve. I had to go ahead and sit on a bunk before I lost it laughing.

"He would," Calder insisted, serious expression never wavering. "He owes me."

I shook my head. *Arthur.* I'd known Calder's family for a decade now, including his spindly youngest brother who was some sort of musical genius. And also terminally hopeless. "You want me to use your too-nerdy-for-band-camp little brother to make Fernsby jealous?"

"He's almost twenty-five now. Not so little. He's been out since high school, so no issues about a public kiss. And Haggerty said Arthur's hot now. Kid went and got all buff in Boston."

"Haggerty said that? And you let him live?" Our mutual friend did like them young and pretty. I had vague memories of Arthur having a riot of unruly hair, far redder than his brothers', and big green eyes, but he'd been barely legal last time I'd seen him a couple of years back. And as I'd already been seeing Steve, and Arthur was Calder's little brother, I hadn't looked too terribly hard.

"It was an observation, not a request to go break his heart." Calder kicked my foot. "Come on. It's perfect. Arthur has always liked you, but he doesn't *like* you."

"Hey!" I should have been relieved that Arthur wasn't harboring some giant crush, not indignant.

"Yeah, yeah, you're a catch." Calder fiddled with the strap on his bunk. Everything got strapped down on a sub, even us. "But he's always said he'd never get involved long-term with someone military."

"I don't blame him." This was why I was never doing another relationship myself. Romance and the navy simply didn't mix, especially not submarine personnel. We were bad relationship bets, and I could admit that.

"See? This is why he'd be good for this. He can fake it long enough to get Steve and Fernsby off your back, but it's not like he'd actually date you."

"Of course not."

"Plus all that experience as a dorm RA has him good at shit like signs and banners and cutesy gestures. And he's been back in Seattle a couple of months now. He'd do it."

"I can't believe I'm actually considering this. How are you going to get a message to him anyway?" The last thing I needed was anyone else getting wind of this ill-advised plan. There was no such thing as privacy on a sub.

"Trust me. I've got my ways." Calder's voice went from confident to hushed as voices sounded near the front row of bunks.

"Dude. Did you hear about Fernsby?" asked one of the youngest chiefs, a Nuke with a chipped front tooth and no filter. I couldn't see him or his buddy but his surfer-boy drawl was unmistakable.

"Yep. Fox is gonna be so pissed." The other person had to be Beauregard, who worked with me in Weapons. The Southern accent gave him away. "It's a wonder they haven't murdered each other this whole deployment. If a crew member stole my girl—or guy—I'm not sure I could stand the humiliation."

"Shush." A third voice sounded farther back, and then there was a lot of fumbling around before Beauregard slapped his bunk.

"Okay, okay, here's my new deck," he announced as the three of them exited the quarters.

"See?" I gestured up at Calder. "It would be justifiable homicide."

"It would. But wouldn't revenge be better?"

"I dunno. Fernsby's head would look pretty great mounted on my wall back on base." I groaned as I thought about returning to my little room in the barracks. I'd let Steve keep the apartment, because I was such a nice guy and all. Damn it, I was tired of being nice. Tired of being taken advantage of and pitied and gossiped about. Fuck it all. "Okay. Whatever. See what you can arrange."

"Leave it all to me." Calder straightened to his full height, which came just shy of the low ceiling. "You won't regret this."

"Oh, I'm pretty sure I will." Dread churned in my too-empty gut, but it was a distraction from all the weeks of hurt and anger I'd been stamping down. At least we had a plan.

# Chapter Two

*Arthur*

"This should be easy." I hefted my large cardboard sign out of the trunk as Sabrina laughed.

"Uh-huh." She flipped her cascading bluish-purple hair over her shoulder. She'd prepared for our day on the docks at base with the hair, a shimmery blue top, and a skirt with scales on it. Her whole look gave her the air of a mermaid prepared to lead some poor sailor to his doom. "If this scheme is so easy, why again did you need me?"

"You have a car." We had the kind of ride-or-die friendship built on insults and inside jokes.

"True." After checking her lipstick in a fancy silver mirror, she snapped her purse shut as I carefully removed the bunch of balloons next.

"And you have more social media followers than a minor Kardashian."

"Also true. I'll get you trending." Somehow Sabrina had turned a secret obsession with fashion when we were teens into a successful sideline as an influencer as her alter ego The Makeup Witch with followers hanging on her every post.

"Counting on it." I adjusted my load so that the balloons weren't in imminent danger of escape.

"We'll drown out this cheating loser dude who got first dibs on kissing."

"Your strong opinions on cheaters are only one reason why I love you, Sabrina."

"And my car." She shut the trunk with a gold-tipped finger.

"Yup." I headed in the direction of the community center where the families and friends waiting for the return of the sub were gathering to await buses to the docks. "Anyway, it's a stupid tradition, but like everything else, the navy takes it super seriously. My mom and dad got the honor at least once, and there are a ton of pics of it. It was when he was stationed in Hawaii, and she got flowers and the boat was decorated with a huge lei. It made the *Navy Times*."

"We can do better than some small-time publication." Sabrina laughed as her heels clicked on the sidewalk.

"Everything is small compared to you." It was true on multiple levels because she was big in notoriety and personality as well as stature. Even as we joined the throng of people entering the community center, Sabrina still towered over most of the crowd, commanding far more attention than I ever could, even with my giant sign and balloons.

But the sign that had looked so gaudy back at my place with all its colors and glitter was only one of dozens here. Tons of pretty young women in fancy sundresses toted catchy signs proclaiming how many days it had been since they'd seen their guys, and little kids had smaller signs announcing how much they'd grown. Proud Navy Mom T-shirts were everywhere, and more than one guy my dad's age sported a Navy Veteran hat. The kids raced around the big common room while clumps of people greeted each other with hugs and excited squeals.

"This is something else. They've even got balloon animals happening." Sabrina gestured at a kids' area set up in the far corner with crafts and a couple of costumed entertainers.

"Yup. When I was little, they had face painting."

"Tell me you asked for something embarrassing that made your big brothers cringe." Sabrina bumped my shoulder.

"I asked for a three-fourth scale viola. I got two music notes and a heart instead."

"You? Ask for something obscure? Never." Her laugh echoed in the large space, mingling with all the other conversations swirling around us. Outside the large picture windows, a row of buses awaited the signal to load up.

"Quit laughing at me," I grumbled as I glanced around to see if any of the uniformed event coordinators were herding people toward the buses yet.

"It's all love, baby." She gave me an air kiss.

In my pocket, my phone vibrated, and I shifted around my armful of stuff so I could fish it out of my skinny jeans. I was waiting to hear about a big freelance job, so I was more eager to check the messages than I might otherwise have been.

But I should have saved my enthusiasm.

Guess what? We caught an earlier flight! We'll probably miss the buses, but we should see you at the docks. Can't wait to see Calder. And you, of course.

And me. Of course. Calder got the bulk of my mom's enthusiasm, as always. And damn it, this was a complication I
hadn't counted on. All I'd told Mom was that I was going to
greet Calder and Derrick. Calder had sworn me to secrecy
on the fake homecoming plan, not that I would have fessed
up to Mom under any circumstances. Telling Sabrina didn't
count in my estimation because we operated in a judgment-
free zone of total honesty. Unlike my parents.

"Fuck," I muttered.

"What?" Sabrina deftly saved the balloons as I juggled
things to pocket my phone.

"My parents are gonna be here."

"Oh." She blinked her thick lashes a few times. "This
should be interesting."

"Very." There was nothing I could do other than hope
they missed the whole playacting-with-Derrick thing. I
stepped aside as a pack of dressed-up kids zoomed between
us. Then one of the personnel from the community liaison
office signaled that it was time to load the first bus. I hurried
to make sure Sabrina and I were in that line. Any distance
from my parents would help.

"So… Derrick?" Sabrina waited to speak again until we
were seated on the navy bus, which was essentially a school
bus made over for military use. "Tell me what he looks like
so I can help you spot him. Is he gorgeous? Why is it that all
the gorgeous guys are the ones who get cheated on? You'd
think they'd have better luck."

"Quit trying to write a romance novel, Sabrina." I moved
my sign to let a family pass as more people filled the bus.
"He's quiet, but when he does talk, people tend to listen.
That sort of commanding voice. Tall. Not as tall as you in

your heels, but taller than me. Big shoulders. Dark brown hair. And a face like one of those old Hollywood heroes. So, yeah, he's hot. But this is a favor. Nothing more. Honestly, I'm not sure he even noticed my existence previously."

"Aw." She patted my shoulder. "The big bad sailor squashed your tender feelings."

"Save it for your fan fic. I was a kid last time I saw him in person. And even if I wasn't, I don't do military."

"And yet here you are." Gesturing at my sign and balloons, she gave me a pointed look.

"Here I am." I adjusted my balloons so a teen girl with an even bigger bunch could settle in behind us. "As a favor to my brother."

Who had loaned me money on more than one occasion while I'd been in school and broke, but even Sabrina didn't need to know *everything*.

"Uh-huh. And this hot, older, silent man whom you might get to plant one on." Sabrina braced a hand on the seat in front of us as the bus got moving.

"I feel sorry for the guy, that's all." Sure, teenage me had found Derrick beyond attractive, but even then I'd known better than to get a crush on a man in uniform. "He got a bum deal with his ex. I met the guy once when they first started dating. The sort of high-maintenance dude who tries too hard to be hot and comes off fake instead. Terrible voice."

"You can't keep picking men simply because they have the right pitch of baritone."

"You never know when a musical number might come up." I laughed.

"With you? That probability is higher than it should be.

I'm still not over you leaving that *fine* hookup simply because inspiration struck for your latest composition."

"Eh. He wasn't that hot. Kinda nasal. And the composition won four awards, which is more than I could say for his kissing."

"And this level of picky is why you're still—"

"Hey, look, we're on base." I could usually handle Sabrina's teasing and give as good as I got, but I didn't need to be reminded exactly how pathetic my love life was right before I went and rescued Derrick from his.

"Oh my gosh, the ships are huge."

It was always fun watching a civilian see the big ships for the first time, and Sabrina's face as the bus turned onto the road that rimmed the docks was no exception. Her wide eyes and slack jaw reminded me of my excitement as a kid, waiting for my dad or uncles to return and taking in all these ships the size of a small city. As always the docks were bustling with activity. Uniformed sailors were everywhere, dwarfed by the giant equipment like cranes and the boats themselves.

The community liaison personnel herded us carefully off the buses and into a cordoned-off waiting area where we had a great view of the Sound and the empty dock space where the submarine would moor. I scanned the crowd but didn't see my parents. Maybe they were stuck in traffic. That would be helpful. I did, however, spot Derrick's sleazy ex right near the front of the barricades, talking to one of the sailors working crowd control. Probably lining up his next hookup.

"Tell me I'm hotter than him," I whispered to Sabrina after discreetly pointing him out. Normally I didn't care at all what I looked like, and clothes were an afterthought at best, but today I wanted to look good in a way I wasn't sure

I ever had before. To that end, I'd let Sabrina mess with my hair before she picked out black skinny jeans, chunky belt, and a white pullover shirt with a subtle rib that made it hug my chest.

She gave me an exaggerated once-over. "Much. Lugging heavy instruments around Boston agreed with you."

"I also discovered that unlike the horrors of PE class, weight rooms and cardio machines are excellent at focusing my brain for composing."

"You undoubtedly miss all the cute gym bunnies trying to flirt with you because you're debating C flat versus F sharp." Sabrina shielded her eyes as she directed her gaze toward the water.

"Guilty." I laughed right as a murmur went through the crowd.

"I see something!" a kid yelled.

I'd been here before, on the docks, waiting for a ship to appear on the horizon, but even so I couldn't help the tremor of excitement that raced through me too. The energy was contagious, and few sights were as impressive as a naval submarine arriving in port. Sailors with life jackets over their gleaming white dress uniforms stood up top, waving. More stood up in the crow's nest where a giant American flag hung. Not a single person wavered as the ship moved toward us, their footing way surer than mine would have been. The boat churned through the water as smaller ships, the size of fishing boats or small ferries, moved into position to help guide it into the bay and assist with the disembarking sailors.

Even as the ship docked, the sailors were too far away for me to spot either Derrick or Calder. One of the uniformed liaison personnel directed three young women holding tiny babies to step forward as tradition said that any new fathers would be among the first off the boat. Derrick's ex also got called to the front. Ugh. He was attractive with bleached-blond hair and chiseled features along with a slim body that would have been at home on any swim team, but his entitled attitude ruined any appeal for me.

The crowd whooped and hollered as a brash young lieutenant was first off the boat and gave him a very showy kiss. Lots of cameras flashed and clicked. *Bletch*.

"I'd bet my new eye shadow palette that they're broken up by next week," Sabrina whispered. "Think you can beat that?"

"Oh yeah. That looked fake, even to me," I agreed even as my pulse sped up.

Three teary enlisted men were next, greeting the women with babies as cameras clicked, and the crowd cheered again. Then more sailors were released and the crowd became increasingly disorganized as people jostled to greet them. I still didn't see Calder or Derrick, but then the crowd parted slightly and familiar broad shoulders and hazel eyes moved into view.

Damn. How had I forgotten how swoon-worthy Derrick was? My stomach wobbled as my racing pulse reached Indy-500 levels.

"Derrick," I called out.

Beside me, Sabrina clicked away on her phone camera, but I was only marginally aware of anything other than Derrick's face as he spotted me. He didn't smile, but his eyes went wide and locked with mine. If this had been a movie, the music would have swelled right then, a beautiful crescendo, and I wanted to memorize every note so I could use this moment later. I'd never experienced anything quite like the energy arcing between us.

And then his purposeful strides carried him closer. His gaze intensified, if such a thing were even possible, equal parts terror and excitement in his expression. Or maybe that was all me, the way my legs shook and my back sweat.

I had to swallow hard simply to get enough spit to speak. "Welcome home."

# Chapter Three

*Derrick*

Arthur turned out hot. That was my first thought when I spotted him after I heard my name called. *Derrick.* My actual name, not Fox, not Chief, and outside of Calder a couple of times, I hadn't heard that name in months. And definitely not like that, all eager and excited and *happy.* On the sub, hearing my name inevitably meant that someone needed something right that minute, but the way Arthur said it didn't inspire dread at all.

I'd already been caught up in the energy of the day. Homecoming day was always exciting, even if I didn't usually have someone waiting. The whole crew was jostling about, getting into our dress whites, making sure everything from our cover to the chest candy of ribbons and medals to the gig line was perfectly straight. Getting chosen to be on deck as we came into port was an honor, one that I usually let others, especially those with kids, fight over, since there was still plenty to do belowdecks in preparation and support. As the chief sonar tech, I was responsible for working with the A-gangers from engineering and the operations department to help navigate us in. Adrenaline was contagious, and by the time my department was cleared to disembark, I had enough energy to rival the reactor that powered the sub.

And then I heard my name.

I recognized Arthur's red hair right away. But the rest...

*Wow.* Arthur had grown hot. Still shorter than me and skinnier, but wiry now, each lean muscle defined under a thin white shirt and tight jeans. No signs of his ever-present too-big nerd-humor tees. Same startling green eyes as before, though, and a new, more chiseled jaw sporting the perfect amount of fuzz. He'd grown into his long regal nose, and the hair that had seemed to have a life of its own when he'd been a teen was sculpted now, this perfectly styled wave that made me want to mess it up. His hands, which had always seemed too big for the rest of him, were clutching a giant sign.

For me.

And for a second—a literal instant when our eyes met and time stopped—I forgot it wasn't real. And in that moment, I wanted it to be. Someone smiling that broadly for me. Had Steve ever been so happy to see me? Hell, I wasn't even sure the poodle my grandmother had let me keep had been that happy. Arthur just radiated pure joy. The kid was one hell of an actor.

"Welcome home." Even his voice was different. Deeper. Sexier.

"Hey," I said because I was simply that brilliant at conversation. I reached an arm out, instinctively going for a handshake, but Arthur shifted his sign and met me partway, coming in for a hug.

A really tight hug.

Damn, he felt good. Amazing really. Solid muscle against me, hair tickling my nose, exactly as silky as it looked, strong arms able to haul me in and hold me tight. He smelled like mint and green tea, two things in short supply on a boat that tended to smell like old socks on a good day. *Sweet.* I inhaled deeply as his lips brushed my ear.

"Calder said to kiss you," he whispered. "And I want to. But you gotta tell me you're good with that first."

*Was* I good with that? Hot guy who smelled like a concoction I wanted to drink every day for a month wanted to kiss me. And ordinarily, the friendship code would put Arthur far, far off-limits, but here was Calder telling us to kiss. It was a free pass, the sort I'd be a fool to turn down.

I wasn't a fool.

And what harm could a peck do?

"Yeah." My voice was a rough whisper, and I didn't have a chance to brace myself before Arthur was sliding his mouth over from my ear to mouth. A double shot of tequila would have had less punch than the first brush of contact.

And okay, not a peck.

We were kissing. Arthur and I, which should have been weird but somehow wasn't. At all. Someone whooped behind us, but almost all of my attention was riveted on Arthur, like I was on watch and every sense was heightened lest I miss something vital.

Like how soft his lips were. Full too. Or the bristle of his scruff against my cheek. I'd done a submarine shave that morning, not my best job, but close enough that the rasp of beard felt electric. Our chests were pressed so tightly that I could feel his heart pounding. Or maybe that was mine, blood zooming to places that had been in deep freeze for months.

"Wow." Arthur pulled back, leaving me dazed and still clinging to him.

"Damn." The statuesque purple-haired woman he'd been standing with laughed loudly and thumped Arthur's shoulder. "Is that the best you can do? Your man has been at sea how many months?"

*Your man.* If only. If he were actually mine, we'd be racing across base, a mad dash to find a room with a door. But he wasn't and all we'd ever have was this moment. A potent mix of want and resolve raced through me as suddenly I was determined to make this count.

I pulled him back to me, and this time when our mouths collided, I was ready. Ready to taste. Ready to absorb every single detail. Ready to seize control and kiss like the world might be ending.

And it could have. Not sure I would have noticed. Everything faded away. The crowd. The docks. The balloons Arthur had been clutching and his sign both as his strong hands clung to my shoulders as we kissed in earnest. He tasted like he smelled, sweet and minty, and his tongue against mine was like floodlights coming on.

"Welcome home," Arthur breathed against my mouth as the sound of applause gradually pulled me back into awareness of our surroundings. Applause. Whoops of laughter. Clicking cameras. But still I couldn't seem to look away from him.

"Your balloons escaped." Arthur's friend was laughing harder now.

"So they did." Arthur turned his gaze skyward where the colorful balloons were racing to the heavens.

"And posted! Man, this video is *so* going viral." The friend made a triumphant gesture.

"Wait. Video? Viral?" Shaking my head, I tried to clear my muddled brain, but before I could I heard my name again, more urgent this time.

"Arthur! Derrick!"

Stomach cramping, I slowly turned my head, like that could delay the inevitable. Sure enough, though, Arthur's parents—two people I had mad respect for, especially his retired master chief father—strode toward us with huge eyes.

"Your parents came?" I whispered to Arthur as I released him.

"Not part of the plan." He shrugged like this wasn't a huge fucking problem. "It was a surprise to me too. Mom texted earlier, but I was hoping they'd miss…the excitement. Oops."

"Yeah, *oops*. You could have said something."

Arthur blinked. "Exactly when?"

He had a good point, so all I could do was sigh.

"What is this?" Arthur's mother, Jane, didn't seem angry, more perplexed with a furrowed forehead. *Me too, Jane. Me too.* This was fast becoming a clusterfuck. I really didn't want to confess to the petty jealousy that had led to me agreeing to Calder's crazy plan, but maybe—

"Damn. Way to go, Fox."

*Oh fucking hell. Kill me now.* Seriously, a lightning strike would have been welcome because Steve and Fernsby were right there. And yeah, that was the whole point, for them to see the kiss I was still reeling from, but now I was trapped.

"Hey, Mom." Arthur didn't even spare a glance for Fernsby or Steve, doing an impressive job of actively ignoring them.

"You and… Derrick?" Jane continued to tilt her head like we were a mystery to figure out.

"Yup." Arthur answered before I could. "Surprise. I didn't tell you—"

"No *surprise* there. You don't tell me much these days." Jane's mouth twisted. As always, her husband was more of a silent presence, but he too looked befuddled and also distinctly uncomfortable. "But how long has this been a thing?"

Arthur gave an easy shrug. "A while. We didn't say anything because Derrick was still on the rebound from his total snake of an ex. But, I wasn't going to miss the chance to welcome him home."

Oh, he was good. Exactly enough vague truth there to be convincing, and he managed a dig at Steve to boot.

"Calder? Did you know about this?" Jane asked as he strode over, trio of friends trailing behind him. "Derrick and Arthur?"

"Oh yeah." He was as good a liar as Arthur. "Isn't it great?"

"Uh-huh." Jane's eyes were too wide and her mouth too tight. "Great. We made reservations at your favorite place for an early dinner. Arthur, you and Derrick will come."

*Bad idea.* I glanced at Calder, hoping he'd give me an out of some kind, but he just grinned, enjoying this way too much. Deceiving Steve was one thing, but the Eulers were good people. They didn't need to get unwittingly roped into my fake homecoming plot.

"I'm not sure I'm hungry," I hedged.

"Liar." Calder chuckled and bumped my shoulder. "We all know you can't wait to get alone, but you can do dinner."

His father went distinctly pink at the mention of Arthur and I being *alone*, and my sputtering noise wasn't much better.

"We'll be there." Arthur linked arms with me as if I might be about to flee into the crowd. Which, honestly, might be the better option than dinner with the Eulers, but I still nodded. He stretched like he was going to kiss my cheek, but instead whispered in my ear, "Trust me."

The absolute worst thing was that I might not have a choice.

*Don't miss* Sailor Proof *by Annabeth Albert,*
*available now wherever books are sold.*

*www.CarinaPress.com*